IF

BY

SPENCER MICHAELS

Evatopia Editions

Library of Congress Cataloging-in-Publication Data

Names: Michaels, Spencer.
Title: If / by Spencer Michaels.
Description: [Danvillle, Virginia] : Evatopia Editions,
    a division of Evatopia, Inc., [2016] | Series: [Twin
    flames series]
Identifiers: ISBN 978-1-63099-110-4 (paperback) |
    ISBN 978-1-63099-108-1 (mobi) | ISBN 978-1-63099-109-8
    (ePub)
Subjects: LCSH: Entertainers--Fiction. | Clairvoyants
    --Fiction. | Man-woman relationships--Fiction. | Mafia
    --Fiction. | Good and evil--Fiction. | LCGFT: Romance
    fiction. | Fantasy fiction.
Classification: LCC PS3613.I34 I4 2016 (print) | LCC PS3613.
    I34 (ebook) | DDC 813/.6--dc23

Epigraph

This is a work of fiction. Names, characters, businesses, places, events and incidents are either the products of the author's imagination or used in a fictitious manner. Any resemblance to actual persons, living or dead, or actual events is purely coincidental.

PROLOGUE

Light always shines greyest when you can't seem to think of the words. When you can't seem to think of, well, anything. It makes the room feel like its colored with winter when, in fact, the weatherman has been saying "spring is here" for weeks now. Grey light, a leaden haze, a foggy sort of luster is the only thing that pours in through the windows. Grey bed sheets, grey walls, grey hair, grey… Old Mr. Banos looks down at his yellow legal pad (also grey in the light) to read the first line he has written.

It was a dark and stormy night.

"God dammit," he mutters, crossing out the cliché line in one swoosh of his red pen. "Got to be better than that," he says. But no one is there to hear him. Just shadows of grey fading into the dusty walls. Bay View Nursing Home was the same as all the rest, shellacked with the last gasps of walking corpses, varnished with the wheezing death-rasps of geezers who finally gave up trying to be black or white, strong or weak, alive or dead. This place was the home of the forgotten.

With his blue pen, Mr. Banos scribbled down a new first line. "Gotta catch 'em with the first line," he said to himself, "gotta hook 'em in quick."

Though I am gone, may my story yet be told.

Reading over it, he liked the way the words felt in his heart, but when he said them out loud all he could think of was some two-bit Shakespearian butchering the prose with a melodramatic delivery. Out comes the red pen, and so disappears another opening line.

Old Mr. Banos catches sight of a tremble in his hand. Normally no one looks at their hands. They're always in sight, but your eyes just don't take notice of things that they see all the time. Mr. Banos' eyes were no different, they knew the routine by now. Drooping thin flesh, liver spots, bruises that appear as mysteriously as the stigmata, and wrinkles. Thousands of wrinkles. But it's when things begin to fall apart, when our bodies start to betray us that we take notice.

A tremor.

What does that mean?

"Great, now I got fuckin' strokes to look forward to, for shit's sakes?"

For some reason, Old Mr. Banos heard his voice echo through the greyness, reverberate from the fog of oblivion. He had gotten used to talking to himself over the past few years, but, every now and again, he would hear his voice and mistake it for someone else's. Not because it sounded alike, but because of some note, some emotional undertone that would go unnoticed by untrained ears.

Today the voice sounded of desperation.

He put the pen to the paper once more. One more time. *Remember me.*

The blue ink shined grey and spoke everything it needed to. Mr. Banos didn't need to read it out loud. This one would stay. Suddenly, he felt tired, the weight of the pad and pens were too much for him to hold. Blaming his hand or the medication or the ulcers or the...he always found his excuse.

Discarding the writing implements for the day, he reached over to his small nightstand drawer. Inside were nothing but old envelopes, bank statements, a letter opener, some spilled denture cream, but under the false bottom…

Old Mr. Banos checked his watch to make sure none of the orderlies would be buzzing around for a while, then deftly removed the hidden bottle of scotch from the inner drawer. He remembered a time when he still cared enough to pour his Macallan into a rock glass with four ice cubes and a fresh lemon twist. Even in his confinement here at Bay View, he insisted that his contraband be classy and refined. Now, all he needs is an airplane bottle, some privacy, and the continued ability to swallow.

Make no mistake, Mr. Banos did not drink to become a better writer in some hopes of being a geriatric Hemingway or Hunter S. Thompson on wheels, no, Mr. Banos drank because the golden amber hue of his liquor was the only thing that didn't shine grey in his life. And so long as he could keep his "nectar" flowing in, he wouldn't be extinguished by the encroaching nothingness either.

He downed the tiny bottle. Stars buzzed behind his cataracts, and the ticking of some invisible clock rattled in his head. The words he had written, the words he knew deep down he might never be able to pair with any others, hummed from the bowels of his nightstand like some fading engine.

Remember me.

ଔଔଔଔ

Chapter 1

You ever hear someone vacuum so long that you forget what silence sounds like? Almost as if they just keep scouring the same, exact, spot on the floor. And they bump the damn thing into the same, exact, spot on the wall. So, for hours on end, all the old man hears is the *RREEeeeaarr, thud, RREEEEEeeearrr, thud,* over and over and OVER again.

"Shit-birds!" Mr. Banos shouted, "Quit pretending to do work and just hide quietly like the stoners that work here!"

But no one hears him. No one ever hears him unless they think he's drinking booze or trying to wire the cable-box to unscramble the Playboy channel. Or if he's trying to escape.

Bastards.

"Good mooorrrnninnggg, Mr. B!" The vacuuming stopped just long enough to hear the clattering melmac plates jostling around on John's cart. "How are you this fine day, my friend?"

Making his eyes as wide as he could, Old Mr. Banos said, "Oh I'za beez finer than a frog hair split four ways massa!" As he spoke he wiggled in his chair a little and rolled his head around. "It's hard at my age, but for your monkey-ass, John, I try to put a little shuck and jive into it."

He just shook his head. "My breakfast rounds just wouldn't be the same without the minstrel show, thanks pal." John reached down to make sure his latex gloves are pulled up tight before reaching for a dish. "All right, just what the doctor ordered, Mr. B."

John slopped the plate onto the wheelchair's folding table.

Dry toast. Prunes.

"Now ain't this just some sorry looking shit," said the old man.

"Now, now, watch your language Mr. B or we'll have to take away your day room privileges again."

"Oh no, massa! I'za promise I be good! Please don'ts go 'n puts me in no hot box no mo'!"

John rolled his eyes and pretended like he didn't want to choke out a geriatric.

Mr. Banos tried to laugh but all that came out was a cough. "See," he said, "when you get past seventy-five, everything changes." He took a sip of water to clear his throat. "Can't even laugh at coons anymore. Hell, even farts are different. Used to be when I accidentally shit my pants I'd have a mess for somebody to clean up. Worked really well when you used to piss me off with your sass, Johnny boy!"

John growled something unintelligible, fidgeting with the dishes in his cart.

"But now, I can't even fill a diaper load for you to wade through! All that comes out is a cloud of brown dust, like I'm just one big goddamned urn."

"Language Mr. B, if I have to say it again—"

"Seriously, John, go ahead, disbar me from ever playing checkers with Eustace again. Brain-dead fuck always eats the pieces anyway."

"Look," said John, losing his patience in record time, "You know I gotta sit here to watch you eat at least some of this. With your diabetes and stomach ulcers this is the best we can do."

"Toast calms the stomach, prunes coax out the toast. It's all just a cycle of shit John, all of it."

"Maybe so, but either you eat it like a good curmudgeon, or I gotta shove it down your throat like I would for a sick cat. You know the drill, so eat the prunes." He folded his arms, trying to look intimidating.

But the old man pushed on, long since unafraid of idle threats. "You call these prunes? Can't fool me John, I know you had those long dreadlocks not too long ago. What happened, huh? White man really keeping you down or you just like serving me hairballs in the morning?"

"So help me I swear—"

But before he could paw at Mr. Banos' sweater vest, the old man distracted him. "Heyyy! Speaking of dried prunes, look who it is!"

In his routine banter with the orderly, Miss Sally Skizdale snuck up to the room.

"Hi, Mr. B," she said in a voice that lasted much too long. "How are we this morning?"

"What, do you think I have a pet mouse in my pocket? Or do you have me mixed up with the schizos on the third floor?

"I just want to know how you're feeling. How are your spirits?"

"Well my spirits are just fine when I can drink them," he said, "but other than that, *we* suck!"

"He's unusually chipper today, ma'am," John said, facing the Nursing Home Administrator.

"Hell, I'm down-right jovial! I'd do a little jig for you but, well, my legs don't work so good Lieutenant Dan."

John wheeled his cart towards the door in defeat. "He keeps giving me a hard time about the *cuisine* here," he said with a sigh. "Like I'm the one cooking around here." Turning back to face me but still addressing Miss Sally he said, "Time and time again I've told him that this is what the dietician recommended, but he just won't listen!"

Like so many other things, John's voice irked him. So the old man chucked a nappy-headed dog-turd prune at him.

The pitch was pathetic, but it smudged his clean white shirt. *That's a win in my book*, the old man thought.

"Mr. B! You must learn to control yourself." Turning to John she said, "Go ahead on your rounds, I'll take care of Mr. Cranky-Pants here." Miss Sally took great pains to bend down slowly, dipping her back with the grace of a giraffe drinking from a pool. Her heaving breasts pushed their way up and out of her low-cut blouse, as they always do. Old Mr Banos found himself suckered in yet again—tracing his eyes up from her high heels, past her stockinged legs and knee-high skirt concealing toned thighs, and landing square-ly on her perfectly rounded breasts floating right in front of his line of sight. Miss Sally loved making every fallen prune a production, and Mr. Banos never got tired of throwing them.

But just like every other time, the moment was ruined when she tried to seductively lift her head and flip her hair. See, Miss Sally had a flawless body, one that aged like wine, topped with one small flaw of the femme fatale — a face. You know, one that ages like milk. Mr. Banos couldn't help but let out a slight, audible "Bleh" as a shiver crept down his spine.

Walking slowly towards the wheel-chair, eyeing every-thing in the tiny room as if she'd never seen any of it before, Miss Sally said "Now just what am I going to do with you?" She tossed the prune in the garbage and placed one hand on each arm of the wheelchair to lean in. "Don't make me have to get…*physical* with you Mr. B."

Miss Sally thought the look she was giving the old man was a coy pose of carnality, but all Old Mr. Banos saw was a pocked face spinster. "No, please," he said, "anything but that!" Not without a paper bag anyway, that's what he always told Marty when he stopped in for a visit. The old man start-ed chomping down on his toast and chewing with a smile.

Seemingly satisfied, Miss Sally backed off and walked towards the door, swinging her hips like a pendulum.

"Sexual harassment is what this is. You just can't stop thinking about the cock rocket in my pocket."

"What was that?" she turned to ask, revealing that hideous face. "I couldn't understand you with your mouth full."

Catching sight of that grotesque monstrosity once again, Mr. Banos just closed his eyes and shook his head. "Oh, nothing." But even after she quit staring him down, he could still hear Wilson Picket playing in the background of his mind.

All you really wanna do is ride, Sally, ride!

Just when you think she's gone from the room, she always remembers one more thing and pops right back in, like some sort of feature in a haunted house to scare little kids. "Oh, one more thing," she'd always say. "Don't forget your physical therapy this afternoon. Between this healthy diet and a little moving around we can really get those juices flowing, hmm?" She curled an eyebrow in his direction.

"These fuckin' prunes do the job just fine." He wanted to also say that her face was a natural laxative but decided to not push his luck. "How many times I gotta tell you two, exercise at my age might as well be the setup for a bad prison movie. I mean, *me*, on a bike? Really?" Mr. Banos looked down at his pitiful little plate and moved a prune around with his spork. "Feels like Bubba's searching for the soap every time I sit on the damned thing," he grumbled. "And I can barely feel my own ass!"

"I told you he was in rare form this morning," John shouted from the neighboring room.

"So don't feed the fuckin' animals!" Mr. Banos raised his voice to project to wherever John was hiding. "Maybe one of these days they might bite your fuckin' hand off!"

"Now, now," Miss Sally chided, "Mr. B there will be no more *fuckin'* in here."

"First time in my life I have to agree with that," said the

old man.

Slightly blushing, Miss Sally lowered her voice to try and mimic something genuine. "Just remember that we only have your best interest at heart. Say, there's bingo this evening! Maybe that will cheer you up?"

Mr. Banos sighed and shook his head. "Yeah, great. But I've already got your number Miss Sally. O fuckin' 69."

With that little quip Miss Sally finally stormed out the door for the day.

With a grin wider than her hips, Mr. Banos said, "Bingo!"

And then the room was quiet. After tossing the cheap plate outside his door for John to pick up without disturbing him, Mr. Banos wheeled around to the window. And he waited. The room had a TV but he hardly ever turned it on. Occasionally on nights when he couldn't sleep he'd throw on the History channel to remind himself that there were things in this world older and lonelier than himself, but other than that, the room remained quiet. He had a small book shelf with an even smaller collection of reading material. Couple of novels by a friend he used to know, young writer named Spencer. And, of course, his trusty Destroyer series sat on the shelf collecting dust. But it had gotten to where Mr. Banos couldn't stand staring at the tiny print for too long, so he read even less than he watched TV. The room had no landline in it, so he bought a cell phone, but nothing irritated the old man more than talking on the phone. He could never hear, and, inevitably, whoever called would always get cut off because of bad service.

So he waited. Alone.

But around 2:00 o'clock, Mr. Banos' one true companion made his daily visit.

"Hey, Sonny!"

The young man walked into the room and hung his coat up. "Hey there, Big Guy!"

Mr. Banos felt the sting of irony in the nickname. It used

to be that he lived up to it quite well. But these days, being only four feet tall because of the chair and having his muscle mass whittled down to a whopping 135 pounds made the once endearing title into a bitter joke. "Glad somebody still sees it that way, I guess. Come on in and sit a spell. What's up?"

"Well, you are, big guy!" The portly younger man laughed in the middle of their routine joke. "I mean, since I didn't see your name in the obits this morning! Must be a good day, huh?"

"That's right. I'm hoping it's about to get better here presently if you…" Mr. Banos leaned in his chair to peer out the open door and into the hallway. Then in a lowered voice he said, "If you brought my *special* medicine that is!"

Sonny laughed in a way that was familiar. When he smiled too much, it would force his blue eyes to squint until they nearly shut. Mr. Banos thought of how the boy's grand-mother used to laugh the same way, but her eyes were so much darker, so much more mysterious.

"Big Guy," he said, "you know I'd never come here emp-ty-handed." The now thirty-something reached into his satchel that he always carried to work and pulled out a small paper bag. "Not until the market dries up anyway."

"I don't know how you stand all that number crunching nonsense," Mr. Banos said. "I tried to study statistics and calculus once a long while ago just for shits and giggles." He let out a snort. "It fried my brain circuits!"

"Haha! I remember, Big Guy. I used to sit in the living room with you at the old house and watch that goofball on YouTube explaining permutation formulas."

"Oh that's right. You did, didn't you?" The old man stretched to reach the bag that his buddy snuck in for him. "Well then I reckon you have me to thank for all your suc-cess!"

"I guess that's one way of looking at it."

Mr. Banos reached into the bag and pulled out an airplane bottle of Macallan. "Yep, and another way of looking at it is that your investing in scotch futures, ha-ha!...Mine!" He unscrewed the tiny cap with the dexterity of a much younger man and downed the smoky smooth liquor in a single gulp. "Ahhh!" Much better than all the goddamned prunes."

"Hey, watch your language gramps! Or should I say grumps? What would Jesus say?"

Mr. Banos laughed a little and lowered his eyes. "Yeah, well," he cleared his throat, "I'll be dealing with his ass soon enough."

Rolling his eyes, Sonny sighed. "You just never quit, do you?" Trying to change the subject he said, "Talked to Marty lately? Has he come by since last month?"

"Yeah, get a load of this." Mr. Banos tossed the empty bottle into the trash without looking. "Calls me the other day and tells me about how I can help my ulcers, right? We're in the middle of talking about the good old days of cleaning out the bars and he says to me, 'You should drink some milk before your scotch.' I told him, 'Marty, the good Lord only gave me a 32 oz. container, you really think I'm going to waste 8 of that with fuckin' milk?'"

Sonny laughed a little but shook his head. "You know that stuff is going to kill you, right?"

"What? My special cough syrup? You're a mighty fine lad and all but you'd be a Grade-A dongle if you really thought that this golden nectar of the gods is doing me any more harm than sitting around this dump."

Sonny just shrugged, he could almost feel a rant coming on.

"Besides," the old man said, "Bread killed me years ago."

Caught off guard, the younger man choked on a laugh, "What? Bread? Bread's good for you as long as you eat whole wheat. What is wrong with you and bread?"

"Not bread, dumbass," he said, "*David just shoot me in the face* Gates and Bread, the band, and their stupid ass song."

"You sure have become the cantankerous type these days," Sonny said. "I remember a time when I wouldn't have believed someone if they said they heard you drop an F-bomb or saw you down a shot."

"Well, that's life Sonny boy. We can't all have the luck or livers of Keith Richards. Hey! Now there's an idea, let's bust outta here and dig him up so I can get a liver transplant! Then I'd be able to drink for another good twenty years or so!"

"Big Guy," Sonny said with a note of confusion, "I don't even know who you're talking about."

"What? How do you--"

"And besides," Sonny cut him off, nose deep in his iPhone, "Wikipedia says he's still alive."

"Well I'll be damned. I guess that shouldn't surprise me. Suppose he wouldn't be too keen on the idea then." The old man wheeled around to a shadier spot in the room. "Ah, who am I kidding anyway? Even if you bought me the best scotch in the world, which you do a damned good job, don't get me wrong, I don't think—" He paused and looked down at his shaking hands. "I don't think I'd want to spend another twenty years drinking it. Not in here anyway. Hell, probably not anywhere."

"See, that's what I'm talking about." Sonny shot up out of his chair and walked closer. "For the past few months now especially you've been spouting off this half-hearted death wish shit and I'm getting a bit sick of it. What's really eating you? And don't say *Bread* or I swear I'm not going to sneak in another drop of contraband."

"Just leave it alone, Sonny."

"No!" The young man turned the wheelchair to make Mr. Banos face him. "I'm serious, you owe me some answers here."

The old man hesitated, but finally said feebly, "It's a long story."

"I've got time. I've always had time for your stories. Even when I've heard 'em a thousand times before." Sonny sat back down in his seat. "So spill."

The old man sighed in defeat. "Just don't laugh, all right?"

His little buddy nodded in agreement.

"See that drawer over there?"

"What your booze drawer? Yeah, Big Guy I know that—"

"Not that one. Next to it. Open it up and get my legal pad."

Sonny retrieved the item and put on his reading glasses. "What's this?"

"Well, I've been thinking a lot lately about the old days. I just wanted to get it all out there on paper before, well—"

"What is this, then? Like a memoir?"

"I guess so. The beginnings of it anyway. I've been working on it for a long time now and I guess I've run into a little writers' block."

Sonny studied the document. "Well how much more do you have than this?"

Mr. Banos cleared his throat. "Uh, well, that's it."

"Big Guy," he said, "this is just one paragraph! You've been working on this for how long?"

"On and off for something like—"

"How long?"

"Maybe four—yeah four years now."

"What!"

"Yeah—" Mr. Banos let his head fall in shame. "I just don't want the thing to open up with some frilly-boring fluff shit like 'the summer wind whistled across the grassy knoll,' or 'my life is one of many ups and downs and a few side-to-sides.'" He thought for a minute. "Hey, actually that second one wasn't half bad, maybe you could write that down for me?"

"I'll make you a deal," said the young man. "I'll write a

few more things down if you just take the time to talk to me. Why play this secret agent game when you could just open up to me?”

“Hmm—well I guess it’s worth a shot. But I’ll see your offer and raise you one trip to the courtyard. Take me out there and light up one of them New Awlins cigars that you got for my birthday and I’ll tell you everything you want to know.”

Sonny agreed and started to wheel Mr. Banos out of the room. “Gotta be quick though, can’t have the sentries coming out there with their cattle prods.”

“Don’t worry, they know who pays the bills around here.”

Stuck in his own mind, and a little more excited than he was willing to let on, Mr. Banos said, “If we’re going to do this, it’s got to be right. I don’t want a publisher picking this thing up and thinking *nobody gives a bird’s turd about your wrinkly ass!*”

“I gotcha, Big Guy. I just hope you can tell a story better than you can write one!”

“I don’t know about stories, but I can give you the old Joe Friday treatment. *Just the facts ma’am!*” He coughed up a laugh. “As best as I can remember them anyway.”

Just the facts.

C3C3C3C3

Chapter 2

The waves crash against the North Carolina shore, spouting mists into the early morning fog. Water vapor commingles and blends sky and earth, the blue grey of the sea becomes one with the blue grey of the horizon. A young woman soaks in the early morning sun, relishing the calmness of solitude. This is a feeling she hasn't known for some time now. A recent high school graduate, the bronze-skinned young lady had become inured to the typical stresses of being a teenager, among other things, for the past four years. Needless to say, her senior year wasn't at all what she expected. But really, whose life is truly as glamorous as they expect it should be?

As she walks she notices a small boy and girl finishing a sand castle. Getting ready to leave they join hands. And as they start to walk off she overhears the boy ask, "Will you marry me?" The little girl giggles and whispers, "Yes, of course I will."

She stands for a moment, a gentle tear falling down her face, the soft rays of the morning, contemplating the taste of salt air on her skin. Trying so hard to release, to let it all go. The water ebbs and flows, and with every return of the tide, she feels a stronger swell of peace within her soul. The white sands of Atlantic Beach didn't have the high volume of sea shells she expected to see. But resting near her foot was a starfish, nearly dried out, sitting on the brink of death. How painful it must be, she thought, to dry up and die when what you need to survive is within arm's reach. The young woman bent down to pick up the creature, and with a strong toss, she cast it back into the sea. Hoping, beyond all else, that it would find new life.

After quite some time, she began to walk into the path of the sun, still though she wouldn't take her eyes off of the ocean. It was as if she almost expected that starfish to wash right back up where she found it. But, as we all know, the danger of keeping your eyes locked on where you've been, is not being able to see where you're going.

Crash!

Nearly lifted off her feet, the blonde-haired girl jolted into a more wakeful state. Before she knew what had happened, she felt an arm around her back, gently cradling her weight. Looking up, she saw the face of a young man, not much older than her, smiling. "Oh my god, I am so sorry!"

The young man helped her back to a more fixed standing position.

"I was just so focused on the beautiful sights, I haven't really been here before, see? And I, well, I'm sorry, I just wasn't—"

"Whoa," the young man said, "It's all right, I understand."

She shaded her brown eyes to get a better look at who she was speaking to.

Laughing a little, the young man said, "I don't normally run into such a beautiful sunrise either." He made a gesture with his eyes as if to admire her alluring figure draped in a black bikini."

She blushed a little, but returned an almost impish smile, even though she was still apologizing.

Almost cutting her off, the young man stuck out his hand and said, "I'm Tom. Tom Marks. And you are?"

Taking a breath, only now realizing how much she had been stammering, the young lady said "Anna. I'm Anna Sopoulos."

"Whew, that's a mouthful!" He laughed at his own joke. "Are you here on vacation or do you just make a sport out of tackling other beach-goers?"

Her eyes widened and she almost screeched from embarrassment before realizing he was kidding with her. "You, Tom, are not very nice to girls you just meet, are you? If you must know I'm on a sort of vacation. I'm here with my parents." She brushed her long hair from her face. "What about you?"

"Nope, not me," he said. And as if he were going to leave it at that, Tom began to walk in the direction from which he came. After taking a few steps he turned and looked over his shoulder, "You were coming this way right?"

Anna smiled and walked to his side.

"No, I actually work down here. Which, hey, you can't really get much better than that right? I get to live in this wonderful place looking out at the ocean, take a swim or work out anytime I want, and occasionally I get knocked head over heels by a beautiful young lady named Anna Sopoulos!"

"You're funny," she said. "But I'm pretty sure there aren't as many Greek girls knocking you over as you might let on."

"That's true, you might be the first." He winked at her.

She returned his wink with a playful shove. "So where do you work?"

He motioned with his head, "Right over there at the resort."

"Oh really?" She couldn't hide the excitement in her voice. "That's where my family and I are staying!"

"You don't say?"

The Ramada Inn stood tall among the underdeveloped motels and cottages on this side of the beach. Seven floors of newly renovated vacation space housed most of the out of towners in the area, and the Ramada Inn boasted nightly entertainment to keep them coming back year after year. As the pair came closer to the towering monolith, they noticed an old man further up the shore.

"There's Melvin," Tom said, "setting up the beach chairs and umbrellas as he does every morning."

Anna looked at the red-haired man struggling with all the equipment, fumbling with the heavy load all by himself. "Do you work with him?"

Tom laughed, "Funny thing is, I technically work *for* him."

"Tom! You should be helping him right now then, what are you doing talking to me?"

"No, you don't understand, it's not like that." He paused for a minute and then finally said in a lower tone, "Melvin owns this joint. The whole thing."

"What? You're pulling my leg."

Tom held up three fingers. "Scouts honor." Clearing his throat Tom he added, "And if you turn to go back to your room now you may never know the rest of the story!" He took off in the opposite direction in a mock sprint.

Without hesitation, Anna chased after him. "Wait! Whoever said I was planning on going back upstairs?"

"Well then I can tell you more of the nitty-gritty then, can't I?"

"Oh, well, whoever said I was going to walk with you?" She turned in the opposite direction and pretended to walk away. But after a few steps she turned around, enjoying the way shock was written across Tom's face. "Gotcha!"

He laughed and said, "You know how to keep a guy on his toes Miss Anna, that's for sure."

"That, unfortunately, is something I have had quite a bit of practice in, but have never fully mastered." She paused and kept walking for a moment, studying the way her toes disappeared into the sands with every step. Quickly changing her tone back to a chirping excitement she said, "So finish telling me about Melvin!"

"Oh, that's right. So, this guy owns the Ramada Inn outright, it's all his. And he sets ups those chairs and umbrellas every single morning at the crack of dawn. I asked him one day why he doesn't just pay someone to do it for him."

"What did he say?"

"Nothing really, it was kind of odd. He mostly just grunted and said something about being useful. I don't know, maybe the old coot is starting to lose it. Funny thing is, he was the one that looked at me like *I* was the crazy one for asking!"

Anna laughed at how Tom told the story, how he gestured with his hands and affected his voice. Then she remembered, he had never answered her question. "So what exactly is it that *you* do at the resort, other than pester the owner and not help him with the chairs?"

"Nah, you first. I've talked enough already. Any more and you might realize that I'm boring." He smiled and the sun seemed to beam from within him instead of reflect off his skin. "How about you tell me where you're from and what brings you here?"

"Oh, you're no fun!" She stuck her tongue out at him. "I'm from Columbiana, Ohio and I just graduated from high school."

"Hmmm," he said, "I travel a lot, but I've got to admit I don't know Columbiana. I've been through Columbus. Is it close?"

"No, it's farther than that. We live right on the Pennsylvania line, nearer to Pittsburgh."

"Ah, now Pittsburgh I'm familiar with. Went to a few Irish pubs there. Never really felt welcomed, that's for sure. I don't know, must be an ethnic thing up that way."

Anna just nodded and walked on.

"Well, Columbsy Anna, tell me more."

"Am I going to have to hit you?" she said drawing back her fist."

Laughing Tom said, "No, no—I'll behave."

"So, this trip is a sort of graduation celebration then?"

Anna tried to answer, but her voice cracked. She felt a heat behind her eyes. "Not exactly," she finally said.

Tom looked over and saw the beautiful girl he had just met nearly in tears. "What's the matter?" he said. "Did I say something wrong?"

She shook her head, "No, no, it's not that." Laughing nervously and forcing a smile, Anna finally replied, "*Celebration* just isn't the word I would use. That's all." She sighed and walked along, studying the ocean's waves. "It's been a tough year. Sometimes you just need to escape, you know?"

Tom nodded. "Now *that* I understand." He took a deep breath that made his cheeks puff up and then exhaled like a tea-kettle. With wide eyes he said, "I know all about tough years. It's like nothing seems to work well as far as work or money goes. Past few years have been fine, smooth sailing even. But then I went to Canada for two months—"

"Canada? Did you go to Montreal? Toronto?"

"Oh no, not at all. I got to spend my days in the wonderful wilderness towns with dirt streets and moose that wandered up and down them all day and night. Let's just say that a compass would call that area the Arctic Circle."

"Wow," is all Anna could say.

"Yeah, *wow* is right. I did see the Northern Lights, but that was pretty much the only beautiful thing. They look like someone throws paint up in the sky and it keeps drizzling down."

"That does sound beautiful. Who knew I was talking to such an adventurer?"

Tom laughed and shook his head. "Who? Me? I'm just trying to work is all. So when things went south I decided I would too. Came down here to take advantage of the resort opening and I'm just trying to figure out what I'm going to do next."

They walked along in silence, each of them heading toward forever on their own pathways, yet somehow conjoined.

Anna saw the endless beach and the limitless seas as the for-ever that lay before them, but Tom felt something deeper, something unseen. He kept thinking about the Northern Lights, how the colors looked like they were falling from the sky, but would stay in motion forever. Together though, walking so closely and meditating on such a similar idea, they appeared as twin flames, illuminating something that would otherwise remain ethereal.

"Not to be nosy, Anna, but, I'm curious, what would have you in such distress?"

She looked over at her new companion and smiled. "I guess I'm just like you, Tom. I'm trying hard to figure out what to do next."

With that, they stopped walking and stood to admire the glistening ocean. Suddenly, Tom felt this tingling sensation in his left ear.

All he wanted to do was kiss this girl he had just met.

All she wanted to do was kiss him back.

At once, the two of them leaned into one another and shared a kiss warmer than either had ever experienced. In that moment, Tom felt like he was no longer on that beach in North Carolina. He felt like he was in a place he had never known, and he was seeing a young lady that had not been revealed to him before. And in that same moment, Tom felt a nakedness he could not understand.

Then it was over, and they were both embarrassed.

Tom stammered and carried on, and Anna tried to keep up the small-talk. Both tried to avoid whatever it was they had just experienced. Finally, to cut through the awkward moments, Tom said, "Would you like to have dinner with me tonight?"

And finally, feeling like her true self again, Anna said, "Yes, of course I will."

"5:30?" he asked.

Caught off guard, Anna said, "My you eat early!"

Smiling, he said, "Nature of the beast. I work tonight."
She nodded eagerly with a smile.

"Then I can't wait to *run into you again* this evening, Miss Sopie. I'll meet you in the lobby."

"It's a date," she said, waving as she ran up the beach towards the resort.

Tom stood there, admiring her body one last time before she disappeared. But all he could think about was that sensation. He wondered, *who is this girl?*

ෲෲෲෲ

CHAPTER 3

A thin trail of sand snaked its way from the threshold of the hotel door, across the linoleum floor of the well stocked kitchenette, past the freshly installed wood-paneling of the living room and into the small second bedroom. Anna had kicked off one flip-flop half-way to the bathroom, tossed her bikini top over the shower rod, and fumbled her way to the small closet of her room. Frantic hands flipped through blouse after blouse, dress after dress…she only had five hours to prepare!

"What in the name of—" A squawking woman filled the once quiet rooms with shrill discord. "Anna? Is that you?" Heavy footfalls traced the sand trail from the front door to the bedroom. "What's all the racket about? You think this place was cheap, huh? You don't slam doors like this at home!" The older woman's mouth moved faster than her feet but, eventually, she came upon Anna near the closet. "And why in the world would you track all this mess in here? If you think I came all this way to vacuum then you've—"

"Mama!" Anna shouted in embarrassment when the loud woman barged in on her daughter half-naked and in a daydream's trance.

"Missy, you don't have nothin' what I don't know is there!" She laughed a raucous roar and sat down on the edge of the bed. Rubbing her hands down her sides in imitation of some sort of fashion model, Mrs. Sopoulos said, "And besides, where do you suppose you got all of your beautiful curves, huh?" The older Greek woman had a thin frame like Anna, but had packed on the pounds over the years. Her *curves* were a bit more pronounced, despite the bed-sheet sized day gown draped over her body.

Anna had positioned the door of the closet in such a way that she could hide from the gaze of her mother and still indulge her costuming fantasy. Consumed by her own dilemma, Anna said nothing to her mother but, instead, kept pulling dresses from their hangers, holding them over her neck and checking them in the mirror.

"Hello? Oh daughter of mine? You awake in there?"

She poked her head around the door. "Sorry, momma. I guess I just wasn't thinking when I came in."

"Well judging by that smile you were thinking about *something*. Spill."

Even through her deep tan, Anna blushed and disappeared behind the door. "Yellow or blue sun dress? Which one will make me the prettiest?"

"Karlianna Sopoulos, *you* don't need a single thing to make you pretty. You know that, don't you?"

"Mom…"

"What? Can't I compliment my only daughter once in a while, sheesh!" She flopped back onto the bed and spoke towards the ceiling fan. "I just don't ever want you to take your gifts for granted. Physical ones or otherwise."

Anna sighed. "Mom—"

"It's just, I'm glad we can all be here as a family, you, me and your father, but, at this point in your life you shouldn't settle for being alone, not when there's such a nice man back home who can take care of you."

Before she could realize the tension she was carrying, Anna looked down and saw a blouse she was holding crinkled between two tightened fists. Through clenched teeth, the only word she could utter was *please*.

But once Stefania Sopulos set her gums to flapping, they

wouldn't stop until the subject was past the point of exhaustion—a dead and beaten horse. "Your father was telling me that William got that promotion he was up for and got a nice little pay raise." She rolled over to her side and threw her free hand into the air. "It's nice to have a little extra security these days, that's all I'm saying."

All she wanted was a way to shut her up. But Anna learned the hard way when she was nine what happens when you scream at a Greek mother. First your ears take a beating, then your face. And her mother loved costume jewelry—big, gaudy, pointy rings. It doesn't take gemstones to leave scars.

"I just still can't believe you gave back the ring." Mrs. Sopoulos studied the glimmering trinkets on her own fingers and wrists. "It was soooo beautiful. And the license was acquired and I mean, yes Anna, sometimes these things happen you know, I mean, God forbid, maybe you just have the bad genes like my sister but try, try, try again, you know? It's just that—"

"Mama!" The word came out a little sharper than she had hoped, but at least it masked the slamming of the closet door. Anna stood in the corner of the room, redder than any tomato Papa ever gnashed between his teeth. She was no longer embarrassed. Standing there with nothing but a layer of dust and sand covering her body and two dresses screening her breasts from her mother, she said, "Choose."

Mrs. Sopoulos blinked in quiet confusion.

"Yellow dress, blue dress?"

Sitting up and furrowing her face up, Anna's mother started in on another tirade. "What are you trying to get all dressed up for anyway, huh? You cookin' lunch for me and your father wearing one of those?"

"No, as it so happens, I have dinner plans."

"Dinner plans? With who? Why didn't you say so!"

"I've been trying to tell you!" Anna took a deep breath and tried to remember who she was talking to. When she closed her eyes, all she could see was Tom's smile, his chest and shoulders glistening in the golden rays of the beach morning. Relaxing into a swoon she finally confessed, "Oh, I met the most wonderful man when I was walking. He is so nice and funny, Mama, so sweet."

"A man? But who is he? What does he do? Not an official city inspector I bet!"

"His name is Tom Marks and what he does is make me smile."

"Oh, no, no, no, no, no… *that* is what clowns do, missy. Tell me, where does he work, huh?"

"Well, I don't know exactly."

"Uh-huh, and where is he from? Doesn't sound like a strong Greek name to me?"

"I guess I don't know that either but—"

"You don't know anything! How can you know a man if you don't know his family. Now Bakalar, *that* is a family name. Wealthy, Greek, and stable."

"Just drop it, mama! When are you going to start listening to me?" Tears welled up in Anna's eyes and she slid to the floor. A heap of dresses swaddled her like a newborn.

"Oh, Anna," Mrs. Sopoulos lowered her voice to something dangerously close to a kind whisper. Kneeling down near her daughter, she brushed the young girl's hair away from her reddening eyes. "You know you're so ugly when you cry."

Wiping her eyes and trying to calm herself, Anna just shook her head. "I'm not going back to William, Mama. I won't."

"We can talk about that when we get home. But I'm not sure what you're doing now is such a good idea. You can't dig yourself out of a hole sweetheart."

"Please just let me go and have a good time. For once, Mama." She took a deep breath. "Please."

Mrs. Sopoulos stood up and walked towards the door of

the bedroom throwing up her hands in defeat. "Fine, but no drinking and be back by 11 or I'm sending your father."

Anna watched as her mother left the room and came back in with her finger wagging.

"Just don't ever say I didn't warn you this: we Sopoulos women have a way about us that you haven't learned to control yet. I don't want to see you get into any more trouble because of forces you don't understand."

Anna nodded in silence and drew her knees to her chest, staring blankly at her feet.

When her mother walked out this time she spoke without turning her head. "Wear the yellow dress; the blue one makes you look fat."

ଔଔଔଔ

Chapter 4

The rest of the afternoon was that spoiled kind of excitement where you feel guilty for being happy. Anna tried to stay out of everyone's way, especially her father's, until it was time for her to head downstairs for her date. Why couldn't they just be happy for her? Why did she always feel like she was a puppet being forced to act out someone else's life, someone else's missed opportunities?

She wore the yellow dress. That's just the way it was.

But it didn't take her long to forget the stifling atmosphere of disapproval that permeated her family's room. Once she was in the lobby of the resort amid the smiling faces of young sunburnt couples with early reservations for supper, Anna felt as if she might just walk through some ethereal door, one that separated the life she was born into and the life she wanted to live.

Looking around, she didn't see Tom. Plenty of other young men were standing around the lobby. Some were single, some had dates, some were tall and thin, others were short and stocky. But, somehow, none quite had the presence that Tom had. Anna couldn't quite decide what it was. A smile? Posture? Maybe it was something the human eye just couldn't see.

Anna figured she was probably early because of her natural anxiety and need to exit the company of her parents, so she didn't take this as a bad sign. Instead, she began to peruse the flyers and advertisements within hotel. Almost glancing past the marquee, Anna had to do a double-take. A large glossy photograph of a face she couldn't believe. Under the title for "tonight's entertainment" was none other than—

"Good evening. The name's Marks, Tom Marks, and you are?"

Anna spun around, startled, and then let out a nervous laugh. "You!" She looked over her shoulder and then looked back at Tom. "That's you on the poster!"

Tom squinted and looked over to where she was pointing. Then he studied his hands and clothes as if trying to make a match. "Well! What do you know? That *is* me!"

They both laughed and Anna playfully smacked his chest. She noticed she could still feel his muscular frame even through the thick dinner jacket he was wearing. Navy blue looked nice on him.

"I guess I never told you exactly what it is I do here," he said smiling. "Come on," he said, gently taking her hand, "I'll tell you all about it at dinner."

Anna felt as if she were gliding through the air as he gracefully guided her through the now growing crowd of people. Without even speaking to the maître d', Tom showed his glowing date to their reserved table by the window. He pulled out a chair for Anna and then took his seat.

"Wow, we have the perfect view to see the sunset!"

Tom smiled, "Yeah, I thought it would be nice to make the sun jealous for once so I had to sit you some place where it could see you in that dress."

Anna couldn't help but blush. "You, Tom Marks, are just a little too much."

When the waiter came by, Tom ordered them a bottle of champagne without hesitation. When he saw a look of surprise on Anna's face he said, "It's not every day I meet someone as lovely as you. It would be indecent of us not to celebrate, don't you think?"

At first, Anna's only thought was that her mother would kill her. But after a moment in the golden rays of the setting sun, she let herself ease into being that woman she wanted to become and answered only with a coy smile.

After the waiter returned with their drinks and took their orders, Anna finally returned the topic of her curiosity. "So is your show any good?"

Tom laughed and nearly choked on his wine, "It better be! It's how I pay the bills."

"It must feel so exhilarating, standing in front of crowds of people like that. What do you play?"

"It has its moments." He took her hand from across the table. "I can play almost anything on the piano and organ, some guitar and other odds and ends, but when it comes down to brass tacks, I'm a singer. You should come to the show tonight and see for yourself!"

"Oh, well, I don't know if—"

"Come on, I'll save you a seat right up front. You can even bring your family if you'd like."

She smiled. "Ok, well, I have to be home by eleven. I don't think my parents would be much interested though."

Tom wanted to ask why she had to be home so early, he wanted to take offense as to why her parents probably wouldn't like his show, but, instead, he decided to redirect the conversation back to his lovely date.

"Well they're more than welcome to come. And if not, I'll be happy to have at least your smiling face looking back at me from the crowd, even if you must leave before your carriage turns back into a pumpkin or whatever."

She laughed and eased back into her chair.

"So what about you, Miss Sopie? You seem like a musical soul yourself."

Shaking her head she said, "Not even. Well, I played baritone horn in marching band for a few years, but not enough to make any sort of life from it."

"A horn is a horn, my dear, and it means you have the music in you. I can see it in the way the light reflects in your eyes."

Anna lowered her head and felt herself starting to tear up. But why? She was having the time of her life.

Tom sensed something was amiss so he said, "I tried tuba once in marching band. But I had to give it up because it rattled my brains around too much." He demonstrated by putting a hand on each side of his head and shaking violently.

Anna laughed, and any mist of tears was swallowed by her smile.

The food arrived and the couple sparkled in the orange glow from the window. Their conversation never lacked, their excitement and passion only increased as the fresh shrimp disappeared.

Tom told Anna about his many successful tours as a nightclub entertainer, album deals, great times with the bands.

Anna told Tom of the many faces and places from home, how her grandmother could only speak Greek and taught her how to make spanakopita, and how she wants to one day have a meal just like this with him in Mykonos, sitting next to a window that looks at the other side of the sunset and discussing how they met on the other side of the world.

Before either one of them knew, they were ankle deep in the sands of what each would call *our* beach, walking the trail that led them to one another earlier that day.

The sun had faded away entirely now, and the two walked under the light of the full moon that had come to take its place. Very much satisfied from dinner and to be in the pleasant company of one another, the two walked along in blissful silence for quite some time. The only words that were said were the ones that needed to be said, and these were only whispered between the lover's palms. The walked hand in hand until the dark and empty beach became a space of quiet confession, a melancholy meandering. Something about the darkness of the beach and the constant lull of the rushing sea breeze made us feel like they were actually alone, not just there, but in the universe.

"Being a showman isn't all it's cracked up to be," Tom said in a low voice.

Anna looked up, but said nothing.

Still staring straight ahead as they walked, Tom continued. "Before I took the job here I was touring with a couple guys in Canada and, well, I guess things just got real ugly real fast." He paused for a bit and sighed. "Me and the guitarist had a falling out over something petty. I was frustrated with the weather and lack of profitable venues, so I called it quits. Basically just ran out on a lot of folks that were depending on me."

The crashing waves in the distance filled in any gaps of silence that might otherwise make the conversation awkward, so Anna just continued to listen, not interrupting the pace.

"Now I'm here, I'm warm, and I've got a handful of financial backers who are at my throat. Even my agent is ready to write me off unless I can make something happen pretty quickly." He ran his free hand through his hair and shook his head. "I guess the crazy thing is that what bothers me the most isn't the debt, it's that I just up and quit like that. I like to think I'm a man with more of a code than that but, it's like sometimes my heart pulls me so hard in a direction that it's hard to say no." He laughed a little under his breath. "I'm sorry, I'm not sure why I'm saying all this and ruining our evening."

"No," Anna finally said, "I like to hear you talk." He still didn't look at her, so she took it as being her turn. "I didn't want to talk so much about it this morning, not because I'm ashamed, but maybe because I want to pretend that none of it's real." She cleared her throat and said, "A month ago I was engaged to be married."

That got his attention, but Tom didn't interrupt. He

wanted to listen as patiently as she had.

"His name is William Bakalar and my parents desperately want me to call him my husband because he comes from a good family and because he works for the city and because…" she took a deep breath and let it out. "I don't know," she said, "maybe I want that life of stability and the old ways but, I guess I'm like you, sometimes I feel my heart pull me harder than I can resist."

It felt like they were playing peek-a-boo with the skeletons in their closet. Tom let go of Anna's hand and wrapped his arm around her waist so they now walked as one four-legged being, their eyes staring in the same direction, and their heartbeats almost in sync.

They stopped to admire the undulating ocean of ink before them and Anna buried her face in Tom's shoulder. "I thought I had to say yes when he asked me because of my parents and—"

Tom couldn't quite hear the rest. He looked down and noticed that Anna had started to cry. He tilted her head back by putting a gentle hand under her chin and said, "Hey, it's OK."

"No it's not, Tom. I had to say yes because he got me pregnant." She tried to control her tears, but they just kept coming.

Tom could only hug her close to him to try and ease the pain.

"But a month ago I fell down the stairs to the laundry and the whole world changed. Suddenly I felt like I had some kind of choice again, some way to make my life what *I* want it to be."

Tom put his hands on her shoulders and rested his forehead on hers. "You always have a choice, Anna. Always."

She smiled and nodded.

Tom kissed her forehead and wiped the remaining teardrops from her cheeks. "Besides, what's life if you don't have a bunch of people constantly pissed off enough to try and kill you."

She laughed and ran a hand through her hair, trying to calm herself and return to the safety of his arms. And after a few moments, they reached a quiet stability, staring out into the shining twilight sea.

It's funny, you never think of darkness as having a luster, but the way the full moon glistened off the murky waves proved that even the blackest of things can have its own sparkle. Anna guessed the same was true of the secrets they both let fester within their souls. How beautiful it was to find that one person who you just knew had the strength to share that pain with you? Suddenly neither of them was suffocating—both could breathe in each other, darkness and all.

Soon Tom felt that same strange tingling in his left ear and, somehow, he felt like the strong gusts of the surf formed a hand that gripped the back of his neck. He found himself forced into the exact place he wanted to be, with his lips softly pressed against hers. Pale moonlight bathed the young couple as they swayed to the rhythm of the rolling waters, dancing in the solitude of heaven's embrace.

But even sooner still did Tom feel the pain of realization, time was not on his side. "Oh no!" he said. "I hate to do it, but if we don't head back now there won't be a show tonight, not in the lounge anyway!" He smiled and whisked Anna away, through the dusky sands and back to the warm light of the resort.

ःःःः

Chapter 5

The evening that followed was nothing short of a dreamscape for Anna. A trail of mystery and wonderment that had all come undone by the unyielding hands of the clock and the stern roar of her father.

Panting from running up the hotel stairs, Anna stood in the doorway of her room petrified, staring straight ahead at two very angry Greek parents.

"You're late," is all her Papa said. He stood with his arms crossed, wearing his flannel robe, a cigarillo hanging from his lips. Tapping his foot nervously, he repeated himself in a lower, more serious tone, "You're late."

Not as choosy about her words, Anna's mother nearly screamed the curlers out of her hair. "My God," she said, "we were worried sick." Stefania rushed over to her daughter to hug her tightly to her breast. "Are you all right? What happened?"

Anna breathed a sigh of relief and started to smile again. "Oh, Mama, it was so wonderful, I had the most lovely eve—"

Smack

Anna was interrupted by the swift slap of her mother's hand. "Don't you ever disrespect me and your father like this again," she said. "Out doing God knows what with some stranger while we, *your parents*, are up here wondering if you've been tied up and thrown in a trunk somewhere."

"But, Mama," Anna started to say weakly, rubbing a hand

across her lips to check for bleeding. Thankfully, her mother had already stripped her hands of jewelry and lotioned her skin.

"No," her father interrupted, "no buts Anna. Your mother is right. No one eats dinner for six hours. Where exactly have you been?"

Anna moved in to the room a little more now that she was halfway sure she wouldn't have to run back out of the door. "After dinner we walked on the beach and Tom invited me to his show, but I told him I had to be home so I—"

"His show?" Mama couldn't help but butt in. "What, so, he's a clown or something?"

"No!" Anna tried not to raise her voice too much. "He's actually a very talented singer and musician and works here at the resort." Seeing that this detail made no difference in her parent's demeanor, Anna added, "He's really a delightful and sweet man. If the two of you would just meet him I'm sure that—"

"Anna," said her father in his cold steel voice, "your mother and I have no interest in meeting some carnie." He shuffled over to the recliner in the main room and propped his feet up, lighting his stogie. "I hope you two said a nice goodbye because your mother and I have decided that it's best to leave tomorrow."

Anna nearly fell to the floor. "Father!" This time she couldn't help but yell. "I thought we were staying another four days?"

"Watch your tone." Her mother inched closer like a snake preparing to strike.

"I think we've been here quite long enough. I hoped that this trip might help your realize the importance of family and tradition." He took a long puff from his cigarillo. "But, instead, it's done nothing but encourage you to go gallivanting around the surf with some drifter and hang out in night-clubs like a two-bit whore!"

"Father…"

"So, yes, we're leaving tomorrow. The sooner the better."

"You can't do this! It's not fair!"

This time Stefania reeled her arm back for a full swing, smacking Anna onto the floor. She crashed and splashed in a pool of her own frustration, tears flowing freely now.

"I *can* and I *will*," her father announced as he leaned up from his seat. "That's final! Now get cleaned up and go to bed, I'll hear nothing else about it."

Anna crawled away, stripped of any dignity she thought she had left.

C8C3CECS

That night, she lay awake in her bed, tossing and turning, sobbing and screaming into her pillow. She couldn't quite decide on one emotion so she chose them all. After an hour or so, something strange happened. Anna didn't feel as if she were asleep, but rather as if she were dreaming. In her mind's eye she could see every detail of her evening with Tom, she could even smell his cologne. Escaping the hostile prison of her bed, she felt like a time-traveler, existing only in the happiest moments of her life.

Her excitement was fresh when she heard the announcer in her ears just as she had at the lounge that night. "Ladies and gentlemen, put your hands together as The Castaways Club is proud to present Mr. Tom Marks!"

And then he appeared—dazzling under the spotlights, cutting through the expectations of the crowd with a velveteen voice. Tom paced the stage in long strokes, dominating the room with the twists of his body and the range of his melody. At times, Anna could hardly hear the music for the roar of applause. So many people, so many hands making a joyful noise for the man whom she felt such a strong connection.

Anna was amazed at how realistic this dream state was—she could consciously look around the lounge, study all the faces, objects, phrases said, and even the feel of a cocktail napkin between her fingers. She remembered watching in amazement, wondering if this is how Tom looked at her, even though she wasn't on stage. Just when she found herself hoping for a sign that she wasn't some fool with a crush, she heard Tom speak from the stage in between numbers.

"Thank you all for coming out tonight, you're such a beautiful crowd. But, I have to say, there's one particularly beautiful woman here tonight to whom I'd like to dedicate this next song." He winked at Anna and said, "This one's for you Sopie."

Anna felt her cheeks flush as one of the stage lights beamed a golden circle around her and people cheered.

"If a picture paints a thousand words, then why can't I paint you?"

Tom was singing her favorite Bread song. How did he know? Had they even talked about music that day? Anna savored every syllable, trying to slow the memory down in her mind.

She remembered singing along when Tom got to the line, *"If a man could be two places at one time I'd be with you, tomorrow and today."*

Anna felt the tears as they formed in her eyes anew, and resisted that same urge to climb up on that stage and suffocate her love with an embrace. Just as she was about to stand up and come to him, she watched as Tom descended down the stage stairs and glided over to her table. Still singing, he pulled a single red rose from the lining of his coat, kneeled and gave it to her.

"Then one by one the stars would all go out, and you and I would simply fly away…"

Anna let the rose fall to the floor as she scooped up her man, nearly tackling him with a kiss. The microphone fuzzed and she cut off his last few notes, but the crowd hooted and cheered as the stage lights dimmed around the happy couple.

And then, the lights went out in her own mind. Just when she could feel his lips pressed against her own, just when she could feel the strength of his arms wrapped around her, she saw him float away. "Wait!" Anna called out to a slowly fading Tom, running after the man who was dissolving into a specter. She ran and ran, but never caught up and he never said a word. Anna felt frantic, running in place, her feet gaining no ground and the lights disappearing around them. Her heels served only to trample the discarded rose—the only color left, the bloody petals of beauty passed.

"Wait!" She shrieked. Anna sat straight up in bed, soaked in her own sweat and panting. Had she really been asleep? She felt so aware of time and her bed…but the dream was so tangible, so realistic. The bedside clock said it was barely six in the morning. There was no way she could get back to sleep, so she just sat there for awhile.

When the pang of realization finally sat in that this was her last day, Anna held her head in her hands and began to cry. But, before long, she decided to sneak away in the early hours for one more walk upon the beach.

Our beach she thought.

Of course, the only person in sight was Melvin, struggling to set up all the folding chairs and umbrellas. All by himself.

Anna walked aimlessly, feeling like the ocean was her home and the rest of the world was the looming threat that sought to drown her. Just when she thought she should turn around, she noticed a figure in the distance running in the sands. Without a second's hesitation, Anna ran towards him. She ran, just like she had in her dream, but this time, she would find her mark. By the time she reached the jogger, her eyes were red and filled with sand and mist, but she jumped into his arms anyway, knowing beyond knowing that this was her Tom.

"Well good morning to you too, darling." Tom laughed at the unexpected surprise, but then he noticed the crying girl he was holding. "Hey, what's wrong, little one?"

Anna let her fears and worries pour out onto Tom, not at all concerned that it might unsettle him. She knew better.

Tom sat the two of them down in the sands so she could catch her breath.

"I have to—" She paused to wipe her eyes and clear her throat, "I have to leave today."

Tom cocked his head to the side. "But I thought—"

"It's my parents," she said. "Ugh, they just make me want to scream sometimes."

"It's ok," Tom said, "I'm sure something just came up is all. I understand." He smiled the smile he'd like to see on her face.

Anna sighed. She wanted to unload on him, she wanted to completely deny and abandon her parents, but she knew she couldn't. "I don't have much time," she said instead. "Here, I brought this in case I *ran into you* again." She smiled and handed Tom a photograph. It was one of those dated wallet sized pictures of Anna in a simple black dress. Her senior picture.

Tom held the photograph in his hands like it was his only possession. When he finally noticed writing on the back he said, "What's this?"

Anna laughed for the first time that morning. "It's my phone number, silly. You should call me, if you want to."

Tom smiled. "Uhh, yeah! I think I'll want to!" He put his arm around her and hugged her body closer to his.

"Of course," Anna said, "I suppose you could throw darts at it or something when I'm gone. Whichever you prefer."

Shaking his head and snorting a laugh, Tom said, "Now who's being silly?" He playfully shoved her over into the sand.

"Hey! Watch it pal, or I'll show you how they fight in Ohio!"

Tom stood up and taunted her. "Oh yeah? What do they do, huh? Joust with snow shovels on the back of tractors?"

"Oh, you're dead." Anna jumped up and chased after him until he spun around and picked her up, slinging her like a sack of potatoes over his shoulder.

"Is this me being dead?" He carried her like this despite her constant wiggling and smacking of his back.

"Let me go you, big bully!"

"Not yet," he said. "If I had my way, I'd never let you go, but since I have no choice, I can't let you leave empty-hand-ed now can I?"

"What are you—*oomph*!" Before she knew it, they were back at the resort and she was right-side-up again. Collecting her balance, she saw Tom motioning for her to follow him. After what seemed like a maze of hidden corridors, the two of them arrived in front of his room.

"Come on," he said as he unlocked the door, "I want to show you something."

Anna stood there, wondering at the time, hoping her parents were still asleep, and thinking of a thousand other reasons why she shouldn't walk into this room. "Tom…"

"Anna, I assure you," he crossed his heart with his index finger, "my intentions are completely honorable."

She sighed, still not convinced this was a good idea, but she held her breath and stepped over the threshold into his room. It was everything you'd expect out of a single guy's beach hotel suite. There was a filthy hot-plate over in the corner next to a small coffee pot, dirty clothes littered the floor, and Cup-O-Noodles lined the edge of the desk.

It was lovely.

Tom sat Anna down on the edge of the bed and returned after he pulled a small wooden box from the depths of his closet. When he sat down beside her, she could see it was a puzzle box, one where you had to slide the pieces on the top in the exact right order to open it.

"This belonged to my Grandmother," Tom said as his deft fingers quickly unlocked the complex puzzle. "Her father built this box to keep it safe and, needless to say, it did its job." He laughed as he was still cracking the coded chest. "Anyway, she gave it to her daughter, my mother, and she trusted me with it for some reason."

Finally a rusty click emerged from the box in his lap. Anna leaned in closer, anxious to see what was hidden inside.

When Tom lifted the lid, Anna saw a sparkling golden circle staring back at her. "Now," he said as he lifted the treasure from its home, "I want you to have it." A gold coin dangled from a simple chain and shined in the light of dawn.

"Oh Tom, I can't—"

"Oh Anna, you must!" He unclasped the chain and hooked it around Anna's neck.

"It's so beautiful, are you sure?"

Tom smiled. "I've never been more sure in my life."

Anna looked down and twirled the coin between her fingers. "It has two faces," she said.

"That's right. It's to remind you that no matter where you may be, I'll always be there."

He took her hand in his. "My mom always told me that the right person always feels like the other side of the coin, you know? So even when we're not together, we never have to be alone."

"I love it," she said, "and I'm never going to take it off."

Tom laughed, "Well you could do that, or you can throw darts at it or something after I'm gone. Whichever you prefer."

She shook her head and kissed him one last time, holding her face against his for as long as she could before she heard herself say, "I'm sorry, but I have to go now."

Tom stood up and led her to the door, hugging her without too much protest. "I'll talk to you very soon," he said, kissing her once more on the forehead.

As the door closed, Anna placed a hand on her necklace. He was right, even though she couldn't see Tom's face, she felt him with her. Somehow, it made the inevitable trip back north a little more bearable. But, she couldn't help but wonder, would she ever see Tom again? Or would the last twenty-four hours be cast in a golden memory? Would she be able to craft the life she desired, or forever be unable to glimpse the other side of the coin?

CBCBCBCB

CHAPTER 6

Old Mr. Banos hadn't talked this long without cursing another human being in nearly four years. In fact, any passing attendee at Bay View Nursing Home would have sworn Mr. B and his guest were listening to some Harlequin Romance book on tape. While he continued telling his story, Sally Cock Rocket popped her head in the door in shock, but even she had the decency not to interrupt such a beautiful story from the normally foul-mouthed old man.

"Those few hours on that beach were enough to change my life, Sonny boy." The old man leaned back in his wheelchair to soak it all in. His guest wasn't the only one surprised by the story being told. No, the way old Mr. B wore his face suggested that even he hadn't revisited this particular tale in quite some time.

"What's the matter, old man? All this sentiment giving you indigestion? Or are you just getting soft in your old age?"

The old man scoffed. "The only thing soft about me is my shit. And unless you want to experience that yourself by wiping my wrinkly ass, then you best wheel me over to the turdlett ASAP."

Sonny chuckled and complied. Getting Mr. B in and out of the bathroom was a common task for him with all the prunes they pump him full of. Roll him to the bathroom door, boost him out of the chair, and hobble him over to the toilet with the raised seat. One thing he learned early on though is to never, ever, reach to try and undo Mr. B's pants for him.

"What are you some Bourbon street hooker in a hurry?" he'd always scream. But today, the old man was too wrapped up in reverie to make a fuss one way or the other. So long as he took a seat on his throne and got to keep telling his story.

When the young man closed the bathroom door he took a temporary seat in Mr. B's wheelchair.

"After she and her family left," he spoke louder than he needed to from behind the closed door, "I spent a day in torment. It's that waiting period that just killed me. Did she love me, was it all just a dream etc. etc."

"So what happened then? You called I assume?" The young man rolled back and forth in the chair as he spoke.

"You're damn right I called! Hell, I was dialing those numbers before she could have possibly driven back to Ohio, I didn't care." The old man paused for a minute to grunt inappropriately loud. He knew that the air vents let sound travel a good distance in the nursing home and if he timed it right he could interrupt the cliffhanger on *The Bold and the Beautiful* with his shit sounds.

"Come on gramps, tell the story."

"I am! Anyway, yes we finally talked on the phone. And when it happened, it was like there was no break in between us seeing each other. That's what was so special about her, nothing was ever awkward, everything was just as matter-of-fact as it could be." As if his body had a natural inclination towards spoiling sweet moments, the bathroom was filled with the clap of a wet fart and the splash of watery shit in the bowl. "Phew!" he screamed, "thar she blows!"

Sonny just pinched the bridge of his nose and shook his head.

"We talked everyday, sometimes twice a day. I didn't want to do anything else. And see, you can't relate to this, but that was the only connection I had with her. No texting or emails or emoto-whatever-the-fucks, in those days it was just Ma

Bell and Snail Mail. That's it!"

Sonny was going to say something, but got cut off by another torrent of explosive diarrhea.

Typical.

"Problem was," the old man continued, "long distance calls weren't cheap. Hell, after a couple weeks everything I made went towards my room bill. But I can honestly say it was worth it."

He paused for a moment. Maybe it was to reflect and smile, maybe it was to wipe his ass. But the young man could swear he heard a timber of tenderness in his voice that wasn't there before.

"One day I called and gave her the same cute line of 'remember me?' even though we had just spoken hours before. Hell, I think I can remember every single word of that conversation."

"Well give me the highlights here," Sonny said in jest.

Disgusted, Mr. B snorted. "You kids, always in a rush. Sure, fine, here you go. I'll bullet point it. We talked about how we were both sad that we couldn't hold each other. We discussed the cruel fates that Greek parents subject their children to. She told me about how they wanted her marry a nice Greek boy from a good family. I told her how Greek papas all think they're the best cooks in the world and Greek mamas only want their daughters to suffer the same charade. Vicious cycles and all that jazz."

"That's the short version? You know the human body only has a set number of heart beats right, old man?"

"Will you shut the hell up so I don't clock out on mine then? Sheesh!"

Mr. B's loyal guest just laughed and waited for him to continue.

"So then she says, 'They just don't realize that I'm fully capable of choosing who I love.'"

The young man could hear that sound again, like the old

duff was actually choking up or something.

"And I trapped her, see? I said, 'Well, who might that be?'" He laughed and asked, "And you know what she said?"

"Paul Simon?"

"You jackass, me! She said she loved me!"

Sonny could hear the toilet paper rolling freely now from the spool so he stood up to help Mr. B from the toilet when he called him in.

"You remember that weird tingle I was telling you about in my left ear? Huh?"

"Yeah, sure, right before you kissed her?"

"That's right," he said, "well, I felt it again that day on the phone." He cleared his throat. "So I asked her to marry me."

"You what!?"

But the only answer that echoed from the bathroom was the roaring flush of the toilet.

The young man couldn't stand it, so without even asking he busted back in through the door. "Marry you?"

"Well hell son," the old man screamed, "you might as well now that you've seen all my goods!" He laughed himself nearly off the seat of the throne. "Now help me off this thing before my ass goes numb again."

Sonny was still in shock from the story that he didn't even understand that the crippled old man was making a joke. "What did she say?" he asked as he hoisted Mr. B from his seat.

The old man raised his eyebrows at what he clearly thought was a stupid question. He then sat solemnly in reflection for the longest time. Then he softly said, "Yes, of course, I will." His tone was not of his own voice, but of her's, just as he had heard it so many years earlier. "Of course, I will."

ೞೞೞೞ

CHAPTER 7

Two weeks passed and Tom found himself with a simple gold band in hand, at Anna's request, driving seventeen hours north to Ohio for a two-day stint.

A 1973 Dodge Tradesman 300 gets roughly nine miles to the gallon on the highway. It has a gas tank that holds about twenty-five. Tom remembered stopping at least four times on the way there, effectively devouring around a hundred gallons of gasoline from Carolina to Columbiana. To put it in perspective, he had an 8-track stuck in the dash that played on repeat anytime the car was cranked. During that drive he heard every song on that recording fifty-one times.

Fifty-one.

The worst part was that it was some random demo tape he had picked up out of the recording studio's slush pile some time back. But that doesn't really matter. Take your favorite album and listen to it fifty-one times back to back and tell me you're not ready to drive your car off a bridge.

Tom was a little more excited when he entered Youngstown, even though it appeared to be nothing more than an even crappier extension of Pittsburgh. Gray skies. Towering steel mills. There was one odd little difference though that always struck him as odd. A huge sign, almost as big as a billboard read: HOME OF GOOD HUMOR ICE CREAM.

The sign that mattered most to Tom, however, was a small green one that you could barely see unless you were searching for it for seventeen straight hours. Columbiana was just up the road. Only fifteen more miles to go…

Finally, he found himself crawling out of the van on Westwood Street. Oblivious to the world around him, he shambled over to the house with the green door. And even though he was a jittery-zombie, Tom knocked on the door and greeted Anna with a smile. "Hiya, Sopie!"

She stood in the doorway, grinning as if to say, *What took you so long?* She kissed him and threw her arms around his shoulders. "Come in," she finally said. "You look so tired."

"I was but…" Tom paused long enough to build up some kind of suspense.

"But what?"

"But now I'm not!" He rushed over towards Anna and scooped her up onto his shoulders, spinning her around and filling the house with laughter.

"Put me down, put me down!"

The two of them both felt as if they were reliving a beautiful moment from their past, and when Tom set her down, they kissed as if they had known each other for a thousand lifetimes.

Anna smiled and said, "Mama and Papa will be home from church soon. I can't wait for you to meet them." She didn't quite know what to say or do, so Anna just kind of jumped up and down repeating, "I'm just so happy you're here!"

Tom leaned over and smothered Anna with kisses. Each one said *I'm happy to be here too.*

Then her parents arrived.

"Mama, Papa, I'd like you to meet Tom." Anna stood slightly in front of him and gestured slowly like a game-show model. Her hands were shaking only enough for Tom to see.

Mr. and Mrs. Sopoulos stood in the doorway like silhouettes, haunting the threshold by pausing there long enough. Mr. Sopoulos wore a modest gray suit and tie that was a little too short for him. He'd probably worn it to church since he was a teenager. Mrs. Sopoulos wore a lightly patterned lavender dress and stockings. The clothes looked like something she might have taken from Anna's closet that morning.

When it was clear they weren't going to be the ones to make the first move, Tom rushed over to greet them. "How do you do, Mr. Sopoulos…Mrs. Sopoulos. It's great to finally meet you both."

Mr. Sopoulos gave Tom the once-over like he learned everything he needed to know in the matter of a few seconds. He nodded and gave a polite half-smile, one that his wife imitated quite well. And without much talk, the parents suggested they all sit down in the living room off the main hallway.

Tom barely had time to even notice his surroundings. When he pulled up to the house, he did take note of how similar it looked compared to all the other houses on the block. In fact, most houses two and three streets over looked about the same. Tom supposed this had something to do with the steel industry. As he was walking into the den, he felt a strange reminiscence of his grandmother's house. The walls and furniture all spoke of some older world that Tom could barely connect with.

"So," Tom said awkwardly from the couch, "Mr. Sopoulos, what's your line of work?" Tom noticed that Anna was sitting at arm's length from him on the sofa. Even though she was smiling, her anxiety was something tangible although unseen. Her nervousness was like an odor that quickly filled the room.

"Like 90% of everyone else around here," the older Greek man said with a bit of annoyance, "I work in the steel mill. Youngstown Steel and Tube." He cleared his throat and pulled a worn wooden pipe from his jacket pocket. From the looks of it, the thing was more for chewing than lighting seeing as how it had hundreds of bite marks but hardly any black around the edges. "Tough job, dirty work. Around here, clean air means no dinner. You breathe in dirt, you work in dirt, and, if you're lucky, you get to bring it home with you."

No one had anything to really say as Mr. Sopoulos retreated into his melancholy pose in the armchair. Finally, Tom piped up and said, "Well it pays the bills, right? So I guess that's why they call it *pay dirt!*" Tom looked over to Anna. She was still smiling that desperate smile that couldn't even begin to cover up her discomfort.

Mr. Sopoulos leaned back in his chair and clenched the pipe between his teeth. He said nothing and didn't really laugh at the joke so much as let out a sharp snort.

For a moment that felt like an eternity, the room was a symphony of odd noises. The occasional squeak and creek of furniture, the interspersed cough or clearing of a throat, the constant click-tick-ticking of the wall clock in the other room.

Finally, the silence was broken when Mrs. Sopoulos said, "Anna, dear, why don't we head into the kitchen to make some dinner and let the boys get to know each other, huh?"

Anna nodded to her mother and looked to Tom with a silent question. Tom nodded as if to say he would be all right and the women left the living room.

Mr. Sopoulos leaned back in his chair and stared at his guest through half-shut eye lids. Chewing on his pipe, he let out a grunt. Or was it a snort? Hard to tell.

Tom's body felt inclined to do the opposite. He leaned forward on the sofa, as if he were being pulled by a leash, and watched his hands nervously fidgeted in his lap. Tom's stomach grumbled loud enough for both men to hear and he laughed a little to see if Mr. Sopoulos would say something or possibly just acknowledge his humanity in some other such small way.

He did not.

Clearing his throat, Tom felt compelled to speak. "So…" was all he could muster. Despite the fact that he was a born entertainer and had worked hostile crowds in cities all across the country with ease and skill, Tom felt himself suffering from stage fright.

What could he say? What did he know? What would be polite?

"You have a lovely home here, Mr. Sopoulos," is all that emerged.

Shit, Tom thought. He wondered if he were repeating himself or if he had only imagined saying that already and decided not to. What time was it? How long had he been here?

The afternoon light filtered into the room through dingy curtains in such a way that you could see dust floating through the air as if each speck was a fleck of gold. It was at once beautiful and terrifying in its stillness. If the two men were friends the room would be a calm place of mutual contemplation. As it stood, Tom felt like he was being hunted and Mr. Sopoulos was waiting quietly in the mist for the most opportune time to spring his trap.

The Greek father just sat there, staring down his nose at Tom. Barely breathing, only moving enough to not raise alarm that he might have stroked out. His silence was the lure that kept Tom wandering into the thick of it until *whap!*

"What are your plans for work?"

There it was. Just when Tom was whittled down to the point of giving up on trying to make conversation, just when he was praying for the father to say almost *anything*, he had to say *that*.

Caught off guard, but at once ecstatic that he was actually being spoken to, Tom quickly replied, "Oh, well, I own my own business performing shows as a nightclub entertainer. That's how Anna and I met—I currently work as the house performer for the resort you and your family stayed at in

Atlantic Beach."

The father, still leaning back in his chair, nodded his head slowly for a long time, bathing in the silence he loved so much. "And what about after that? What will be your real job?"

Tom winced a little at the way Mr. Sopoulos enunciated the words *real job*, but trudged on nonetheless. "Sir, that *is* my job. I am a nightclub entertainer."

And then, the silence.

But after a few moments, Tom thought maybe he could find some compromise. He was here, after all, for Anna. "My true passion is music, Mr. Sopoulos. But I'm not an unreasonable guy, I mean, I know that everyone gets too old to perform at some point. I could see myself opening a store." Tom looked down at his feet as he said this because he wasn't sure he could handle the look of disapproval Mr. Sopoulos was sure to be wearing. "You know, to sell instruments and give singing lessons and things like that. So long as I can stay with the music—"

"Where will you live?" The father's voice cut straight through any kind of sentimental dreams Tom might be trying to conjure.

"Pardon me?"

"As an entertainer, where will you live? How long do you plan to make this your only source of income?"

"Well I live in the hotels. Resorts really. Like the one your family stayed in. And I'd like to keep this up for another ten or twenty years I suppose. Heck, I'd like to still be performing at your age Mr. Sopoulos!" Tom smiled and tried again to warm up his host to no avail.

The father started to laugh though. Only, this was clearly a dismissive snort. Tom certainly felt laughed at rather than laughed with.

Raising his voice a little more than before Mr. Sopoulos said, "And when you're scraping your pennies together going from town to town singing your songs in the nightclubs, you expect to take my Anna along with you? Is that what you believe? Where would my daughter live?"

Tom leaned up in his seat and felt the hairs stand up on the back of his neck. "Uh, if she were with me she would live in the hotels."

"My daughter forced to live like some transient. That is every father's dream, am I right?" He took the pipe from his mouth and sat it down on the table beside him. His hands fumbled around in his jacket pocket until they found a matchbook. "Do you know what sort of home Anna has always dreamed of? Has she told you while the two of you are running up the phone bill night and day?"

Tom felt his face flush a little, but he tried to calm himself before speaking. "She has not."

Mr. Sopoulos put the pipe back between his teeth and struck a match to light it. After a few quick puffs to make sure the ember was hot, he sucked in a mouth full of smoke and filled the den with a cloud to conceal his face. "Since she was a little girl she has always drawn these pictures of a Cape Cod style home with a nice white picket fence."

Tom spoke more sharply now. "And if she and I are to be together I will make sure she has that home." He paused for a moment and added, "someday."

Mr. Sopoulos brushed the smoke away from him and leaned forward. "What day? What day exactly do you believe that you can provide that type of life for her with the kind money you make?"

"I do just fine for myself actually. This year has been a little rough because of some small setbacks, but typically I have a very high income potential."

Mr. Sopoulos snorted again. "Can you put food on the table with *potential*? I don't think so. I've seen guys like you all around here. Everybody thinks they have it all figured out how to cheat the system and get rich quick and yada yada

yada. But here's the breaks kid—being a man is about learning responsibility. And responsibility is knowing exactly how much money you're going to make on a paycheck and exactly how much of it you have to shell out every month. Until you can do that day in and day out, until you can sacrifice the things you want for the needs of your family, you're just a little boy chasing a dream."

Tom stood up from the sofa in a rage, ready to let this pompous grease-ball know exactly what a little boy could do.

But before he could, Tom heard the words, "Supper's ready!" Mrs. Sopoulos walked in from the kitchen. "Oh, jeez, I thought you weren't going to smoke that silly thing in here any more George."

Tom looked over towards the kitchen and saw Anna standing in the doorway. Suddenly he realized that his fists were clenched. When he saw her in that moment, he felt his whole body relax. He remembered why he had made this terrible drive and entered this terrible town to begin with. The remaining smoke in the room, the light shining in through the curtains, the floating dust all created some phantasmal screen through which to view his love. Anna shimmered in that air like a dream, and reminded him that they could one day transcend this place. And everything with it.

"Come on then, Tom," Mrs. Sopoulos said, tugging at his arm, "We don't want it to get cold." She smiled up at him with a mask he couldn't read. "Oh my," she said as she ushered him into the dining room, "This one here must work out, Anna. So strong."

"Stefania," grumbled Mr. Sopoulous from behind them.

Nothing else needed to be said. Anna tried to smile at Tom, but it only made him feel worse. The dinner conversation was much like the warmth in the house—non-existent. For thirty long and solemn minutes, the only sounds were the scrapes of forks against plates along with the occasional clearing of a throat. Tom thought he had complimented the food, but his voice seemed to get lost in the silent void of his own unimportance.

After dinner, when Anna suggested they go to a local nightclub favorite called *The Apartment,* Tom tried to casually say, "Sounds good to me." He didn't want his true feelings of THANK-YOU-LORD-IN-HEAVEN to shine through too much for fear of offending.

But Anna didn't have to be a mind-reader to know that something had upset Tom. As she drove the two of them to the downtown club, Anna said, "Please forgive my parents. It takes them a while before they warm up to new people, especially non-Greek people."

Tom chuckled and shook his head. "If they gave me a chance I might just surprise them!" He sighed and grinned. "We will get along just fine so long as I don't have to live with them."

Anna laughed and said, "You know, I feel the same way sometimes."

At the stop sign Tom leaned over and kissed her. Somehow that made everything right again.

At *The Apartment,* Anna introduced Tom to her friends Joey and Roxanne. She looked prim and proper like the girls apparently should in this town, but Joey was dressed in a fashion that Tom could identify with a bit more. His loose fitting V-neck shirt and long hair betrayed that musician's sensibility that Tom had come to know well in his time on the road.

"Guys, this is my fiancé, Tom."

Fiancé. That amazing word of partnership, cooperation, interconnection. Somehow, hearing it out loud, hearing it come from Anna's lips, it changed Tom into more of the man he wanted to be.

"How do you do?" asked Roxanne, extending a dainty pale hand.

"How's it going man?" Joey said in a more laid-back way.

When Tom shook his hand and felt the permanent calluses on the fingers, he already confirmed what Anna was in the middle of saying.

"Joey is also a musician and plays a mean guitar." Her voice was like an echo of Tom's own thoughts. "Maybe you guys could get together and play sometime," Anna said.

"Oh that would be fun to see," Roxanne chimed in.

Tom agreed. "Well, as it so happens, I'm looking for a guitarist to do a session with me right now. My studio guitarist broke his wrist and will be out for months." Tom tilted his head as if to study Joey. "You any good?"

The kid laughed, "Well, some people think so. We'll get together tomorrow and you can see what you think."

Tom nodded. "Sounds good. But what I think right now, is that I need a scotch. Bad!"

After he had gotten a shot or two down, Tom felt like he were back at the beach. The room started to feel and sound like those ocean waves, and Anna wore the same smile she had on that day in the sun. When the music slowed, he whisked her away onto the dance floor to hold her close. Tom couldn't stop thinking of how much he loved this girl, how little time had passed since they met, and how sure he was that he wanted to have a life with her.

"I love you, Sopie," he whispered in her ear. "And I will always take care of you."

On the drive home he couldn't get that promise out of his mind. He kept hearing the disapproval in her father's voice and the desperation in his own. As he tossed and turned on the couch that evening, his mind raced with all the ways that he could do exactly what he said he would—Tom wouldn't rest until he could be the man Anna needed him to be.

જીજીજીજી

Chapter 8

In his dreams Tom saw Anna walk to his side, cup of coffee in hand, the idyllic house-wife smile on her face as she kissed him saying, "Good Morning, Sweetheart." It was a perfect picture, one he hoped to marvel every day for the rest of his life.

When he awoke that morning, he found the half-sipped mug on the table next to the couch. He picked up the faded yellow cup and studied it. It was real, it was in his hands, but he couldn't really believe it. Stretching and yawning, Tom stumbled up from the lumpy sofa to pour some fresh coffee—technically his second cup. As the steam rose to his face and his eyes blinked into waking life, the wall clock caught his gaze. Only after a few gulps did the numbers make any sense.

"Geez," Tom groaned. "Seven in the morning?" He looked around the kitchen as if someone should be there. Tom figured Mr. Sopoulos would be grinding dirt by now or whatever he does. He didn't expect Anna would have to be at the department store so early…and her mother? Where was she?

Staring out the kitchen window at all the other empty houses on the block, he caught himself wondering just how bad of a trade it would be. He could grind dirt. At least he wouldn't have to work on weekends, wouldn't have to travel all the time.

COOKOO! COOKOO!

"Holy—" startled, he jumped and spilled coffee all over his shirt. "How many clocks do these people have?"

After cleaning up his mess and finding no sign of Mrs. Sopoulos, he decided to do what any self-respecting road musician would do if he found himself awake this early—watch *Captain Kangaroo*. That is, only until Mr. Rogers came on.

Barely into the first neighborhood adventure and only half-way through his coffee, there was a knock at the door. He got up, but then hesitated. Being a guest and all, he wondered for a second what the etiquette was for opening someone else's door. But, being a little ambivalent as to how he might offend his new out-laws, he decided to make himself at home.

When the door swung open, there stood Joey, it looked like he hadn't even gone to sleep. "Come in," Tom told him. Laughing, he said, "you failed the audition…what kind of musician are you to be up at this ungodly hour?"

"You're up, aren't you?" Joey kind of bounced a little when he walked, his long hair bobbing up and down with every step. "Can I get a cuppa that, man?"

Tom nodded and gestured towards the kitchen.

When Joey had a hot mug in hand and took a few sips he said, "Ahh! Now I'm alive again. Just needed a little kick-start."

"You and me both. Anna woke me up before the sun was up I guess. Crazy bunch of worker ants in here."

"What's a matter," Joey teased, "Prima donna needs his beauty sleep?"

"Cute." Tom moved over to the dining room table and sat down. "I'm just more of a nocturnal animal, Joey. And from the looks of it I'd say you are too."

Joey bounced over to the table and sat down his mug. "That's where you're wrong my friend. I hate sleep. Been trying to kick that habit for awhile now."

Tom laughed. "Are you serious?"

"As a heart attack from forty-thousand feet my friend." Joey turned a chair around and straddled it. "Dig this—Leonardo da Vinci taught himself to sleep in two hour spurts. He'd go to sleep and then stay awake for like three or four hours. He saw all the parts of the day instead of just half of it but still got his full eight you see?"

Tom just drank his coffee and listened.

"See he was bending the rules, challenging the norm you know? But I say, why bend 'em when you can break 'em?"

"Now you're speaking my language!" I made my eyes real wide to try and let him know I was being sarcastic. He didn't get it.

"Exactly man! So there's this swami or something who lived in a cave for something like a hundred years. No water no food no sleep. He broke all the rules."

"Now you're just pulling my leg."

"No! Really, get this. I've been reading all about meditating your body into a state of rest while waking. If you gradually wean yourself off of sleep as we know it and supplement it with delta-wave yoga then—"

"Ok, I got it, guru." Tom laughed and said, "How long have you been without sleep right now?"

Joey looked like he didn't understand the question. "Three days now maybe?"

"Holy shit! You've just been drinking coffee and praying or—"

"*Meditating* man…there's a difference. It's all about being able to take the involuntary and making it voluntary. Don't let your body control you, you know?"

"I guess." Tom downed the rest of his coffee. "But for my money, I still prefer sleeping off a hangover than chanting a mantra over it. Just personal preference I guess."

Joey held his hands over the steam of his cup and then slapped them over his eyes. "You're a funny guy, Tom! I can see why Anna likes you."

"Yeah and you're a nut! But I've always been partial to pistachios so I guess we can be friends."

Joey shot up from his chair. "All right! Chop, chop, we've got a full day planned."

"Is that right?"

"Yep. Anna tasked me with giving you the tour of the town!"

The room fell silent as Tom waited for the punchline.

"Yeah, you're right," Joey said, "that should take all of three minutes. But then we get to jam so let's hop to it!"

Tom stood up and took Joey's mug to the sink to rinse it out. "Whatever you say, boss. Let me get some clothes on that haven't been washed with Folgers."

"Make it quick man we—" Joey noticed for the first time that the TV was still on. "Oh, Mr. Rogers is on. Take your time." He jumped over the back of the couch and plopped down.

After about fifteen minutes Tom had showered and changed clothes and, to no surprise, he found Joey drooling in a deep sleep, leaning halfway into the floor.

"Ok," I shouted, "Up and at 'em little Buddha buddy."

Startled, Joey gasped and squeaked out a yawn. "I was, where? I was just resting my eyes, man. Let's hit it."

Tom found that riding around in Joey's mustang wasn't the worst way to spend a morning. He was right though, it took no time flat for him to drive by the Mill, the local watering hole, and the downtown market.

"Hey, how about we surprise Anna at work? Where's her department store?"

"Ha, you really *do* want to impress her parents huh?"

"What do you mean?"

Anna's boss is one of Mr. Sopoulos' good buddies and he's a total hard-ass. You wanna get Anna in trouble and have to hear her old man lecture us freeloaders for the rest of your visit then be my guest."

"Hmm… you've got a point there."

"I've always got a point. That's why I'm taking us back to my apartment."

Soon they were parking outside of a little duplex on the other side of town.

"Come on, music man," Joey called, "Let's wake the neighbors!"

Tom climbed out of the car and followed Joey through the grass-patched yard littered with old beer cans and through the front door that seemed to be held in place with duct tape. "I'm always down to play, but I sure am starved. Got anything to eat?"

Joey led them in through the kitchen and tossed his keys onto a wooden crate with chairs sitting next to it. "Great minds think alike." He smiled, "I got some frozen pizzas that are calling our names."

"Breakfast of champions."

After they'd had their fill, Joey took Tom to the basement and uncased an old Les Paul.

'Nice ax," I said. "Play something."

Joey plugged into a small amp and let fly some of the most amazing riffs Tom had ever heard…at least live anyway. When he'd finished he said, "Man…where in the world did you learn to play like that?"

"Here and there," he said nodding towards a box of Staxx Records."

I felt my jaw hit the floor. "You're kidding, right?"

Joey smiled and started to crack up. "Yeah, but I had you going didn't I?" He slapped his knee and laughed himself silly. "Come on, I've got a Hammond over there in the corner. Show me what you've got. I need to know you're worth the drive before I make the trip to lay down tracks with the likes of you."

Wasting no time, Tom started the organ. It was an M-3.

Not a great one, but it did have a 122 leslie connected to it. He began to play a vamp and said "Blues in G."

Joey hoisted up his guitar and nodded.

"One, two, one-two-three-four…"

And from that one count they set off jamming for the biggest part of the day, never tiring, never stopping. They learned more about each other in this way than they ever would have by shooting the shit and swapping stories. He could tell that Joey had probably busted some knuckles in his day based on the way he made his A chord. Joey could tell that Tom was a perfectionist by the way he would repeat phrases until he thought they were tight enough. But their little idiosyncrasies complemented one another well, so Tom asked him to do the session with him.

"I could come back for you in two weeks, put you up at the beach resort, and even feed you. May not be eating high on the hog like that frozen pizza up stairs, but I'll keep you fed." I laughed and stood up from the organ bench. "What do you say Joey? You wanna be a star?"

His face crinkled as he brought his hand to his chin. "Hmmm… I want a per diem plus an hourly rate, 20% royalties, and 50% merchandising featuring my likeness."

Tom stood frozen for a minute, trying to figure out if he even had enough money set aside for the studio time.

Joey busted out laughing. "Look at your face! Tom, I'm kidding man, you had me when you said beach resort." He stepped towards Tom and slapped an arm around his shoulders. "You've got to lighten up dude. For a guy that's got so much positivity floating around in his life right now you sure do sport that grim reaper glare more often than not."

"Shut up, you just caught me off guard. And I'm always serious about my work—when we get in the studio it's not all fun and games like down here."

"Yeah, yeah, I know, but right now we're not in the studio, boss man. Come on, it's getting late."

They climbed back up the rickety basement stairs and headed out to the car. "Wow you weren't kidding," Tom said, "it's already four o'clock. Anna will be home in a half hour."

"Don't worry man, I'll take the shortcuts through town. See? There you go again getting all anxious."

They hopped in Joey's car and Tom sighed. "It's just her parents, Joey. I mean, I really love Anna more than anyone I've ever met, but those…people."

"I don't get it," he said, driving with one hand, "so they don't like you. What's the big deal? You and Anna are the one's making a decision about your future, not them."

Tom rubbed his hands across his face. "Yeah but it would be so much easier if they approved. I just know that if I work hard and prove myself that they'll accept me…accept us."

Joey took a deep breath and let those words settle as he drove. "Sometimes Tom, you can't train the universe. You have to just adapt and be flexible for when the world shifts into something you can't recognize." He turned and looked at Tom, despite the narrow streets. "Or else you're going to drive yourself crazy man!" He laughed and slapped Tom's shoulder. "I can see it now, you blow a gasket and suddenly can't remember who you are, they roll you around in one of them wheelchairs in a nuthouse or something. Probably feed you prunes and toast all day. Is that really what you want?"

"You're insane, so I guess this advice is coming from ex-perience?"

"There he is! Funny Tom is back in the vehicle."

"All I'm saying is that her dad really got me thinking yes-terday. I've got to figure out a concrete plan for how I expect to provide Anna all the things she deserves. Not for Mr. Sopoulos' sake and not really even for Anna's—but for my own. I don't know if I could take it to know that I'm a dis-appointment to her."

Joey slammed the brakes and fishtailed for dramatic effect.

"What are you—"

"Stop. Just stop it for a second man. If you live your life fearing to disappoint, then you're sure to do it. Anna didn't fall in love with you because of your last name or them white picket fences you could pull from your pants. Anna loves you for deeper things, like your good looks and half-way decent personality."

"You ever consider being a guidance counselor? You know, consult children on a daily basis?"

"I'm serious here man, you've got this storm cloud following you around, but it's a sunny day!" He moved the car from the middle of the street and parked it with one tire on the curb. "Now smile and go say hello to your fiancée."

Tom sat there for a minute. Then he finally said, "You know, for a flower child zombie, you're all right, Joey. I'll let you know when to pack your swim trunks."

"Right on man, looking forward to it."

He stepped out of the car and closed the door. Speaking through the window Tom said, "and Joey, thanks."

He just winked and said, "Don't scratch the paint job, lover boy."

Laughing as he walked towards the house, Tom started to think that maybe Joey was right. Maybe love was enough and so long as he started thinking of himself and Anna as a team, maybe that's all he needed to make things work. Her parents would come around…in time.

All he needed to know right then was that it was a sunny day and he was ten steps away from kissing the woman he loved. Tom walked up the stoop and saw her standing behind the screen door.

He smiled. But she didn't return one. Nor did she open the door for him. "What's wrong?"

"Tom," she spoke through the door, "I've…I've been thinking a lot today about you and me, and I—"

"Anna? Let me in so we can talk about—"

"No! No…I'm sorry Tom," she started to tear up, but quickly cleared her throat. "I just don't think we can make it."

His hand was on the screen door handle. He couldn't understand why it wouldn't open. He could see Anna, her face was right there. But he couldn't touch her. He started speaking without even paying attention, as if he were watching the whole conversation from the sidewalk.

"Not make it? What are you talking about?" he heard himself say, "This morning you were so in love and now, now what? Now you're trying to break it off or…?"

"Please…" she said in the softest voice, "It's for the best."

Tom studied her face through the screen, searching for any sign of hidden meaning. "Is this about what your dad said?"

She remained silent.

"No…it's about that Billy Baklava or whatever his name is, isn't it? Did he come around and convince you not to marry me? Is that what this is? Please, Anna, just let me in."

"His name is William Bakalar and…," she spoke slowly and deliberately, "He is a very important man with a good job."

He kept his hand in place, hoping the screen door would budge. Her face was so close, but still he couldn't touch her. "A good job. Oh, ok, I get it." Finally, he let go of the door. "Fine," he said stepping down the stairs, "See ya!"

Stomping down the sidewalk, he saw Joey's car was still there. Joey got out of the car when he saw Tom coming. "Hey man is everything al…*oomph*"

"Move," was all Tom said when he shoved him out of the way."

"Jeez, Tom, what happened?"

He could feel himself losing it more and more by the second…how could she? This…this couldn't be real. Tom's foot found its way to the van door. Over and over, and over again. "Fuck this!" he screamed.

"Hey calm down, man. You want the cops showing up?"

Opening the door and fighting back frustrated tears, he blurted out, "Joey, if you are ready to go to the beach then pack it up—we're leaving now!" Tom slammed the driver's side door and cranked the van. "I won't be back in this piece of shit town in two weeks or ever!"

"Wait, wait, Tom!"

But his only answer was the sound of tires squealing and a cloud of kicked up dust.

ଔଔଔଔ

CHAPTER 9

"Bullshit!" Old Mr. Banos screamed out the word over and over again. "Bullshit," he said.

Startled, Sonny who had been such an eager listener asked, "What's wrong? What's bullshit, Big Guy?"

"All of it." He slunk down into his chair, hiding from the light of day in the courtyard, retreating into himself like a turtle in his shell.

Sonny parked the wheelchair near a rosebush. Sitting across from Old Mr. B he asked, "What do you mean? I know it can be upsetting but—"

"No, you don't understand," he said. Sighing, the old man continued. "None of this ever happened. It's all just a pack of stories and foolishness."

Sonny laughed and said, "No, you can't back out of this now. There's no way you'd be telling me all these details without it being real, just no way. So if you don't want to tell me anymore that's fine but—"

"You're not listening!" The old man's voice cut through the afternoon and scared the birds from their nests. "You're not listening," he said again, more quietly.

Sonny relaxed in his chair and waited.

"I can't…the truth is…well the truth is that I don't know the truth. I can't remember most anything."

Sonny smiled. "Come on Big Guy, I mean, you're in your nineties. It's only natural that—"

"I may not have your brain, but believe me when I say

I can remember every conversation, every birthday, every phone number of everyone I've met in my life." He rubbed his eyes. "But for the fucking life of me, Sonny, I can't remember the beginning of this story."

Seeing the old man on the verge of tears was not something his companion was accustomed to. "Big Guy—"

"I have these fragments. Like faded photographs. I see us walking on the beach and I remember her coming to my room—but that's all. Everything else was just how I hoped it happened, it's what I dream of most nights."

"So the date? The conversation before the show?"

"I don't know. I don't know if any of it's true or if it's just the way I've wanted it to have been for all these years."

"But what about marrying her? Was that just fantasy?"

"No. I remember her voice on the phone…and my own. I proposed and she said exactly 'Yes, of course I will.' I can hear every pitch, every syllable, the rhythm in her speech, the emphasis on every letter…"

"What else do you remember for certain?"

"Little things," he said. "I know she asked specifically for a gold band instead of a diamond. I remember buying it in South Carolina but I couldn't tell you whatever happened to it. Pieces of Ohio…two trips instead of just one." The old man started shaking his head. "Stupid little things, Sonny. I remember waking up on her couch after driving all night. She said 'Good morning, Sweetheart' and handed me a cup of black coffee. She had large calves."

Sonny snickered just a little at the obscurity of that particular image, a mistake he soon realized.

"You think this is funny? You think having some hole scooped into your brain is a cute little joke?" He leaned forward out of his chair as if he were going to leap out and attack the young man. "I've been chasing down parts of my own mind for SEVENTY SOME FUCKING YEARS!"

By this time, some of the orderlies had caught wind of

all the commotion. A couple of them made their way to Mr. B's chair.

"Wait, stop," Sonny said, "He's fine, just upset."

"You know the rules, Mr. B. Keep scaring everyone out here and we have to give you something to calm you down." One of the attendants was poised and ready with a syringe of sedatives.

"I promise," said Sonny, "we're just talking, ok? I'll bring him in soon and make sure he's not disturbing anyone."

The orderlies nodded and backed away into the building.

Mr. B didn't even take the time to make a racist joke or spit at them. He was too preoccupied.

"I'm sorry," Sonny said, "I'm just not used to you being so open and serious. I don't think this is funny…I'm always on your side Big Guy. OK?"

The old man sighed. "It's just hard, Sonny. It's really, really hard. When I think of the dinner with her folks, that's just kind of a blank picture. No emotion. But I remember that second trip…that fucking screen door. That one hurts every time."

"Maybe something happened in Youngstown that your mind just couldn't handle. That happens a lot with Post Traumatic Stress."

"Maybe. But I don't feel like that's quite it. I have a pretty strong mind and I know how to relax it to find answers. But nothing has worked for years, including hypnosis. Besides, it's strange, I know it wasn't long after this whole ordeal that I moved out to L.A. And the one time I saw Joey after I came back from the west coast, he talked a little about an Anna. I'm sure he didn't say much because he didn't want to hurt me…but all I could think was *Who the fuck was Anna?*"

"Why didn't you ask him?"

Mr. B laughed. "That's the thing, Sonny boy. I've wondered that for years now. Fact is, at that time, not a year or two after being engaged to this girl—I didn't remember that she existed."

"What? How could…"

"That's the mystery, kid. If I would have known to ask Joey then and there, problem solved. Maybe I wouldn't be the crotchety old fuck that sits here before you. Fact is, I didn't even know to ask. And now Joey is completely off my radar."

"There's got to be something more. Something else."

"Oh there's plenty of little snapshots lodged in this twisted mind of mine. And over the years I've placed them in little pockets of narrative to help make sense of it all. Like this letter…I remember getting it sometime after Christmas. I tell myself it's because I sent her a card on her birthday. December 29th sticks out because I still remember numbers and dates, but all I can recall from the actual letter is one stupid line about 'mending white picket fences' or some such garbage. It's just all so fuzzy."

"Have you tried reaching out to someone who might know something you've forgotten."

The old man looked tired. He leaned back in his chair and said,"It's been decades. You can believe me when I say I've tried *everything*. The only thing I know for certain is that after L.A. I didn't remember shit, and no one could seem to help me. Every few years a new piece seems to fall into place, but it's a puzzle I don't think I'll live to see completed." He took a deep breath. "Sonny, every time I try and remember that one summer, it's like more thoughts seem to disappear from my head instead of reappear. And I've been trying for a long time."

"But you said you've been trying to write it all down, right? That you've never really told anyone else the story? Maybe that's it, maybe if you just keep talking, maybe we can uncover it all together?"

The old man lowered his head. "Not right now," he said. "I feel a migraine coming on so…" His voice trailed off and he retreated into himself. "Let me rest and I'll, well I'll see you tomorrow. OK, Sonny?"

The man nodded and wheeled Mr. B back into his room. Their walk was solemn and their goodbyes simple. The old man found his way to the bed and a restful peace overcame him. Sleep washed over him like death.

ೞೞೞೞ

"Good morning, Mr. B!" Yet again, another day where John's shrill, overly cheery voice served as a nightmarish alarm clock. "How are we this bright sunshiny day?"

Disappointed to open his eyes, the old man said, "I don't know how *we* are, but *I* feel like shit…" He rubbed his eyes and sat there for a moment, John staring at him, almost as if he were expecting something.

"Well," he said, "what the fuck's for breakfast?"

ೞೞೞೞ

Chapter 10

Anna went to bed that evening still savoring her night out with Tom. He got along so well with her friends. He danced with her until last call, never losing interest, never looking for an excuse to leave. She could tell that it really made him happy to make her happy and, honestly, she had never felt more so.

The more she thought about the night they had shared, the more she combed through every single detail, the more she could clearly see his face, feel his palm on the small of her back, the heat of his breath on her neck until she finally succumbed and fell asleep.

Anna awoke, or thought she awoke, around 3 a.m. Her eyes were open, but she felt as if they were closed in the darkness of her bedroom. The image of her lover was above her. Not just his face, and not just some dreamscape, IT WAS TOM.

A kiss lighted on the base of her neck, something which she could measure against the softness of Tom's lips and the gentle strength of his jaw. From the site of the kiss, a haze of warm energy spread across her skin, blanketing her nerves, radiating like another body resting atop her own. This sensation was a slow one, almost imperceptible, but the next feeling was more abrupt, more forceful. Electricity crackled down her spine and sent a tingling to her extremities. Instead of fearing the foreign exchange, she embraced it, fed it.

She felt the presence of *something* else within her. What

began as a faint kiss, what transformed to a more noticeable bolt of ethereal bliss, quickly escalated to more concrete sensations. Anna's nipples stood erect, responding to the swirling mists encompassing them, teasing them with gentle caresses.

She remembered specific moments now, the impact of her body against his that first day on the beach, the night they both shared tears in the cover of dark, how it felt to hug her truelove after his long journey to see her.

And with every memory she studied, her physical responses increased. Her body arched towards the ceiling, and the passionate storm followed the curve of her body, inching lower to her navel, tickling the soft skin above her hips.

She heard the melodies of Tom's song, heard him sing for her and her alone in a language only spoken between their hearts.

The rose he handed her at the beach, its petals tickled Anna's inner thighs, its thorns scratched down her back. Everything was throbbing now, every muscle every tissue, every fiber of her being. Every vibration was an explosion within her, her breathing shallow, her skin ablaze, it was too much.

And then the world vanished into a single sound.

"I love you Anna. Will you marry me?"

"Yes, of course I will."

ჱჱჱჱ

The universe flooded back all at once and Anna felt the weight of shadows strangling the life from her, pressing her to the mattress with a strength she couldn't fathom. She moaned or thought she moaned, screamed or wanted to scream from the terrible, delightful dread upon her, within her, without her, in the place where her spirit should reside—

An eruption of insight, an explosion of realization. For the briefest of moments she saw the corporeal world as a well-maintained illusion, a lie we tell each other.

But only for the *briefest* of moments.

Then the ultraviolet hue of metaphysics retreated, and Anna gasped in the familiarity of her bedroom. Her eyes shot open, though she had thought they were open the whole time. She trembled, limp with ecstasy.

Was it a dream? It had all felt so real. Had Tom not been right here, in the grasp of her inviting body? Panting, confused, and exhausted, Anna collapsed into the soaking wet sheets and drowned into the oblivion of dreamless, perfect, sleep.

Cश्Cश्Cश्Cश्

The next morning, Anna woke up feeling like a new person. She tip-toed through the den where Tom was still sleeping and poured a cup of coffee. Even though it was half-empty already from her father filling his thermos for work, the pot was still hot enough to not need reheating. Anna cradled the steaming mug and walked back into the living room. She stood above the couch and watched Tom for a moment. His body was all twisted up in a mess of blankets, one foot propped up on the arm of the couch and one hand sprawled out onto the coffee table. Anna couldn't help but giggle at how loudly he snored.

"Good morning, Sweetheart," she said as gently as she could.

He rolled halfway over and kept snoring.

Anna nudged him a little and sat down by his feet. "Sleep well?"

Tom opened one eye and looked up at her, studying her face, seemingly unsure of exactly where he was. He groaned. "Sure did." Wiping his face with both hands, he repositioned so Anna had enough room to sit comfortably. "How 'bout you?"

Anna blushed a little. "It was the best ever."

Much too early for this to arouse any sort of question, Tom asked, "So, what's up for today?"

Smiling still, Anna said, "I have to go to work in a few minutes, but Joey will stop by shortly. He's going to pick you up and show you the town."

Tom grumbled something about how the whole tour might take less than five minutes and Anna just laughed. As fun as it would be to tease him this early in the morning, she didn't have time to poke the bear. It was almost quarter till.

"I'll be home around 4:30, ok?" She leaned over to put the coffee mug nearer to his reach and kiss him on the forehead. "I'll see you then."

ೞೞೞೞ

Anna didn't even notice the unusual amount of traffic on her way to Swanson's that morning. All she could think about was this unfaltering feeling of serenity and happiness. Since her strange experience the night before, her body felt more like a home instead of a prison and, for once, she felt at ease about her place in the world.

For once, she knew everything was going to be all right.

Her morning was pretty typical: she arrived about three minutes early, spent a few hours folding clothes and hanging dresses until customers started coming in. Then she worked a register until about lunch. Normally her feet hurt around noon and couldn't wait to sit down for a break, but today, it felt like she'd been gliding on air all day. She couldn't stop thinking about coming home to find Tom there, and this thought kept her fresh and alive. At one point in the afternoon, she found herself staring at the clock, wondering if Tom and Joey were having a good time. Maybe Tom would want to stop by and surprise her.

"Miss Sopoulos." A voice cut through her reverie.

Anna was startled and nearly jumped into a nearby mannequin. "What? Oh, sorry. Yes, Mr. Peterson?"

"I just got word that they want to see you upstairs."

"Upstairs, Sir?"

"Yes, Miss Sopoulos, that's what I said. Mr. Figerino wants you in his office right now."

"Mr. Figerino?" Anna was curious what the store manager could want with her. She had never even met the man. "Do you suppose I'm in some kind of trouble, Mr. Peterson?"

Having already delivered his message and gone about his business, her supervisor turned back with a furrowed brow. "If you aren't already, you certainly will be if you choose to keep him waiting. Get a move on, Miss Sopoulos."

Anna was confused, but not necessarily nervous. As she pushed the button for the elevator, she found herself thinking positively. Maybe this was the promotion she had been working towards. After all, she had never had a complaint lodged against her and next month would mark her second year at the store.

When the elevator door opened it revealed a very darkskinned man in a red velvet vest. Having never ridden the elevator, she was a bit taken aback.

"Afternoon Ma'am," said the attendant. He could sense her momentary apprehension. "Don't worry, Miss, I've been here long enough to know not to bite, step right in."

Anna smiled and said, "Sorry, I'm just a little jumpy today I guess."

"Quite all right Miss. Where to?"

"Mr. Figerino's office," she said.

"Oh," the attendant said in a higher pitch. He smiled. "Well I suppose I'd be a bit jumpy myself." He closed the rolling cage and pressed the button for the fifth floor. "If it were my first time meeting with the boss man."

Anna laughed. "And how do you know I've not met him

before?"

The attendant grinned. "I been here every day for the last seven years ma'am. Never a sick day once. And in all that time, I ain't never seen your face in this elevator." He stuck out a hand. "My name is Phillip."

"Anna," she said in return.

"It's quite a pleasure, Miss Anna."

She took a deep breath before the ride ended. "Do you have any advice? I mean, have you met him?"

"Yes to both," Phillip said. "Mr. Figerino is a man who doesn't like to hear the word 'no'. Usually he's not allowed to say it himself if you catch my drift." Phillip winked.

The elevator dinged and stopped at the top. Phillip pulled back the rolling bars and gestured with his hand that it was safe for Anna to exit.

"Thank you," she said. "And it was nice to meet you, Phillip."

He laughed. "Smile and speak that sweetly to Mr. F and you'll be just fine, Ma'am. His door is the last one on the left."

Anna turned and walked down the hallway full of cubicles and ringing phones. Secretaries all repeated, "Thank you for calling Swanson's Department Store, please hold," and the occasional uproar of men laughing from hidden rooms rolled through the floor. As she approached the end of the hallway, a secretary asked Anna, "Can I help you, Miss?"

"Yes, I'm here to see Mr. Figerino."

"Anna Sopoulos?"

"Yes, ma'am."

The secretary pressed a buzzer. "Miss Sopoulos to see you, sir."

A crackling static answered back. "Send her in."

The secretary pointed to the door over her shoulder and motioned for Anna to show herself in.

Anna couldn't get over how different it felt to be on this

floor compared to the base level department store. Her excitement had reached a peak until she opened the door and saw two familiar faces in place of one new one. "Papa?" she said with audible disappointment. "What are you doing—" but before she could finish, another familiar face emerged from the corner of the room. "William?"

Mr. Sopoulos quietly stepped behind his daughter to shut the door. "Hello, sweetheart," he said softly. "Here, have a seat. This is Mr. Figerino," he said pointing to the older man across the desk.

Anna was too shocked to even consider shaking her boss's hand. She fell into her seat, trembling at the thought of what these three men might have in common.

Mr. Figerino grumbled and nodded towards her.

Too petrified to respond, Anna just sat deep in her chair, motionless.

"Anna," Mr. Sopoulos began softly, "I had hoped that you wouldn't allow this to come so far, but here we are."

All Anna could do was speak her worry through trembling eyes. Was this really her father in her boss's office? Why was William smirking in the corner?

"I tried to warn you in Atlantic Beach," he continued, "I tried to let you know that this was not the way things will go for you in this world."

"Papa—" Anna finally felt words escape from her lips...a desperate whisper to ward off the approaching evil.

"Let's cut to the chase, shall we Mr. Sopoulos?" Mr. Figerino leaned forward in his chair, visibly annoyed by the whole ordeal. "It has come to my attention, Miss Sopoulos, that you are currently involved with a gentleman from North Carolina. Is this correct?"

After a confused pause Anna said, "Tom? This is about Tom?"

"Ah yes, that's right, Tom. Well, you see, Miss Sopoulos, this little tryst of yours has gone on long enough and must come to an end. Simple as that. It's a matter of business, you see?"

Anna couldn't believe what she was hearing. "Papa, how can you let this man say these things to me? Who I choose to date is a discussion for family, not my boss."

"Please show Mr. Figerino respect and speak to him when he addresses you."

"It's all right," Mr. Figerino said, "Your daughter is naïve. She doesn't understand that we are her family here and family knows best. Now, you will end things with this outsider and apologize to Mr. Bakalar here."

Finally Anna felt more furious than nervous. "Apologize? To that monster?"

"Lower your voice Miss Sopoulos! This is an office not a circus. The fact is, William Bakalar is a good man. He is someone that your father and I and others in the family can approve of. Your marriage to him will ensure the strength of this community and it will further our interests—simple as that."

"I…I don't understand."

With a sigh, Mr. Figerino said, "What's not to understand, young lady? Were you not to marry this man? Do you not already have a license for marriage?" The next few remarks were punctuated by the thud of his meaty palm on the desk. "You will honor your commitment to this family, you will marry William and that's that!"

Standing from her chair, no longer paralyzed by fear, Anna shouted, "And what if I refuse?"

From the shadows, William Bakalar broke his silence. "Hard to marry a dead man."

"What is that supposed to mean?" Glaring at William was like staring into the eyes of a snake. She turned to her father. His face resounded with shame.

"Anna, my darling…sometimes accidents happen. You should listen to your boss and trust me it's for the best." His head was lowered and his voice was calm.

"Papa, are you suggesting?"

The look in his eyes confirmed her suspicions.

When she took a breath, Anna could taste death on her tongue. The stale odor, the image of Tom in a ditch, it all came together at once and she fell to her knees. "Please," she begged no one in particular, "You can't hurt him. Please."

Mr. Figerino took this opportunity to say his final piece. "We can do anything we wish, Miss Sopoulos. The sooner you realize this, the better." He stood from the desk chair and looked to Anna's father.

He knelt down next to his daughter and spoke softly. "What happens next is entirely up to you. If you truly do love this man, you know what must be done."

"I'll…I'll call the police," she said to him in desperation. "Whatever they're doing to you Papa, we can fix it."

"No," he said in a gentle whisper. "No, we can't." His hands on her shoulders and his forehead pressed against hers. "This is how our life is lived. Everyone here, from the police station all the way down to the lowly steel mill workers like myself, we all know it. And it's time that you know it too." He rose to his feet and offered Anna a hand. "Now speak no more and do what is expected of you—like we all must."

The room became punctuated with the sound of her tears, but she felt her heart dim like a fading candle. The life and passion within her faded out, the love drained from her.

She could barely hear Mr. Figerino's voice from the depths of her own fog when he told William "Go with her and make sure she ends it. If she doesn't, you do."

Anna didn't feel herself walk down the narrow hallway, didn't see or hear the friendly elevator operator, didn't remember driving back home from work. The only thing she saw was Tom when he stepped out of Joey's car. The only thing she felt was the barrel of William's gun pressed into the small of her back.

Her father's words rang in her ears.

If you truly do love this man…

She counted his footsteps as he approached the screen door. Every bend of his knee, every bounce in his gait, every muscle twist in his face when their eyes met for what would have to be the last time.

You know what must be done.

"Hi," Tom said. "Aren't you going to let me in?"

The screen door felt like a window between two dimensions. Anna and Tom could see each other, they could hear one another, but certain realties would never translate. They were within the reach of a whisper, but at the same time, light years away.

"Tom," she spoke through the door, "I've…I've been thinking a lot today about you and me, and I—"

"Anna? Let me in so we can talk about—"

"No! No…I'm sorry Tom," she started to tear up but quickly cleared her throat.

William's gun dug deeper into her spine.

"What's wrong?" Tom said.

All she wanted to do was scream, to touch him, to rupture the divide between their two lives and allow love to collapse the space-time continuum, to implode in a singular quantum of a macabre embrace.

Instead, she chose to save the life of the man she loved.

"I've been thinking a lot today about you and me," she said, "and I just don't think we can make it."

Tom recoiled in shock. "Not make it? What are you talking about? This morning you were so in love and now you're…what? Trying to break it off? Why? This just doesn't make any sense!"

"Please don't be mad," Anna said, choking back her urge to scream. "It's for the best."

"No…it's that Billy Baklava or whatever his name is, isn't

it? Did he come around and convince you not to marry me? Is that what this is? Please, Anna, just let me in."

Anna felt the gun begin to slide. Slowly it came away from her body, slowly William threatened to make good on his assigned task. She had to get Tom out of there fast.

"His name is William Bakalar and—" she spoke slowly and deliberately, "He is a very important man with a good job."

"A good job. Oh, ok, I get it." His hand was on the door, and then he let it go. "Fine," said stepping down the stairs, "See ya!"

She watched him stomp away, watched him shove Joey and shout in the streets. But when she watched him get in the van, she heard the squealing of his tires harmonize with her own wild shrieks. Instinctually, she began to run to him, to burst through the screen which divided them, to rebuke any and all ties she had to her own world—but a sinister force grabbed her by the hair and pulled her back into the house, slamming the front door behind her. Any hope or vision of a future in another world was eradicated, drowned in the darkness of her parents home, suffocated by the un-wavering stranglehold of her future husband—William.

Anna ran to her room and locked the door behind her, spiraling down to her bed and nearly fainting from the weight of her own grief. But before she escaped into the abyss of her dreams, the only thought resounding in her head was— *will I ever see Tom again?*

CdCdCdCd

Chapter 11

What does heartbreak look like? What does it feel like?
For Tom, heartbreak was everything beautiful. It felt like the
sun was beaming down but never quite touched his skin.
He was back in Atlantic Beach now, back in a routine that
seemed familiar. Play a show, meet a pretty girl, walk on the
beach, take her back to his room.

Rinse and repeat.

Night after night it was the same thing. But every beautiful thing, the ocean, the sands, the women…they all left him
emptier than when he arrived. The luster of this place was
killing him, taking away his love a little at a time. He knew he
had to escape, leave this place behind him before he became
yet another sad fixture at the beach tavern with a burnt out,
broken heart story.

What does heartbreak look like? What does it feel like?
For Anna, heartbreak looked like beady eyes, dark hair, olive
skin—her devastation was made manifest in William Bakalar. What it felt like…well, for Anna, heartbreak could feel
like the simplest touch of a hand upon her cheek, or it could
feel like the tightest grip around her wrist. Either way, sadness was the touch of another, the touch of someone who
didn't belong beside her.

In the days after Tom left, she felt herself a shadow—
only existing because of someone else's ability to stand in
the sun. Perhaps she was trapped between one world and
another, but she had to let all hope of escape drain from her

in order to keep her love alive, to keep from becoming yet another hollow Greek mother, parroting the sentiments of her betters for no greater purpose than self-preservation.

It was the winter of '75, the winter when Tom decided to head west, the direction of death. He didn't exactly want to die, but he sure as hell was ready to put an end to the life that plagued him. When an old high school friend approached him with her plan of driving to California, Tom saw this as providence. This was surely his shot to put all this tragedy behind him and move on with a new life. This was his chance to escape the cycle of beautiful sunrises and sunsets sparkling over all the coastal beauty he had called home.

The decision, like most of them that year, wasn't one that Tom put a lot of time into. Joy showed up in Atlantic Beach one week because, well, because Joy is the type of gal who just shows up when you least expect. Usually when you least need her, too, but, that's a different story.

After the show that night and a couple drinks, she said, "I'm going out to L.A. and I need a ride. What do you say? Split the trip?"

Tom finished his quart of Schlitz and burped out a "sure."

And that was it. A complete life 180…3,000 miles…essentially a transformation of worlds from the time it took that last bit of warm backwash to travel from his mouth to his gut.

In Tom's mind, though, there really wasn't much to think about. The truth is, with his parents dying a few years before, he didn't have anyone to truly love. He didn't have anyone to take care of except for himself. Sure, there were people on the line who he owed money to, owed time to…but fuck 'em.

It only took a couple of days for Tom to burn the necessary bridges, gather up his belongings and as much cash as he could get his hands on, then the two were off on the open road.

"I'm so happy you said yes to coming out with me, Marcus. You're really going to love the west coast. Everything is so much more relaxed. The people are just…more free or something, you know? They really get it."

Tom glanced over and just nodded. They got an early start and he was content just sipping his coffee, cruising toward I-20 and trying his best to pretend to care at all to what Joy had to say.

"Look Joy, I changed my name to Tom a few years ago as a stage name and that is the name I use now, so if you don't mind, please get used to calling me Tom."

"Ok, Marcus. I mean *Tom.*"

"I was watching Johnny Carson the other night and he had Capote on…have you read him?"

Tom could barely shake his head before Joy kept on prattling.

"Oh you just have to read *Breakfast at Tiffany's*, Marcus… Tom, I mean, you'd really love it. But Capote was talking about L.A. and even though he's always just such a sass—he was spot on. Did you catch it?"

"Nope, I don't watch television much unless it's early morning."

"Oh, you're such a dope. Still sobering up to cartoons?" She took a short break from talking as she munched on her breakfast of M&M's and Vienna sausages. Joy always hunched over her food in a weird way…kind of like a trash bird eating roadkill. Every bite was prefaced by her flipping her wiry brown hair back and adjusting her Bonnie and Clyde sunglasses.

"I don't know how you can stomach that shit," Tom would always say. But, the truth is, Tom could tell the kinds of circles Joy ran in and he was pretty confident she was used to putting much worse in her mouth on any given Sunday.

"Don't judge, don't judge. Very bad karma, Tom, you know that. When I was working at Capitol Records the last time I was out west, we always kept karma jars at the desk. People put little notes and well wishes and just nice things. Lots of M&M's too, so I guess that's where I got addicted."

She kept talking about all the jobs and all the things she'd done the last time she was in L.A. How she had her apartment all set up and how Tom was going to love their neighborhood so much more than the Carolinas. Blah blah blah, William Morrison agency, blah blah blah, Peterson Publishing…everything boiled down to how she was eventually going to be famous and, the supposition was that she would do the same for Tom and his career.

It felt like hours before Joy actually said something that Tom cared to hear—"Mind if I drive for a bit?"

"Sure," Tom said, "but we need to get some gas first." They had made it to Shreveport and only filled up once after leaving. When Tom pulled up to the pump, he asked Joy for some cash.

A long sigh preceded a long search of her purse. "This is all I have left," she said, extending a five dollar bill.

Tom didn't quite understand. The words didn't seem to match up with anything else she had told him. "What do you mean? I thought we were splitting the trip? We're barely a third of the way there!"

"Well, Tom, this is all the cash I have left. I mean, I've got my dad's credit card, but, that's just for emergencies."

Tom felt a vein in his forehead nearly explode. "Last time I checked, gas is an emergency!"

"Hey, don't yell at me, we'll get there just fine. Quit worrying so much!"

Tom slammed the car door behind him after throwing the keys at her. He filled up the tank and did as he was instructed; he quit worrying. Joy took the wheel and drove like a bat out of hell through Texas, burning nearly every last bill Tom had to his name. At least he got something valuable for his money—peace and quiet. After their little tiff at the gas station, Joy thought she was giving Tom the silent treatment. Tom thought he was getting a gift from the gods.

While he had some time to think, he pulled out a letter he'd gotten from Anna a while back. It was a reply from a birthday card he'd sent. It was strange, even as memories of her started to fade, as his emotions for her began to dull and even disappear into numbness, he still remembered dates and numbers so very clearly. December 29th, that was her birthday. Reading over the letter, he wasn't even really sure why he'd kept it in the first place.

Dear Tom,
Thanks so much for the birthday wishes—I'm surprised you re-membered, especially after I had to break it off with you. I guess I just need a little white picket fence in my life. Know that you will always be in my thoughts and prayers and that I will always love you.
Anna

What was it that he kept clinging too? What was it that lodged in him like some sort of shrapnel that was too risky to be removed? The sentiment that she would "always love him"? Was that worth holding on to so much pain? And what did that even mean? If you love someone, and will always love them, how can you leave them in a state of con-stant agony?

The easiest answer was that she was a liar, that the letter was just a nicety, something to placate him, something to make herself feel better…

C3C3C3C3

Somewhere on the 900 mile stretch from Louisiana to New Mexico, Tom opened the car window. And somewhere on that 900 miles stretch of highway, he let the 80 mile per hour winds rip the scented stationary from his hand, tearing away one of his last connections to Anna and tossing it to the gale of fate.

The easiest answer was to forget the way she spoke in a language half a generation older than he did, to put the image of her curling cursive script out of his mind, to keep his eyes heading west instead of in the sideview mirror to watch the flimsy piece of paper tumble in the breeze.

But the easiest answer isn't always the right answer—a new life isn't always different than running away.

But away he went.

 CBCBCBCB

CHAPTER 12

When Tom and Joy finally arrived in Los Angeles, they only had ten dollars between them. Of course, "between them" actually meant that Tom was the only one with money. He'd had at least 2,000 miles of enough western roads to come to terms with this little oversight however, and wasn't as perturbed as one might think. Actually, Tom was too exhausted to care much about anything.

"I'll just be happy to sleep in a real bed tonight," he told Joy as they were stuck in traffic outside the city.

"Yep, same here, Tommy Boy. All we gotta do is head to my complex and talk to the super about getting another room."

Tom felt any bit of energy he had left fade fast from his body. He was almost too afraid to ask but, ask he must. "What do you mean *another* room? I thought your apartment was all set up? That's what you said, Joy—"

"Well, yeah, I mean, I moved out of the one room but the guy knows me so it shouldn't be a problem to just rent a different room in the same complex. Have some faith, Tom, things work differently out here. People just—"

"They *just get it,* yeah, I know Joy. I think I've heard that somewhere before." The old van didn't do but so well with all the highway driving the two of them had put it through, but it especially didn't do well sitting in gridlock traffic. All the pressure and frustrations Tom had been bottling up for the past three days finally bubbled up to the surface. "Come

on!" he shouted. One, two, three, four violent fists crashed
into the steering wheel as he rocked back and forth in his
seat.

"Chill out, man!" Joy recoiled and pushed her sunglasses
up on her forehead. "This is L.A. traffic no matter how you
slice it. This is just something you get used to." She laughed
a little to herself. "You gotta learn to calm it down or you'll
never survive here."

Tom usually considered himself a level-headed individual
but, as he saw it, being stuck in a small space with someone
like Joy for an extended period was a danger to himself and
others.

As expected, when the two of them finally made it to her
old apartment complex, the super looked at Joy like she was
crazy. It's true she did stay there before, but it was also true
that he wanted a new security deposit and a check for the
first month's rent. Seeing as how neither Tom nor Joy had
access to money like that, they were forced to crash at one
of her ex-lover's apartments. Joy introduced him as Jim or
John or Jonas but, all Tom could see was a dead-on imper-
sonation of Wolfman Jack.

The first night they were in the new city, the Wolfman
took Tom and Joy out to eat at Cafe Figaro on Melrose Avenue. As she was a *wanna* be, Joy couldn't help but introduce
Tom to everyone she met as an up-and-coming *somebody*. Of
course, to no surprise of Tom's, no one out west seemed to
give a rat's ass.

After dinner and a few drinks, Joy and her werewolf barely even pretended to care that Tom was sleeping on the floor
outside of the bedroom with no door on it. For three nights,
Tom didn't sleep a wink. For three nights, Tom could pre-
dict with dead accuracy when Joy would fake an orgasm and
when Wolfman Jack would growl out a hot load so gruffly
that he might as well have been taking a shit.

Needless to say, Tom was eternally grateful when the

man—beast decided to "lend" Joy the money they needed for their own place.

After a rough start in a new part of the world, Tom made up his mind to not be dependent on Joy for any kind of support moving forward. He hit the streets looking for prospects in any field he could think of. But every musician he met wanted to *jam* instead of book an appointment, every producer he spoke to wanted to *do lunch* instead of set up an audition, every time he went to the shopping mall people rode up the escalator for God's sake!

Eventually Tom found himself with an inventory job at a local music store. Money was money anyway. Not to mention, it kept him out of the house during the day to avoid interrupting any of Joy's "cummings and goings" as he referred to them.

When he wasn't wasting away behind a desk counting up how many saxophone reeds needed ordering for the next shipment, Tom was wasting away in the driver's seat of his van wondering what on Earth possessed him to move away to Zombie Land. Every single day was waiting in line, sitting still, standing still, being herded from one cattle call to the next. And the front of every single line was just another fucking vampire ready to suck the life from his soul…

But he wasn't without friends or acquaintances. Tom could still play a show at a bar (much smaller scale than he was used to of course) and meet people to talk to. But something seemed so hollow about everyone he met. Every guy that talked shop with him spoke like a pull-string doll, every girl laughed at the same pitch and flipped their hair at the same angle.

One such night, Tom brought a girl back to the apartment. It's not that he forgot her name, he just never even bothered to ask it. Did he like her? See anything interesting about her personality? Was he even attracted to her really? No, no, and no. In fact, one of the biggest reasons to bring dates home was some passive aggressive attempt to get back at Joy. He always tried to time his late night visitors with the opening monologue of the *Tonight Show* to really piss her off.

But this one was a little different than the rest…different, but somehow the exact same. In the throes of fake passion and moaning, Tom was thrusting and approaching his climax.

"Oh God, oh shit," she'd say over and over. "Oh God, oh shit."

Tom closed his eyes and tried to tune out her metallic voice.

"Oh God, oh shit…Oh God, oh shit." Over and over and over…Just when Tom had blocked her out almost entirely, she shouted, "Please! Please tell me you love me, even if you don't mean it!"

Tom tried his best to ignore her, but she sank her nails into his back.

"Say it! Say you love me!"

And, try as he might, he couldn't pretend to care any longer. Rolling over and kicking the covers off himself he just let out some sort of animalistic groan.

"What's the matter," she started to say, "don't you think I'm—"

"Stop," Tom raised his voice, "Just don't, ok?" He stood up and buttoned his jeans. Tossing her a bundled up bra and blouse he said, "Just get the fuck out of here, huh?"

Of course a string of shouted insults followed and, of course, an angry Joy stormed into the room threatening to kill them both if they didn't keep it down.

That was just how it was for about three months. Then Joy got a call about her mom dying of cancer. She split— Tom guessed dear old Dad sent her a plane ticket. No surprise that somehow he got stuck with the whole apartment for the rest of the lease and didn't hear from Joy after that. What was a bit of a surprise, however, is when a mutual friend called from back east to say that Joy was awaiting trial.

"Bobby, what the hell are you talking about?" Tom was hiding in the storage room at work using their long distance minutes.

"Yeah, buddy, no shit, she's headed for the slammer big time!"

"What are you talking about?"

"I'm talking about how Joy was found by the cops in her dad's house with a hammer in her hand, blood all over her clothes, and bits of brain and skull stuck in her hair. Oh yeah, and Herbert's head was bashed in."

Tom felt his knees buckle and he sat down on a palette. "Herbert, as in, her *dad Herbert?*"

"The one and only. He was a fucking mess face down in his birthday cake. Oh yeah, it was his birthday, man! And get this, get this, you wanna hear something sick?"

Tom couldn't even find the words.

"Police found burns on his face…you know what that means? Fucking bitch didn't even let him blow out the candles first!"

This was the moment when Tom knew that something was deeply, deeply wrong with him. Even though he had grown up with Joy, been in and out of Herbert's house, heard him talk to his dad at many a VFW meeting—even though Tom had spent every day for the past few months with a murderer, his first thought was *Well, I guess she got what she wanted. She's famous now.*

More alarmingly, the news didn't seem to resonate in any meaningful way. It's almost as if Tom had developed a layer of plastic around his skin and cardboard around his heart. What could he do but go back to work?

It was still about another month, but Tom finally had a real meeting with a real talent manager from Paramount. The guy, Lucas Freely, seemed to be a straight shooter. The only thing peculiar about him was the accuracy with which people who knew him described his appearance. Ask ten people how to pick Lucas out of a crowded room and nine of them will say, "He's the one that looks like a bowling ball sitting on a sack of shit."

Regardless, he liked Tom's voice and presented him with an opportunity to work with his group as they toured Canada. The goal was to break in the new songs up there and tighten up their material before heading to Vegas in about half a year.

"How much," Tom finally said, cutting him off.

"Five grand," Lucas said flatly.

"Hell," Tom snorted, half standing from his chair, "I made three times that back in Carolina. I don't think—"

"A month," Lucas continued. "Plus room and transportation."

Tom didn't so much sit back down as he fell into his seat. "Holy shit," he said, "Where do I sign?"

To put it in perspective, most folks were lucky to pull in a hundred a week. Tom's dad owned his own contracting business and, even in its heyday, only brought in about one-fifty.

"Look, I think you're talented, kid, don't get me wrong. But this tour in Canada isn't a cakewalk. It's almost exclusively one-nighters with lot's of road travel in between. If you're going to sign on for this I need you in top condition, Ok?"

"You got it, I'll be rehearsing non-stop."

"Not just that, I need you working out, getting in shape. You got a gym around here?"

Tom hesitated for a minute. "Well, I mean, I run a good amount."

"Cardio won't cut it, kid. You need strength. Ever do any martial arts?"

"Yeah, as a matter of fact, I earned my black belt in Tae Kwon Do down in Carolina."

"Perfect, that's perfect," Lucas said as he picked up the

phone. "I've got a guy you need to meet then, good friend of mine."

And after a quick phone call, Tom found himself with instructions to go down to Santa Monica the next day to meet with the infamous Master Bennie Hanna.

ଔଔଔଔ

CHAPTER 13

Walking through the doors of the dojang, Tom bowed to the flags on the wall and the instructors leading class. They noticed him, but did not bow in return. The studio was a large open space covered mostly in gymnast mats. Around the perimeter were a few folding chairs where Tom took a seat to observe. The scene was something out of an old kung fu flick—a bunch of guys in uniform standing stiff as boards responding to the militaristic barking of the class instructor. He was a young, stern looking Asian man with a larger frame than you normally see in martial arts. This guy looked to be a couple hundred pounds of solid muscle. Every time he would shout, the entire group of students would punch. Shout, punch. Over and over and over again. God knows how long they had been doing it.

Before the class was over, a lanky white instructor with a long pony-tail approached Tom. "Hi," he said in an overly gentle voice, "Are you here to inquire about classes?"

Tom stood up and bowed. "Yes sir," he said, "My manager sent me to meet with Master Bennie Hana. I was just waiting for him to finish his class."

The tall instructor paused for a moment and his eyes widened. He looked behind him at the class and then looked back to Tom. "Oh," he said, "that's not Master Bennie. Sa Bum Nim is in the office waiting for you. Come on, I'll escort you."

The two of them walked around the mats toward the

back of the studio. Tom couldn't help but notice the contrast between the two instructors. The bulky one leading class looked like his veins were going to rip through his skin at any moment and the tall one looked like he glided through the air.

"I do apologize," the tall one said, whipping around his pony tail, "I was quite rude in not introducing myself." He extended a hand. "My name is Stephen."

"Tom," he said with a firm shake.

"It's a pleasure to have you with us, Tom. Step right in here and Master Bennie will discuss our classes with you."

Tom reached for the doorknob to the little office door, "Yeah, thanks," he said.

Before he could even walk in all the way he heard unintelligible shouting. "What? They no teach you knock where you from?"

Tom saw a tiny Korean man sitting behind a desk with his face only inches away from a little black and white TV with giant aluminum-foil-wrapped antennae sticking out. "I'm sorry," Tom said closing the door behind him. He bowed and started to introduce himself, but was interrupted.

"What you bow for? Show me bald spot? What you want?"

"Uhh…I was sent here by my manager to train with you?"

"Yeah?" Master Bennie smacked his little TV to turn it off. "Well Rucas know how to knock on door. You know if Fred going to get back into Water Buffaro Crub? Because I don't!"

"Excuse me?"

"Fred Frinstone! How can I teach if you don't even know Fred Frinstone?"

"I do know Fred Frin—I mean, I know who Fred Flinstone is…sorry for interrupting, but I just want to know how much it is to start taking classes."

Master Bennie scooted his chair back and stood up fast

to peer over the desk. "Too expensive for you! You take old Reebok shoes out of here."

"I have the money," Tom said. "Look, I'm only here because Lucas told me to come, Ok? I don't even need classes—just a place to work out."

Master Bennie walked around the desk now to get a closer look. "Oh, what? You know everything? You train before?"

Tom nodded. "I have my black belt."

"And I have brown belt because brack pants are at dry creaners!" Master Bennie laughed so hard at his own joke that he started coughing. He wiped his eye and walked over to a little teapot sitting in the corner to pour a cup. "You good fighter? You spar?"

"I used to compete back east pretty regularly."

Master Bennie took a sip of his tea. "I no ask how many times you get knocked out by chumps. I ask if you good?"

Tom stood up. "Look, no disrespect, but I just want to work out, Ok? Are you going to let me or not?"

Master Bennie raised his eyebrows. "Hmmm…you show me."

"Show you?"

"You go do class. Go, go, go!"

"But I—"

"Take off shoes, go do class. Go, go, go!"

So Tom did as he was told and joined the class in progress. This time when he bowed to the instructor, he bowed back. After that, Tom fell into sync with the other students. He punched when they punched, did push-ups when they did, ran suicides when they did. He even remembered his forms from his training and could practice those with the group when instructed. He was sweating and breathing hard, but everything seemed to be coming back to him. After awhile, Master Bennie crept into the studio to observe. He watched as Tom did everything asked of him, performed every kick with relative accuracy for having not trained in some time, and succeeded when many of the other students began to tire.

When the class came to an end, the instructor bowed to Master Bennie who now assumed the mantle. At once, the students spoke with one voice and moved with one body. "Charyuht," they shouted and stiffened to attention. "Sa Bum Nim kyung nae!" Everyone bowed.

"Shiuh," Master Bennie growled. "We spar now, no contact. Use good control."

Instinctively, everyone paired up and spread out to spar. To be sure, fighting was something Tom was used to and, really, quite skilled at. However, the idea of "no contact" sparring was something that he thought to be kind of useless.

Master Bennie made his way around the mats critiquing or praising pairs as they sparred. Tom looked ahead at a very intense little man who was probably under a hundred pounds. Every time they faced off, Tom would lead with a few roundhouse kicks at about half speed and, when he closed the distance, go for a back fist jab. However, every single time, the little man would scoot around and put a stiff side kick about six inches from Tom's ribs. Every time he did this he would *kihap* loudly and then back away. Tom must have rolled his eyes because before he knew it, Master Bennie was yelling at him.

"This no good for you, Tom? If you think waste of time you leave now!"

Tom gritted his teeth. "Yes, master."

The scene continued and Tom felt himself become frustrated. After a sigh, Master Bennie returned.

"What's matter now, Tom? You think you can beat opponent because you bigger?"

Tom couldn't restrain himself anymore. "Yes, master, I do. No contact sparring proves nothing."

Everyone in the studio stopped what they were doing. The room fell quiet.

"I see," Master Bennie said softly. After a moment he shouted to the class to have a seat. "Master Kim," he said in the direction of the surly instructor, "you spar with Tom. Full contact."

The bulky man stood up and cracked his knuckles like some kind of villain. He assumed a stance and roared out a kihap that shook the walls. Tom put his guards up and centered himself. Instead of yelling, he just shook his head, nearly laughing at how red his opponent was turning.

"Seijak!" Master Bennie shouted.

As soon as the words left his mouth, Master Kim leapt forward with a skipping side kick that hit Tom like a freight train in the gut, knocking him down to the mat.

"Point!" Master Bennie shouted and raised his hand.

Tom stood up slowly and took a deep breath. This guy was as strong as he looked. When Master Bennie shouted again, the instructor jumped forward once more in the same way. This time Tom was ready with a counter. As the kick came in, Tom spun around clockwise and landed a heavy spinning back fist on his opponent's jaw.

"Point!" Shouted Master Bennie.

Tom relaxed and began to bow, assuming that blow was enough to knock out his opponent. But as he turned around, he saw Master Kim charging forward, hardly phased. Tom smiled and fell into a rhythm of trading blows, trying to counter, and eventually assuming the role of the aggressor. The longer the match went, the more confident he felt, the more he felt like his old competitive self. Tom threw a tricky roundhouse kick towards his opponent's head and, when he dodged, Tom whipped his leg back in mid-air to land with a hook kick to the side of his face. For once, this seemed to stun the bulky instructor. Here Tom rallied—jumping into the air he threw a lightning fast crescent kick to back up Master Kim. As soon as he landed Tom leapt forward with a second with the same result. When Master Kim had readied to counter the third, Tom spun around with the full torque of his body to deliver a devastating sweep to the back of Master Kim's calves, knocking him off his feet and sending him crashing down to the mats. In one fluid motion, Tom shot across the floor and mounted his opponent to deliver the final strike to the face.

"Gomahn!" Master Bennie shouted.

The room returned to him, and Tom looked down at a bloody man beneath him. Tom's grip was tight around the instructor's collar and his fist was stained with red.

"Enough," Master Bennie said.

Tom stood up and bowed, panting like a wild animal.

Master Bennie wore a stern frown on his face. "You leave now."

Flabbergasted, Tom said, "but I just won. I thought that's what you wanted to see?"

"I saw plenty. Now go. You no train here." Master Bennie turned his back on Tom and walked toward the back office.

"Hey," he shouted, "Hey, just wait a minute! What's going on here? You don't want me here because I'm too rough on your guys?"

Master Bennie disappeared into the office, saying nothing.

"Fine," Tom said as he wiped the sweat from his face. "It's not like you chuckleheads could teach me anything anyway." He laughed and started to walk off the mat when Master Bennie returned with his teacup in hand.

"Charyuht!" He shouted to the class. The students all lined up and stood at attention. When they all bowed out, Master Bennie said, "Everyone please wait outside before next class. Tom, you come here."

Tom almost had his shoes back on at this point, but he did as he was told. As he came back onto the mat the other students all filed out silently and closed the doors behind them. "What is it? I'm leaving, Ok?"

Master Bennie took a sip of his tea. "You think too hard with fists and feet. No use heart or brain."

"Uh-huh, yeah thanks for that. I'm going now, nice meeting you and this freak-show you call a school."

"You like fight so much, you fight me."

Tom sized up the feeble old bald man with a dainty teacup in his hand and laughed. "Are you serious?"

"Fighting stance!" Master Bennie barked.

Tom shook his head and said, "Look, I'm sorry if I hurt your guy or embarrassed you but I'll just leave, OK?"

"FIGHTING STANCE!" Master Bennie shouted even louder.

Tom sighed. He put his hands up and said, "Are you at least going to put your tea down?"

Master Bennie smiled so wide it closed his eyes. "Me see no need."

And before Tom could even think about throwing a punch, he felt a tidal wave crash into him. When Master Kim kicked him earlier, he felt the foot in his abdomen. Whatever this pressure was, he felt it deep in his bones. A split second later, Tom's back was on the mat and he was staring up at Master Bennie, teacup in hand, still smiling. It felt like he was having a heart attack. Gasping for life, Tom tried to speak.

"Don't do that," Master Bennie said, "you no talk." The old man knelt down to Tom and whispered. "See, no contact useful too." He laughed loudly again like before. But the jocularity quickly faded away from his face. "You no control self, you control nothing. Remember this." Master Bennie stood up and sipped his tea. "Now, you go."

CICICICI

CHAPTER 14

Stupid fucking grasshopper!

That's all Tom could think for nearly a week after his visit to Master Bennie's. It didn't matter much anyway, it was all bullshit. Tom found another gym to work out in, one without all the superstitious mysticism floating around it. He spent most of his days shadowboxing and lifting in the early mornings, picking up a shift at the music store until the early afternoon, and rehearsing with the new band into the evenings. Soon he developed a routine where he didn't have to think too much about life—he could just exist on auto-pilot without any of the messy emotional garbage that people tried to shove down his throat.

One night the guys in the band decided to hit the bars after playing. Normally Tom would just brush this kind of stuff off. He had many a long day ahead of him to prepare for the tour and he just didn't get much out of socializing and partying anymore.

"Come on you pussy," goaded the drummer. Dudley was on odd combination of Leif Erikson and Popeye and would fuck a rock pile if he thought there was a snake at the bottom. "You never come out with us. What are you some kind of religious type? You a monk or some shit?"

"Leave him be." Wayne locked up his bass case and took a slug from his flask. "If da boy don't want to go out and play he don't have to, right Tom?"

Tom just laughed a little.

"Besides," Wayne continued, "That just means they's mo tuna fish for us!"

The guys all laughed as they finished packing up their equipment.

Larry shook his head. "You guys are a bunch of fuckin' pigs, you know that? Not you, Tom, but these assholes."

"Oh give me a break," Dudley yelled, "You're the worst there ever was. 'Faster than a speeding cocktail waitress... Able to leap tall bar stools in a single bound...Look up in the sky...It's a bird, it's a plane...No, it's Larry's *Cock Rocket* looking for a docking station. Hi, My name's Larry. (singing) *You're my Starship. Come take me in tonight...*'"

"I never said that to a chick in a bar!" He threw his hands up as if severely offended.

Wayne didn't miss a beat. "No, you said it to Dudley's mama last week, though."

Tom broke up the bickering with a simple request. "Look, I'll go out and have a drink if you guys agree to shut the hell up."

"All right!" Larry shouted. He clapped a firm hand down on Tom's shoulders. "I know the perfect place over on the strip. New joint just opened up called *The Handle Bar.*" He wore a wicked grin.

"You sure?" Dudley looked suspicious. "Last time you picked the bar we ended up in jail."

"Hey, no one asked you to hump the mechanical bull, Mr. 12 shots of tequila. We're going to *The Handle Bar* and that's that."

So they went. And Larry was right, the place was definitely happening. The dance floor was packed, the bar was a continuous fountain of liquor, and the people seemed friendly.

Really friendly.

"Hey there, Big boy," said a Marlboro-man voice from over Tom's shoulder. "What are you sipping on there?"

Tom looked behind him to see a shaven-headed man in a leather vest and aviator sunglasses waggle his eyebrows at him.

He hesitated for a second. "Scotch and water."

The greased up brawny man leaned in closer to Tom, so close that the hairs of his handle-bar mustache almost reached out and touched him. "My favorite he said in a sultry stage whisper."

"That's great, " Tom said, "good talking to you." He spun around in his stool to face the bar.

He felt a heavy hand on his shoulder and heard the man behind him call to the bartender, "Two more of these, Teddy."

Tom felt the blood rise to his face. He took a sip of his drink and shouted over the disco music. "If you want to keep that arm Mr. Clean, you should get your hand off of me right now."

The leather admirer slid around and sat next to Tom. "Oh, I like the rough stuff." He slid his hand across the bar and put it on top of Tom's. Immediately recoiling and jumping up from his bar stool, Tom yelled without thinking, "Look, I'm not a fucking faggot, Ok? Get lost!"

Everyone around him turned and gasped and started murmuring about this and that. The guys from the band weren't too far off and saw a crowd of people begin to swarm around their singer. Larry ran over first and said, "What's going on, man? Everything kosher?"

"Not hardly," whined the bar fly. "Tell your friend here to crawl back in time to the stone age." He stood up and walked towards the dance floor. That's when Tom and Larry both noticed he was wearing assless chaps. Spanking himself, he called back, "You wouldn't know what to do with it anyway!"

Tom shook his head. "This place is fucked, Larry. What the hell?"

The two of them looked out at the place. A familiar song

came on the sound system. "If" by *Bread* started to play, and at least six or seven men started singing their guts out to each other.

"That definitely does it for me!" said Tom in disgust.

Larry laughed. "Well, you have to admit that it's lively. I just didn't get the memo that this was a gay bar. Whoops!" Larry threw his hands up. "Good happy hour prices though, right?"

About that time Dudley waddled over to join the conversation. "Man, these women here sure love to dance! And boy are they tall. Come on Tom, what's the matter, you scared to dance with the big girls?"

"No, I'm afraid of their adam's apple you dip shit. Look around, Dudley, this place is full of nothing but fairies. Larry brought us to a queer bar."

"Hey, keep it down, Tom, they'll kick you out of here."

Dudley studied the dance floor, squinting at one and then the next. "I don't know guys, I think the ones I was talking to were girls." He chugged the rest of his beer and burped. "Only one way to find out!"

"Fuck this shit man, you idiots have fun." Tom threw a wad of bills on the bar top and started to storm out."

"Hey, come on man," Larry called after him, "Lighten up, would you? Don't you want to feel fabulous?"

Tom didn't look back when he tossed him the bird.

On a stool near the door, Wayne was sipping a Jack and coke. He raised his glass to Tom as he walked out and didn't say a single word.

Once he got out in the parking lot, there was a small group of guys talking amongst themselves, seemingly waiting for their chance at some trouble.

"Is that the guy?" one of them asked.

"Yeah, that's the fucking hate monger right there."

"Hey," they called as Tom walked away. "Hey! We're talking to you pretty boy. What's the big idea coming in here showing your ass like that?"

Tom stopped and actually laughed at that. He turned around and said, "I should be asking you Nancies the same question. Now look, I'm leaving, Ok? Let's not start any shit on top of that, all right?"

"You already started the shit, Mr. Manly Man." The ringleader of the pack pulled a tire iron from his waist band. "We'll show you who's tough around here." In a rush, the guy lunged forward and swung the iron with two hands like a baseball bat.

Tom stepped forward into the strike to close the distance, shot a hard elbow to the attacker's chin, and used his right arm to wrap around his assailant's elbows. With his free hand, Tom snatched the iron and spun around with a hard blow to the guy's temple. He dropped to the pavement like a wet sack of rotten peaches.

The three others stood with open mouths. Tom dropped the tire iron and roared out a *"Who's next?"* to the group. They said nothing, but backed away and ran to the safety of the bar.

ଔଔଔଔ

Tom couldn't believe his luck. The one time he agrees to hang out with these knuckle heads and he has to be eye candy for a bunch of trannies who could suck a golf ball through a garden hose. What's worse, he didn't even get a good buzz going. And yet again, here he was, stuck in the shit hole of Los Angeles traffic. Tom hopped off on the nearest freeway exit and decided to try his luck on the scenic highways. It was hard to see and Tom wasn't quite sure of the right way, but he didn't care. Just so long as he could drive the car instead of sit still in it.

For the first time in a long time, Tom acknowledged his own anger. He took a second to feel his pulse and listen to the amount of cursing he was doing. In a strange flash, he felt like he was this angry once before. It felt like a lifetime ago, in a place he'd never really been. Tom drove by a billboard and swore it said "Home of Good Humor Ice Cream."

In his ears he heard a voice repeating the same two words.

I'm sorry.

It was a woman's voice. Over and over again.

I'm sorry…I'm sorry.

Then, from nowhere, he heard another sound. A screeching, clawing sound, a shattering of glass and the twisting of metal. Tom felt the air in his chest spew out as he spun around in his seat like he was inside a washing machine. A bright flash of yellow light blinded him, and then darkness enveloped the world. Before he faded away, he heard the crunching sound of bones breaking, and the noise sounded like a beautiful name written on his heart.

Anna…

೫೫೫೫

Tom woke up, or dreamed of waking, in Marina Del Rey Mercy Hospital. His voice was his own, but the words didn't make any sense. Men in masks muffled something about a surgery, about "what's left of his leg" and about percentages…

Tom ascended, or dreamed of ascending, above his body on a table. The sound was the same as his high school days in metal shop—buzz saws grinding on stubborn bone and steel. He couldn't feel anything, but every time he watched one of the doctors touch his body, he empathized, he feared, he wondered about the pain. So much blood, so much gore. Another high pitch sound… "CLEAR!"

As the dreamscape faded, the nightmare began with a jolt of searing shock. Every fiber of his body burned and tears streamed down his face. The first words he could understand himself saying were, "I'm sorry…I'm sorry."

ଔଔଔଔଔ

118

Chapter 15

Tom awoke, groggy from the anesthesia—he could feel his limbs throb with pain.

Every time he tried to open his eyes fully the light pierced through his skull and pushed him back. Finally sitting up in the bed, he could tell that he was in a hospital room and could see the cast on his left leg.

Wincing Tom said, "I broke my leg?"

"I'm afraid so," said the nurse. "It's pretty bad. It was crushed in the accident, but you were very lucky. You could have lost it. You have a few broken ribs and a slight concussion, but you will heal if you follow your doctors' orders. You will start physical therapy in about six weeks and then..."

"Six weeks! I'm supposed to be on tour in three."

"I'm sorry, but you will be confined to this room for a least two months."

Just then Lucas, Tom's manager appeared. "Well, you finally came around did you?" He walked over closer to the bed to shake my hand. "It's good to see you conscious."

"How long have I been out?"

"You were in ICU for four days and they moved you here Thursday, so about a week. For awhile I wasn't sure you were gonna make it."

"A week? What about the tour!"

"Tom...I hate to be the bearer of bad news, especially now, but..."

"I mean, we can move some dates around at the very

least, right?" He tried to sit up in bed but the pain was unbearable.

"Easy there, easy. Look, there's no way you are going to be able to tour. There was just too much damage to your leg. Nasty accident. That lady hit you head on."

Tom's face still showed a blank stare of confusion. It wasn't sinking in.

"But don't worry yourself with the bills," Lucas continued. "I am having my attorney handle your lawsuit and financial matters until this all gets cleared up and you get back on your feet."

"Thank you Lucas, I appreciate it—but the nurse, she just said that I would heal. Can't we just postpone some shows and hire a backup for a couple of the early ones?"

"You will heal Tom, and with God's help you will walk again, but not without a cane.

Lucas's voice took on a deeper more serious quality. "But there's something you need to understand—I am afraid your performing days are over."

"Over!" That word hit Tom like a ton of bricks. Over? How can his career, his livelihood just be...over?

Lucas and the nurses started to fade away slowly, the light in the room was a pale white and it seemed to swallow up anyone who stood inside it for too long. Eventually Lucas disappeared altogether, a shadow in the dark, a cloud in the fog. Tom was vaguely aware that nurses would continually prick his fingers or change an IV, but only vaguely. As time went by, he wasn't even quite sure if he had his eyes open anymore. Tom felt like he had stared out into space for so long that he wasn't quite seeing anymore so much as he was imagining. The longer he sat in that bed the more he felt like he was releasing himself from the very nature of time and space. It was calming to be blanketed by oblivion, but Tom didn't realize that he was retreating into the silence of desolation.

Days would go by without him ever uttering a word. Visitors would come and go and think he was some odd variant of comatose because of his lack of response. Tom had woken up, sure, he was conscious, but some important part of him wasn't actually awake. Something inside him decided to roll over, pull the covers tightly around itself, and hide in the darkness of dreams.

Weeks blinked across his vision without a lingering moment…the doctor had ordered physical therapy to start but Tom couldn't even hear the voices of the staff anymore. He was somewhat aware that there were little puppets moving around him all the time, opening and closing their mannequin mouths, but Tom heard nothing.

Not until one day when the room was empty, the fluorescent lights were off, and he was alone. A sound softer than a falling snowflake whispered in his ear.

Wake up…

Tom blinked. Slowly he craned his neck to peer through the darkness of his room. The sound came again.

Wake up…

This time it was a more than just a sound, it was a voice—an angel's voice. Tom registered some small amount of joy and beauty for the first time since his return to the land of the living. All he wanted, all he craved, was to hear that voice again. He closed his eyes.

WAKE UP!

The voice shrieked through his mind and in time with flashing images. The screech of twisted metal, the spark of bones fracturing, the dazzling high beams. The voice rattled his nerves and flooded his bloodstream with a pain he couldn't understand.

And he woke up.

For a moment, Tom let his mind imagine that it was all just a dream. Not just the voice, but the hospital room, the accident…all of it. But he surveyed the familiar scene, the same hospital, the same fluorescent lights, the same cast choking his leg.

Suddenly a gang of white coats burst in the door. "Someone double check that monitor and make sure it's not malfunctioning."

Two or three sets of hands started clambering all over Tom's body, wrestling with him, subduing him.

"Get me 1.5 milligrams of Lidocaine, STAT!"

"These readings are—"

"What? I can't—someone hold him down, I can't hear myself think."

"The readout is correct, administer the anti-arrhythmia."

"Hurry, he's going into shock."

Tom couldn't figure out why so many people had appeared. After a few moments, they all stopped looking like shadow puppets or cartoons…after a few moments they were people again.

Slowly, he could hear a rush of sounds. The doctors barking orders, the squealing wheels of a gurney, the high-pitched beeping from the heart monitor. But there was one sound that was louder than all the rest, one sound that made his intestines tie themselves into knots, made his marrow churn…it was a man screaming. The howling was like a wounded animal, a blood-soaked kind of wail that echoed not only tragic loss, but confusion. It sounded like it would never stop. That sound of anguish was so loud that it shook Tom to his core.

The cage of hands clamped down on him tighter and tighter until Tom realized—this was his scream. This was his waking up.

"Can someone please shut him up so I can get a needle in!"

In the days following, Tom slowly felt himself float back towards reality. He was at least fully aware now what had befallen his body. And at night, he was aware that he felt some unbearable loss that extended beyond the accident, a pain that ran so deep that he couldn't even name it. But he was awake, and he planned on staying that way.

For Tom, physical therapy was a torturous affair, but he was stubborn and determined to perform again. During the time he was confined to his bed, he would work his upper body using small weights to maintain muscle mass and mobility.

"Lucas" Tom shouted as he strolled in. "How are you?"

"Fine" said Lucas. "I just dropped by to check on your progress."

"Not much progress yet, but I'm working on it," Tom said. "Don't dig a hole just yet."

"Well, it's good to see your sense of humor hasn't left you." said Lucas. "By the way, I brought an old friend of mine down to see you. He may be able to speed up your recovery a little."

"Hi Tom," a hauntingly familiar voice said.

"Master Bennie? What the fuck are you doing here?" Tom shouted loud enough for the whole floor to hear.

"Watch language, I come to help." replied Master Bennie.

"The last time you *helped* me, you helped me to the floor and damn near killed me. Did you come now to finish the job, while I can't fight back?"

"No...if I wanted to kill you, you would be dead and ashes scattered. I introduce you to floor because you being plick!" Master Bennie continued, "And you know it all...and interrupt Fled Frinstone! You still be plick and know all it now, Tommysan?"

With a heavy sigh, Tom decided to swallow his pride. Even he knew the way he'd acted the day he met Master Bennie wasn't a reflection of his true self. "I guess you are right." "I did not show you proper respect. I'm sorry," Tom said remorsefully.

"Aye..universe humbles us to show us errors of our ways

when we have much anger and hate. I can help with your recovery while you are here working in physical therapy and help diffuse your aggressive nature. We begin anew," said Master Bennie.

"Begin what?" asked Tom. "I certainly can't do martial arts."

"Martial arts much more than just karate. It is way of life. Your new way of life...but we talk later."

Master Bennie then unrolled a cloth full of long needles. "I have brought treatment with me to help you heal."

"By making me a pincushion?"

"You again, being plick! Be still."

He placed the acupuncture needles strategically around Tom's body. "Leave these alone for 20 minutes or so, then pull out. These will start to heal your body's nerve centers and chakras. I see you tomorrow. I go now. Goodbye today."

Tom lay there as Master Bennie disappeared, looking much like a porcupine. Tom figured what the hell, if it would help him to recover faster he'd give it a try.

The next morning as Tom awoke he noticed the figure of a small man hovering over him. "Good morning, Tommysan. Today I teach you to bleathe."

"Breathe?" Tom asked confused. "I'm pretty sure I already know how to bleathe—I mean breathe."

"No, you take air in and out...not bleathe." Master Bennie said. "I show you. Inhale...exhale...inhale...exhale…" he watched Tom as he spoke. "NO, NO, NO...not like that. Take air in through the nose, blowing stomach up like balloon, then expand chest and hold it and then exhale slowly, again through the nose. Do this five times. Inhale...exhale...inhale...exhale. Good now do five times on own."

Finally, he was satisfied with Tom's meager beginning. "Good, Good...you can be taught." Master Bennie jeered. "Since you just lie here with nothing to do, practice bleathing. Focus on nothing except your bleathe. If thoughts enter your mind, acknowledge them and dismiss them. Practice very important. Now it's time for me to needle you, ha-ha, Bennie make funny."

For the next three weeks, Master Bennie came everyday to assist with the breathing exercises and administer the acupuncture needles. Until they were ready for next steps, literally.

೫೫೫೫

"OK, today we start to learn to walk again."

"Walk?! Hellooo...Have you not taken notice of this thing on my leg. How am I supposed to walk?"

"You walk with mind. When mind is calm from bleathing, start to visualize the image of yourself walking in a pleasant garden. Walk up the glassy knoll, enjoying the gleen plant life and frowers. Stop and smell the frowers and notice their beauty. Walk slowly taking time to notice each step you take...how it feels...the sensations it sends to the other parts of your body. In a few weeks, when they remove your cast, the doctors will be amazed that your leg muscles have not deteriorated."

Then, finally, came that day when he would rid himself of the extra 20 pounds of concrete. As Master Bennie had predicted, the doctors were totally astounded at Tom's well toned muscles in his legs. At first, the only thing that moved were his toes. Even that felt like his muscles were cramping around a hot knife. But eventually, he was able to shuffle on the parallel bars nearly collapsing, but shuffling. Then just a week later, he took his first small steps without the bars, although he had to use a walker. After two more weeks, he was walking on his own with only the assistance of a cane... which he loathed.

He was then released as they had done all that they could. As the orderly wheeled Tom to the entrance, he hailed a cab and helped him into the back.

The cabbie said, "Where to Tommysan?"

Tom did a double take as he again saw a familiar figure behind the wheel. "Oh my God!" he stuttered. "What the—?"

"Not God, Bennie," he said. "Where to?"

"Well, I am not sure. I don't have an apartment anymore since I have been in the hospital for so long."

"I see—" said Master Bennie. "Well, right now I am hungry and I want to show you something. Let's go eat."

"Where?"

"Brown Derby."

"The Brown Derby? Are you nuts?! That place is expensive. I don't make that kind of money."

"I pay...You go. I like the tea."

"Well then, I go."

When they arrived, Tom felt extremely underdressed. There were all kinds of people there...actors, managers, publishers, record execs, anybody that was anybody in Hollyweird.

"No fear. You somebody," he laughed and turned to the maitre 'd, "Table two, Hanna."

CXCXCXCX

"May I take your order sir?" the waiter asked.

"Tea, we'll have tea."

"Tea sir? Hot or Cold?"

"Hot prease."

"And what would you like with your tea?"

"Nothing, thank you, just tea."

"Just tea?"

"Just tea."

"You go now, get tea," said Bennie.

"So, we go to an expensive restaurant to drink tea?" Tom

126

asked.

"Not to drink tea, to learn," said Bennie.

"And what will we learn today?" Tom asked.

"*We* not learn shit...*Me* know. *You* learn."

Tom could sense he was getting a little testy so he shut up and listened.

"Do you see the man in the green leisure suit? Watch. He will turn around to look at us in 3...2...1..."

"I'll be damned...he turned. How…"

"See the lady sitting over there in the bright blue dress? She will not only turn but smile at us in 3...2...1...

"Holy shit, how did you do that?"

"That is what you learn today."

"Here comes our tea. Good." Master Bennie poured Tom some tea and then poured some for himself. "Ah, tea is very good, don't you think?"

"Yes, it is very good."

"If you don't mind me asking, why did you come to the hospital? And why would you try to teach me anything when I was so rude to you at your studio? I thought you were done with me."

"No, not done, just beginning. You have many gifts that you are totally unaware of. This is why I pick you up at the hospital...to continue your therapy. You stay in Bennie's home for awhile. Your recovery will be much faster and you have much to learn."

"Master Bennie, I don't know what to say."

"Say 'Thank you' and drink tea. We talk later."

"Thank you," Tom repeated humbly. He relaxed with his tea cup in hand.

"Now look at the back of the neck of the woman in front of you. Gaze at the base of her neck and envision a fly at the base of her skull."

Tom did what he asked and in about two seconds the lady turned around as if to brush away something from the back of her neck.

"You see, you are merely suggesting that something is there. This is just a parlor trick. There is much more to learn. Imagine if you had instead envisioned a bear behind her or a snake crawling up her spine...I believe the reaction might be a little stronger."

"Let me try."

"No, no, no! As with all things you learn, it comes with great responsibility. Remember when you got your black belt? You had achieved and learned a great deal, however, I hope you did not go to a bar looking for a fight!"

"Well—" Tom muttered, humbling himself.

"As expected," Bennie retorted. "With these gifts that I will show you how to use, you will progress and get much stronger. You will also see a great many things, sometimes private things that you must block from your view."

"I don't quite understand."

"Ok, let's say, once I show you how, you go on a journey through time and space and you happen upon a couple being intimate...surely, you would turn your head? Do as you would in the physical realm and you will be fine. Don't and you could receive a psychic backlash that could kill you. Using your gifts to injure another, even in self-defense can have lasting and sometimes permanently damaging effects. See things you don't like? Just turn your head and walk away... those things will go away, too. Enough for today...let's go McDonalds...your treat!"

 CB CB CB CB

Chapter 16

Tom arrived at Master Bennie's humble abode; a couple of bedrooms and a bath and kitchen, kinda what one would expect from an Asian master.

"This your room, Tommysan." He pointed to one of the bedrooms. "You can put your stuff here. You get rest now. Tomorrow we start hard road to recovery," he said, laughing as he retired.

Unbeknownst to Tom, Master Bennie had already started on his therapy. To truly recover, he needed to block his painful memories of the past to clear the way to his future and his mission in life.

Master Bennie prepared candles, with a white one on the left and right and a red candle in the center. After lighting the candles he meditated. Then lighting a piece of paper with Anna's name on it, he recited the following incantation:

"As Anna leaves his life, Tom leaves behind his pain.

As Tom leaves Anna in his life, he leaves her with his sorrow.

I burn thy name, Anna, so it shall be cast from Tom's memory.

Your memory erased from his mind.

No longer held by the constraints of time.

Knowing the Universe will restore that which is necessary at the perfect time.

I accept this made manifest. So shall it be."

Then he extinguished the candles and went to bed.

೧೮೦೩೮೦೩೮೦೩೮೦೩

The next morning came early.

"Wake up, it's time to start our day," announced Master Bennie.

"Up? What time is it?"

"4 a.m. Time to meditate. Get dressed."

Tom stumbled out of bed and did as he was instructed. Meditation lasted an hour in which they both concentrated on nothing but breathing — no thoughts, just breathing.

"We do this to start every day from now on. From this, you will eventually know how to fill the remaining part of day," said Bennie. "Time we eat."

For Tom, breakfast naturally consisted of tea as well as yogurt, fruit and granola.

"What are you eating?" Tom asked.

"Twinkies and tea. Bennie not sick," he said biting into the filling. "Mmmm....good."

Rolling his eyes, Tom asked, "What's on the agenda for today?"

"New martial art, Ji Pang E."

"My body won't let me do martial arts."

"Not true, just need to make adjustments."

"Adjustments?"

"Yes, adjustments."

"You know," continued Master Bennie, "Just because we are predestined to achieve certain things in our lives doesn't mean we won't have unexpected changes, such as accidents, that require us to make adjustments so that we are able to continue to carry out our missions in life.

The universe plans accidents sometimes to ensure that we focus on what is really important instead of being side-tracked in a direction that our ego leads us. There really are no accidents. Besides, you now have a new weapon in your arsenal."

"And what weapon might that be?"

"Ji Pang E — the cane."

"What?"

"The cane. In Korean we call it Ji Pang E. It very useful in Hapkido. Let me show you..."

Master Bennie then showed Tom a video of a Korean master utilizing the cane as a weapon in self-defense.

"See," said Master Bennie "Now you be better than before."

"I don't think—"

"You no think shit—you not know shit—I teach. Fighting stance. "Ready, Begin!"

And with that Master Bennie opened up a whole new door for Tom and began to restore his confidence. At first, Tom was like a fawn learning to hobble and walk without falling. Having to work very hard to restore his balance. He practiced over and over until he could walk and move blind-folded. Then, he worked on all of the techniques that utilized the cane until he became totally proficient.

Everyday was the same. Get up at 4 a.m., meditate, eat and work on Ji Pang E. This continued for two months until one morning Master Bennie said, "Wake up, Tommysan, wake up."

There, before Tom stood Master Bennie, but not in his usual garb. He was dressed in a khaki vest, summer shirt and trousers and wearing a fisherman's hat with hooks in it.

"What the—" Tom started.

"Come, we go—early worm catches the fish."

"Worms, fish? What the hell?"

"Not hell, gift from sea—we go fishing today."

Before Tom could object, they were zooming down Santa Monica Boulevard to the pier.

Now, pier fishing was something Tom was accustomed

to. He had fished off of the Triple S and Iron Steamer Piers his whole life back in Carolina. He wondered how it would feel with the ocean being on the wrong side.

Shortly, after arriving, Master Bennie said, "You know, Papasan used to bring me here to fish when I was a young boy. We used to hang out with the Chinese who were catching crabs. They always had a pot of salt water on the pier and kept it boiling. When they caught the crabs, they would immediately put them in the pot. By day's end they had a huge crab feast and everyone was invited to eat all they could hold. I would sneak a drink from the Chinamen's bottle and have myself a little party. Great memories."

"Now that is interesting. We in North Carolina have what we call a *Down East Clam Pot*. But we put everything in the pot — crabs, clams, fish, corn on the cob, potatoes, anything that's caught that day. Same thing though—everyone eats and drinks and has a great time."

"Sounds good, Tommysan. Maybe one day I go and try."

ೞೞೞೞ

Out on the pier it is quiet and peaceful. "This is meditation too, Tommysan. A great deal can be learned from the solitude of fishing and of course it has it's own rewards as well. Sometimes you end up with a great supper—sometimes not."

Just then Tom felt a tug on his line. "I think I've got one—a big one."

"Careful Tommysan—play it!"

Before he knew it, he had reeled in a nice size halibut.

"Then Master Bennie yelled, "I've got something, too."

"Careful Papasan—play it."

Looking at Tom with a grin he slowly pulled in a white sea bass.

"Oh, I haven't caught one of these since 1957. They had

a great run of white sea bass here at the pier during what they call an El Nino year. That run lasted for nearly two weeks, and the fish were between 15 and 40 pounds each. Quite a haul!"

"We eat good tonight...Come. Sun go, we go, too."

෯෯෯෯

The next day at the mid-day meal Master Bennie said, "Your physical skills have once again become quite remarkable, however, your inner self is holding you back from reaching your full potential. You present certain spiritual gifts that have not yet been fully developed; therefore, they cause you great pain. Until you get them under your control, you will be in constant conflict. You have many blocks to your achieving greatness. You must discover your true self."

"What do you mean...spiritual gifts?"

Master Bennie said, "Have you ever noticed that when you sleep sometimes you feel like you go somewhere else... somewhere you have never been...meeting people you have never met and yet, down the road you run into these same people and places?"

"Well, yes, on occasion I have. What does that mean? I always thought it was just a weird dream...sorta déjà vu."

"Not dream...It's déjà vu in reverse. You actually can control your own destiny. What do you see in my hand?"

"A pitcher of water."

"That is your perception of reality. If I put the water in a cup, it becomes the cup. It is formless, but becomes what contains it. Water can flow, or it can crash. It can change form or it can evaporate. Be like water."

The master continued his example. "You can shape your reality to be what you want it to be, through your desires. Your desires are fulfilled from your true self. I showed another talented, but impatient student named Bruce these things, but he finally succumbed to his demons last year. Very sad. It is a force that can move mountains."

"Mountains...yeah right—"

"Wait, Bennie show you, again. Fighting stance."

"Huh?"

"Fighting Stance! Begin."

Tom prepared to spar as Master Bennie's body went limp. The last thing Tom remembered was picking his ass off the floor. Where did he go? There was this explosion of energy that hit the center of his body and threw it to the mat. Master Bennie was still standing where he was...just looking on.

"What the hell was that?"

"Not hell, gift from God. Your gift, once it is learned and controlled. It can be used for good or evil...that choice is up to you. But remember, there is always consequence with any choice you make, good or evil. Also, there are many dangers when you pass into these different planes...so take heed and learn."

φφφφ

By the time the day was over, Tom was exhausted. He never realized that using mental energy was more tiring than being physical, and this, Bennie said, was a light work out.

In the following months they worked everyday developing Tom's Chakra and Chi energy to the point where he could basically will people to do simple tasks...interrupt what they were doing and have them do something else. He thought it was all pretty cool, although he had never thought this was even possible.

Master Bennie said, "You have been doing this all the time, but you just haven't recognized it. You are just awakening that which has always been inside you. Every strange woman that you have come in contact with, that was suddenly attracted to you like a magnet came from your inner desires manifested."

"And here I thought it was my singing." Tom laughed to himself.

ଔଔଔଔ

It was soon July 4,1976. America's Bicentennial celebration was here. Everyone across the United States was celebrating and Master Bennie and Tom were no exception. They had made plans to go to Disneyland in nearby Anaheim to see the parades and fireworks. Upon arriving, Tom felt like a kid again, riding rides and eating junk food until it ran out of his ears.

"Be careful, Tommysan. You are not used to eating this type of food. It could make you sick, especially when you shake it up on all of these rides. Gravity will not be your friend if you puke."

"What makes me sick is the four dollars I just paid for this hot dog."

"That's why I brought my Twinkies," chuckled Master Bennie.

"Wow, this is some parade," Tom noted. "All of the floats show a different part of our history and culture. I now get the part about the country being a melting pot. Listen to that music, would you? They're playing *The Glorious Fourth* by the Sherman Brothers. That is really inspiring and makes you proud to be an American."

"Aye, great song, great parade, great friends."

As they stood and watched the fireworks display, Master Bennie couldn't help but smile and reflect that Tom had become much more than a student. Yes, Tom was now the son that Bennie never had.

The next morning, after meditation and breakfast Tom inquired, "Master Bennie...when are you going to teach me that awesome move you put on me awhile back? Man, I would like to learn how to do that!"

"Here you must be very much in control, it is very dangerous."

"Dangerous? How so?"

"When you do this you must leave your body for a short time and you become completely vulnerable. You could lose your life and possibly your soul."

"Sounds serious," Tom said in a jeering fashion.

"Not playtime," Master Bennie snapped and Tom immediately sensed the gravity of all of that was being told to him. "If you use this against an attacker, you must be careful not to let your emotions run wild and end up killing your opponent, for his spirit will be released and could fight you into eternity. The only way to conquer him is to return to your body, and that is not always easy when someone is trying to stop you."

"I see."

"You no see shit. This is serious...listen carefully and take heed."

With that he explained the method used to exit the body and return.

"Practice while you sleep and you will gain skill. Set your alarm for 3 a.m. When it wakes you, go back to sleep, but in a conscious state of sleep. Envision your spirit rising slowly from your body. You will also see a tether extending from your forehead to your spirit's navel. This is your lifeline and will ground you to your body. As you float high above your body, command yourself to go where you wish to be. You will soon see yourself floating higher and higher...be careful though....no spying!"

"Whatever do you mean?"

"You know what fuck I mean! Don't play." And with that Tom was dismissed.

CRCRCRCR

That night Tom lay there with great anticipation, waiting to fall asleep. Promptly at 3 a.m. the alarm went off and Tom did as he was told. After a short while he could feel himself beginning to float...higher and higher.

As he floated higher he thought that he might like to go to the coast where he is from. Quicker than quick he was hovering over the sandy shores of Atlantic Beach looking out over the moonlit shimmering ocean. It was more wonderful than he could ever imagine.

"I feel like Peter Fuckin' Pan!" Tom exclaimed.

Before he knew it he could see the resort he used to work at coming into view. He was approaching the rooms at the resort, but was halted by Master Bennie's warning against spying.

"No fun!"

But, he decided that Master Bennie was so adamant about spying that he would not even peek. Tom decided to return back and floated gently back inside his shell and fell back asleep.

The next morning he felt refreshed and liberated. He finally felt like he had fulfilled a yearning that had been pulling him since he was little. Of course, he had no idea what that feeling was, just that it was frustrating—always feeling like a part of him was missing.

At breakfast Master Bennie asked, "Were you able to project astrally last night?"

"Yes, and I didn't peek."

"It's good you didn't. Come on, we still have much work to do."

Over the next several weeks Tom traveled many places and saw many exciting and wonderful things. Some not so wonderful. One night as he was starting to float a couple of odd things happened. Nobody had mentioned the welcoming committee that he might encounter. Some scary shit out there! Tom just ignored those things and walked away as he had been instructed by Master Bennie, and they went away from him as Master Bennie had said that they would.

Then, he had a visit from his spirit guide who led him to safer waters and instructed Tom on navigating in this realm. He led Tom to a quiet room where he reclined. There he saw a wonderful green light that filled the room.

First, it struck the top of his head and then proceeded down his entire body. As it did, he could feel its gentle warmth heal his body's imperfections and open up his chakras. As he was healed, the guide introduced Tom to many, more powerful possibilities than just soaring through the skies enjoying the view...and then...a sudden jolt.

Tom returned and sat straight up in the bed.

C3C3C3C3

As Master Bennie greeted Tom the next morning he asked, "Did you make another journey last night?"

"I sure did," Tom said. "And this time I met my spirit guide, who helped me understand that there was much more of a use for my abilities than just providing myself a little entertainment."

"Aye."

"But you didn't warn me about the monsters."

"Oh, those...just ignore them and they'll go away. Children's fairy tales had to come from somewhere didn't they?"

"I suppose. It might explain some of the experiences I have had over the last couple of years and the strange dreams. I had a really weird dream recently about people wearing what looked like red and green helmets made out of plastic Lego blocks sitting in two rows of six chairs. Two of the chairs were empty and then it just faded out."

"Not dream…vision. You were being introduced to the twelve twins. Twin Flames that have been reunited and now are ascended masters. One chair is empty as I am here. One chair awaits two souls to reunite and that will be the twelfth."

Just then Tom noticed something that looked quite familiar hanging around Master Bennie's neck. "Hey, my grandmother had a necklace with a coin on it just like that, although I can't seem to remember what happened to it."

"I'm certain that it will turn up. It is the symbol of the Twin Flame."

"I don't understand. What is a Twin Flame and—"

"Me understand—you don't know shit—but soon you will. Goodbye today, you have much work yet to do."

☙☙☙☙

Months pass and it is another routine day for Tom. He meditates, eats and works on his techniques; his average work day. When he finishes, he heads for the kitchen to meet with Master Bennie for his meager mid-day meal before continuing his routine. Tom had forgotten time or the calendar as he was totally immersed in his daily ritual.

"Surprise!" Master Bennie and Lucas Freely yell. "Happy Birthday."

Totally shocked, Tom grinned, "Oh, thank you all. I had forgotten that today was my birthday."

"Not just any birthday, Tommysan, your 21st!"

"Look at that cake! You all shouldn't have. How did you know?"

"Me know much—you still don't know shit," laughed Master Bennie as he and Lucas sang *Happy Birthday.*

"Quick...blow out candles." And as Tom did everyone clapped. "Now open presents. This is from me." Master Bennie handed him a rectangular shaped box.

Tom quickly opened it to find a bottle of 21 Year Old Yamazaki Japanese Whiskey. "I don't know what to say except, thank you. Thank you very much." He leaned over to give

Master Bennie a hug.

"Good stuff, Tommysan. Much better than that Scottish rot gut you have been drinking. Only the best for your 21st."

Lucas handed Tom an envelope and said, "I thought this would be a great time to give you this."

"Thank you Lucas, but you have already done so much."

"Well, I have to be honest. It is not from me. Open it."

Tom opened the envelope and peered inside to find a check in the amount of $1,812. It was the property damage settlement from the accident he had been waiting for.

"Damn Lucas, this could not have come at a better time. I have felt kinda lost without my wheels. Thank you."

"And that is next surprise," said Master Bennie. "We go car shopping...but first we eat cake!"

After they had eaten, Tom and Master Bennie went car shopping down Santa Monica Boulevard. There were hundreds of car lots and Tom was certain it would not be difficult to find a replacement. He thought that maybe this time he would look for a car instead of a van as it would be much easier to maneuver in the city.

As the two were cruisin' along Tom yelled, "Stop here." Out of the corner of his eye Tom had spotted a blue '68 Mustang convertible. "Let's go."

They ambled into the dealership so that Tom could inquire about the Mustang.

"Sure, it's a beaut. A little old lady from Pasadena traded it in and she only drove it to church on Sundays—just kidding. My name is Hank Lewis, pleased to meet you."

"Tom Marks," he said, extending his right hand. "And this is my friend, Bennie Hana."

"You want to take it for a spin?"

"Sure do," Tom said excitedly.

As Tom drove, he almost felt as if he were learning to walk again as it had been so long, but he found that it did not take long to get back in the rhythm. Four in the floor, a 302

Boss engine; this was a dream come true. Pulling back into the dealership Tom asked, "How much?"

"$2100."

"Whew! $2100. Well...I guess maybe I could finance—" Tom started.

"You cannot afford. You no have $2100, just $1500. You cannot finance, you have no job. We go somewhere else, look more," piped in Master Bennie.

"Wait! No need to rush off. I think I can sell her to you for $1,500. Let me draw up the paperwork."

Tom agreed and in about 15 minutes the two were driving back home with Tom behind the wheel of his Mustang.

As they got out of their cars Master Bennie laughed and slapped Tom on the back. "See Tommysan, you now have new car and some pocket change. Happy Birthday. Now let's go break open the birthday present I gave you and see if it fits."

 CICICICI

About a week later, Tom found Master Bennie meditating intensely in the dojo. When he became present, he invited Tom closer. "Come, now is time to focus your inner energy on an opponent. There are two ways—One is the bear."

"The Bear?"

"Aye, Very powerful. Simply envision a large Grizzly Bear creeping up behind your opponent's back. Visualize every gruesome detail of that bear snarling, saliva dripping from his fangs and focus your mental energy just above and beyond your opponent's shoulder, like you would if you were trying to break a board. Make it real using your Chi and he will either turn and run from you or YOU will have an opening when he looks over his shoulder."

"I believe I can see how that would work. That is similar to the visualization exercises you have been having me do."

"Aye, but much more focused and terrifying for your adversary. The second is much more powerful and much more dangerous, because for a few moments you will be completely out of your body. It's called BEE THE BEAR."

"Be the Bear?"

"NO! BEE THE BEAR! You will envision a horde of bees buzzing around his head biting and stinging. Then YOU will leave your body and become the bear, eagerly searching for honey, which you spy dripping from his ass. You quickly jump up his ass and—"

"Wait—are you shitting me?"

"No, but opponent might be. Heh-heh, Bennie make funny."

"I think I get the idea—yuck."

"Very messy for everyone involved," said Master Bennie. "Be prepared to fight his spirit if you ever use it, as no one has ever lived after having a bear shoved up their ass."

"OK, OK! Too much visualization. Geez."

"Enough for today—you go."

ભ ભ ભ ભ

Tom quickly learned that Master Bennie was much, much more than a Sensei, as he utilized acupuncture to heal his body, meditation to heal his mind and introduced him to the secrets that Jesus must have shared with his apostles.

Master Bennie explained the meaning of the twelve that Tom had seen in his vision. He also revealed the origin of Twin Flames and how these souls split to have unique experiences through many lifetimes. They then become reunited, especially during the transition of new millenniums, to accomplish their mission of healing the earth through their emission of higher frequencies when conjoined. These frequencies cause a planetary shifting that prevents meteorological events such as earthquakes and floods from occurring that could easily cause the end of days. It is because of the reuniting of the Twin Flames that this planet has survived for so long. They help mankind by becoming one, more powerful being that directs the future of all mankind, not only in this dimension, but ultimately in the sixth dimension becoming one with God.

Tom was told that one day, he would again encounter his *twin* when he was ready and that they would accomplish these things, but it was not yet time. But the time was drawing near.

It was a lot for Tom to comprehend and he did not fully understand the ramifications nor the importance of all of this, but Tom did now pay attention.

This took up the the remaining part of the year, but by then Master Bennie had molded him into someone who was ready, not only physically, but mentally for the challenges that lie ahead for him in life.

"Master Bennie, the prospects here are very slim for me and I am running low on cash...I think it would be better for me to go home to North Carolina to find out what I want to do with the rest of my life."

"Before you go, I have one last important lesson to teach you." And with that, Master Bennie glided into the air and spun away from him.

"Whoa!! How did you..."

"Air is like water...formless. Yet it fills a balloon. You can't see it, yet it is a very powerful force that can destroy buildings in a hurricane. What is your reality? Do you believe you cannot fly because you have not flown or can you believe with your whole heart that you can fly and do? I say that you have the ability to do whatever it is that you desire and if you believe this desire to be true to your whole self, then it will be manifested. Be like air."

Tom handed Master Bennie a package and said, "Merry Christmas!"

"A gift for me? But I didn't get you anything."

"It's not much. Open it."

Master Bennie fumbled with the paper opening the square flat package revealing a picture in a frame with the two of them wearing Mouseketeer Ears in Disneyland the summer before. Inscribed on the picture was:

"To Master Papasan,
It has not always been a walk in the park.
Love, Tommysan."

"Oh, this is a most precious gift." Bennie said tearfully. "I will never forget it—or you." Wiping his eyes he said, "May God bless you. You will always hold a special place in my heart, son. I will pray for you to have a clear head so that the road before you will be easier, without the baggage from the past. This way you can focus on the future and you will find that your past becomes your future. As my good friend, Mary, wrote in her book, *He who will go forward with his whole mind will obtain what he seeks...Only do not be of two minds."*

As usual, Master Bennie's wisdom was full of riddles and bullshit, of course it was...but Tom knew Master Bennie had his best interests at heart, so he strained to endure Master Bennie's ramblings as he prepared himself for the long road home.

CHAPTER 17

Youngstown, Ohio in 1977 was a year when traditionally black and smog-filled skies faded and cleared. An outsider might think clear air was something the town needed, a breath of fresh air, but the truth is that now this community was suffocating.

"Black Monday" was what all the locals called the day when production at the steel mills ceased that September and thousands of factory workers lost their jobs. One of these workers was a proud Greek man, unafraid of dirtying his hands to provide for his family. In fact, George Sopoulos, despite his constant complaints about his work, took a certain pride in knowing that he exhausted himself to make an honest living. Most folks in Youngstown felt that way. And then they had that taken away—the cornerstone of their lives kicked out from under them. Soon, they'd have to watch as everything they'd built, ugly and rough as it may have been, would come toppling down to its foundation.

"Good thing you're getting married to a man with work," Stefania Sopoulos said to her daughter. "Not too many people these days know where there next meal is coming from."

Anna sighed as if she'd said these words a thousand times before. "But I don't love him, Mama."

Mrs. Sopoulos also spoke as if she'd said these words many times before—almost enough to believe them herself. "Love can grow later."

She walked over to the pantry to grab some spices for the

stew Anna was stirring. "You will have new responsibilities to keep you busy and keep you from pining over that musician." said Mama. "William may be a little rough around the edges, but he will be a good provider."

She nudged Anna slightly out of her way to carefully season the broth. "I don't how but he has managed to keep his job through all of this mess. If that's not God's work I don't know what is."

"I don't think God has anything to do with it," Anna retorted in a low tone.

Too absorbed in her own train of thought to notice, Mrs. Sopoulos continued, "It's a good thing Mr. Figerino gave your Papa a job or we wouldn't be eating either."

Anna felt a twisting sensation in her stomach. How could her mother be so blind? But, then again, Anna would have never suspected the darkness that lingered underneath the surface of her little town even a year ago. She had grown up thinking her father was a simple blue collar worker and her fiancé, although a bastard, was just a bastard who worked for the city, not for the mob.

Mrs. Sopoulos nodded her head as if to agree with herself. "Nice man, your boss. You are very fortunate."

"Yes, Mama, oh so fortunate." Anna wondered when she could, if she could, ever tell her mother the truth. What good would it do? It's true, Anna and Stefania never were best of friends, but they were mother and daughter, and Anna would never wish the kind of pain she felt now on her own blood. So instead of ruining any last warm impressions Mrs. Sopoulos may have clung to in those dark days after the plants closed, instead of destroying the faith she had in her husband as an honest breadwinner, Anna simply stirred the pot, sniffing occasionally and remarking half-absently about more rosemary, more sage…

More thyme.

Across town, Anna's father is feeling an uneasiness of his

own. In Mr. Figerino's office, George Sopoulos feels restless. His hands are in and out of his pockets, he doesn't ever know when to stand or sit, and he feels too self-conscious to chew on his pipe.

It doesn't help that Mr. Figerino is content to sit behind his desk in silence for prolonged periods. He pretends to think very hard about something, but he's really just practicing the art of intimidation.

Inevitably, George Sopoulos buckles, and speaks first. "I have been thinking quite a bit about this forcing Anna to marry William," he said. "It's just, sir, she is so sad all the time and I..."

Mr. Figerino half-closed his eyes and put his hands together in such a way that only his fingertips were touching. "Go on, George, I'm listening."

"Well, I hate to say it but, I have noticed some very troubling traits in William."

Mr. Figerino responded only with a half-cocked eyebrow.

"He seems…angry." George squirmed in his chair, wishing he were back at the mill, back on a schedule he knew backward and forward.

"Well now, George, we're all grown men here. Anger is only natural." Mr. Figerino started to shift his attention to some loose papers on the desk.

"But, sir, this isn't the kind of anger that a rational man has—this is something violent. " He cleared his throat and stammered a little, unsure how to say what he really wanted to.

"George I'm sorry you're having a little buyer's remorse but, really, this all seems a bit trivial and I have to—"

"I have my doubts," George said in a louder more nervous tone, "that Anna fell down those stairs a couple of years ago by accident. In my heart I can feel that something else happened."

Mr. Figerino was silent for a moment, but then leaned

back in his chair and let out a loud belly laugh. "Ok, that's a good one, George. You really had me going there for a second."

George said nothing, but his fists clenched tightly.

"Come on, you're not serious are you? What kind of proof do you have, huh?"

"I don't..." he muttered.

"Didn't we get rid of that musician without killing him? If anything, you owe William a great deal of gratitude for his restraint. No, the wedding will go on as planned."

"She was pregnant with my grandchild—his child—" George was almost whispering now, unsure if anyone in the world could hear him at all. He stared straight through the desk, through the floor, all the way down through the hard, iron-rich dirt that the building was sitting on. He felt a white heat behind his eyes and a voice of defiance rumbling up from somewhere deep inside.

"What if I refuse? She's my daughter, Leonard."

Mr. Figerino leaned back in his chair and grinned. "You won't. *You have no choice.*"

It was a simple enough statement—four simple words. But, the fact is, he was right, and George knew it.

In the days leading up to the ceremony, Anna looked down at her finger. The traditional gold band that she had always dreamed of circled her skin. But every day it shined brighter with a type of luster that she could only look at with malice. The ring tormented and teased her, dared her to try and remove it. She frequently had nightmares where the ring glowed and cut deep into her flesh. Blood would spray out from under it and cover her white dress, but the gold would remain untarnished.

Every time she would wake up, gasping for air, covered in a cold sweat, fumbling in the darkness for a body that wasn't there. Some nights she would even call his name.

Tom...

The blessed day came on October 20, two days after the Lynyrd Skynyrd plane crash. They were one of Anna's favorite bands and, of course, it reminded her of Tom. But then again, what didn't? He was everywhere and everything for her. There wasn't a place or a moment in her life that he wasn't reflected in.

What was he doing? Where was he? And most importantly, why wasn't he here to save her? Part of Anna wanted to be angry with Tom for not riding into town wearing shining armor, but she knew her life wasn't a movie—she had no illusions of a happy ending.

So, Anna was forced to marry William. They had all the pomp and circumstance of a traditional Greek wedding with all of the trimmings. William sent over Anna's bridal shoes on the morning of the wedding with money in them.

"Cheapskate!" Anna shrieked. "He put a $1 bill in each. I guess I should pray to the Virgin with thankfulness that he even remembered to include that. I suppose he did that to remind me of my worth." Anna started to cry.

Mama said, "Let me help you write the names of your bridesmaids on the bottom of the shoes."

"Why? So everyone can see who the next lucky bride will be when the names wear off after a night of dancing. I figure no one will get lucky tonight as the last thing I feel like is dancing."

"Honey, this is supposed to be *your* day. Try to be happy. I know you don't think so now, but everything is going to work out fine. You'll see. You just have wedding day jitters."

After being prepared by her Koumbaras, Anna headed to the ceremony in a zombie-like haze. Most of what happened that day she would later look back on as just a bad dream, fuzzy and incoherent. A grueling hour and a half of wearing the traditional gold crowns was enough to make her feet, and her heart, go numb. The crowns were attached by a ribbon symbolizing that the couple would rule over the house together. It was an old joke that no one bothered to laugh at anymore. They were swapped between them three times and then they moved their rings from the left hands to the right. And just like that, it was done.

Then they began the gala wedding night of celebration with the Kalamatianos, a traditional Greek dance done at weddings. They all danced back and forth in the circle stopping only to eat and drink. And did Anna drink! Anna thought that maybe if she drank enough she wouldn't have to think about the finale of this little charade. All of the guests came up and pinned money on their clothes, as they danced the last dance by themselves.

Then it was off to the honeymoon. They arrived at the Quail Hollow Resort where William had booked them a suite, not out of love for his new bride, but merely because his uncle knew somebody that knew somebody that owed him a favor.

"Isn't this nice, sweetie?" William said as he carried Anna into the room.

"Just loverly," Anna muttered as she staggered toward the bed once William put her down.

She almost fell on the bed covered in cash and rice that was put there to wish the couple prosperity and strong roots. Anna noticed that they forgot to drag a baby across the bed to ensure the sex of their first born, which suited her fine because she had no intention of having a child with this bastard.

William said with a smirk, "I will open some more champagne. Why don't you get undressed so we can get down to business once I find some glasses?"

As William turns to get some glasses from the kitchen, what was left inside Anna's heart sank low beneath the freshly shampooed carpets as she fell on the bed and passed out completely...

"You Bitch!"

Anna's new life soon became more and more unbearable. After the disappointing honeymoon, William was an absolute tyrant and Anna his slave. Her thoughts and feelings did not matter. Everything was about William, his work, his needs. He did not allow her to have anyone over other than her mom and dad.

He was mentally and physically abusive beating her every time she disagreed with him or spoke up. So, she quit speaking...to anyone other than herself. She tried to be what he wanted and make a nice home, although her heart was certainly not in it. She dared not to speak to anyone about what was going on in their home as she knew William would find out and cause her even more pain.

And, of course, she was still in love with Tom. Anna looked on the dresser in her bedroom at her doll collection and saw one comforting reminder of her past.

"My doll, my doll...my little Effie." Anna said sweetly, picking up the toy. "How are you today?" Effie, of course, didn't answer, but seemed to smile with an 'I'm fine' look. In a more serious tone Anna said, "You know, every time that monster I married touches me, it make me want to puke. All I can do is just lie there and think of Tom to get through the ordeal. It's either that or risk another beating. I make sure that I don't get pregnant and hide the birth control pills to ensure William doesn't find out. He thinks I just can't conceive because of the time he pushed me down the stairs and I lost the baby. That's good for my sake as I couldn't bear the thought of raising children in this household."

"You know, Effie, I am not allowed to have friends over to talk to—maybe you and I can talk like we used to. What's that you say—why didn't I just marry Tom? Why did I marry William? I had no choice, well, I had a choice, but he would have killed Tom. He would have had Tom hunted down and killed, I know it."

Anna nearly choked on her water when the front door slammed shut. She fumbled and quickly hid her pills in a tampon box under the sink. She heard footsteps in the kitchen.

"Hey! Where are you?" William opened up a few cabinets and then slammed them shut just to make noise.

Anna took a last look in the mirror and rushed out of the bathroom. "Sorry," she said softly through the hallway. "I was—" She noticed the clock above the stove. "You're early?"

"Where's dinner?" William growled. "I've got people coming over at six and I need to eat. What the hell have you been doing all day?"

"I, umm, I'm sorry, I haven't prepared it yet but—"

"What the fuck do you mean haven't *prepared* it yet?" He did his best to imitate what he thought was weakness in her voice.

"You didn't tell me that—"

A strong slap across the face interrupted Anna's interjection. She fell back into the counter and started crying.

"Don't you even *think* of talking back to me. I just got done working my ass off and I sure as hell don't need to come home to some uppity bitch." What William meant by "working" was shaking down elderly shop owners to make sure they paid for "protection." It was in this way that he worked so hard as a "city manager."

Anna held her eyes low, not wanting to give him the satisfaction of seeing her cry.

"Why don't you try doing *your* job for once, huh?" William opened the fridge and grabbed a beer. Walking into the den he yelled, "Quit your blubbering and fix something quick. Else I'll give you something to really cry about."

Anna stood up from the floor and felt another bruise rise up on her cheek. She quickly grabbed a pan and started blindly tossing in ingredients. Oh how she wished she had a box of rat poison to dump in. The longer she stood there over the simmering pot, the more she descended from murderous rage to a more solemn wistfulness. She liked to imagine sometimes that she was cooking for Tom, that her labors of love were actually for someone she loved. The memory of Tom was really the only thing that kept her going…in all aspects of this situation.

At first, she blamed herself for making the wrong decision. But after the first few months, Anna realized that you can't regret making a *wrong* decision when there was really never any choice in the matter. She did what she did for the safety of the people she loved, plain and simple. And now she did her best to continue that vow.

When the couple sat down to eat, they always said a silent prayer. William's was probably a cursory abbreviation of "Bless us oh Lord, and these thy gifts…" but Anna's—Anna's was much more personal. "Thank you God for this food, may it turn to lead in our stomachs and poison our blood and may your graceful hand separate me from this man for the rest of eternity."

This was just when Anna was angry, though. More routinely she prayed that wherever he was in this world, that God would perform the miracle of allowing Tom to forget that he'd ever met her. She couldn't bear the thought of his heart hurting as much as hers did every single day.

On this night, she thought of the birthday card he'd sent a few months ago. It was a godsend that her parents passed along the letter in the first place and even more unlikely that word didn't reach William. He'd be sure to round up the other wise guys and take a trip to wherever the return address demanded just to make her life a little worse.

Yes, Anna couldn't deny that the thought of Tom kept her going, but she just couldn't handle the fact that every time he thought of her his mind and heart would be clouded with pain and resentment. The only cure she could hope for was a divine amnesia—something to offer him a fresh shot at being the loving and caring man she knew he would become.

William gulped down supper without a word and then got ready for his guests. Anna began wiping down the kitchen and washing dishes. No sooner had she swept the floor did the doorbell ring.

"Hey Guys!" shouted William, "Come on in and pull up a chair." Three men walked in the door bearing a not unremarkable resemblance to The Stooges. Each was bigger and dumber looking than the last. "The game is five card draw, deuces wild." William sat backwards in his chair and hugged the back of it while his friends took off their coats. Tilting his head back towards the kitchen, William bellowed "Get me and the boys some beer, would ya?"

As William drank and played cards, he got louder and drunker and more abusive.

"Bitch can't even have dinner ready when I get home," he shouted as the punchline to a joke.

"Hey! Why's my glass getting dry, bitch?" He cackled like a maniac and elbowed his friends if they weren't laughing.

Anna quietly appeared and replaced the glass with a new, full one. "Please don't talk to me like that," she said very quietly with her back to their company.

William arched his eyebrows and scoffed. "I'm sorry, did I just mishear you?" He looked to his friends and laughed nervously, "Did she just say what I think I heard her say? Huh?"

The guys all shrugged.

William stood up slowly from his chair, but because of the way he was sitting it fell over and knocked over the fresh beer. "Oh, well ain't this fuckin' wonderful? Look what you've done now?" The foamy brown liquid started to stream down the table towards the cards and piles of cash. "You don't want me to talk that way, is that it? What should I say, huh? Hows about this—" William cleared his throat with deliberation and changed his voice to match one of those Leave it to Beaver type husbands. "Honey, would you be a doll and bring me a fresh beer?"

Thinking he was finished, Anna started to say, "Yes, would that be so—"

"Before I yell to the whole fucking neighborhood what a lazy CUNT you are?" He started howling and slapping his knee. "Now clean this shit up and get me another beer before I lose my sense of humor."

Without thinking, Anna turned and said, "Get it yourself."

At this point, it stopped being a conversation and started taking the shape of a match of questions and answers. Anna turning her heels and walking away from her husband was the first question. William answered deftly with a quick grab of her arm. He pulled her back so hard it nearly wrenched her shoulder from its socket.

From the pain and the humiliation, Anna reacted by posing another question. What would happen if she hit him? What would happen if she could make him feel weak and powerless for once? Make him feel the rush of embarrassment she was so accustomed to by now? Her hand came up into a sharp fist, one she wanted to dig into the soft skin right under his eye.

But again, drunk as he was, William still had an answer. As her hand touched his face, he caught her by the wrist and spun her around.

"Look at this shit fellows! I got me a feisty one tonight huh?" He held her by both wrists now and breathed a heavy noxious breath down her neck. "That gets me a little *excited...*" He started kissing and biting her neck despite her writhing and squirming. "'Scuse us, boys, looks like me and the wife need to have a private conversation about minding our manners."

"Maybe what you need is a good fuckin' being the little whore that you are." He grabbed Anna by the hair and dragged her across the living room and into the bedroom where he proceeded to rape her.

Anna couldn't even form words. The screams she let out weren't recognizable as noises a human should make. By the time she'd be pushed into the bedroom, he blouse was torn down the center and William had his belt in his hands.

William just kept repeating the phrase, "Fuckin' whore, I bet you like this" over and over. He became eerily quiet with every repetition. After ripping her pants down and forcing himself inside her, after beating her to a bloody pulp, after Anna could no longer kick or scream or beg, she saw a strange blue light through her teary eyes.

"Fuckin whore, I bet you like this. You want it harder don't you, you fuckin whore—" Right before Anna was about to pass out from the pain and exhaustion, she watched as William's fist stopped in mid-air, and he was propelled backward off the bed. He stumbled and shook his head. "You bitch, hit me will you?" as he lunged forward again.

"But I didn't—" But before Anna could even think about what was happening, the lights in the room dimmed, the strange blue tones flashed again, and William bounced off the wall again as if he were attached to a bungee cord.

Anna felt delusional. The room started to sizzle and fade away, but before it did she saw the ghastly outline of a face that she'd only seen in her dreams for years— "Tom?" She whispered...

03030303

Anna was so humiliated and bruised she couldn't move the next morning. She could barely breath from the beating. "Effie, I have just got to find a way out." She hugged her doll and fell back asleep.

It was lunchtime when Mama came over to pay her daughter a visit. "Oh my God. Jesus, Mary and Joseph! What happened?"

"Nothing, Mama." Anna put a mug of coffee down on the table for her mother. "One or two sugars?"

Stefania didn't even bother to answer. Pushing the mug aside and reaching up to her daughter's face she said, "It doesn't look like nothing. It looks like you were in a car wreck! Are you okay?"

"I'm fine Mama."

"Did William do this?"

"I don't want to talk about it." Anna walked back to the counter and poured her own cup. She lingered there and looked out the window. She saw her mangled face, a nearly transparent reflection staring back at her. It's like she was barely even in this world anymore.

"It was him, wasn't it? You need to go to the police."

Anna shook her head slowly. "Believe me, that is the last place I should go."

"What do you mean?"

It was a question she'd been able to dodge or redirect for so long at this point, a lie she had told herself for so long that it didn't seem like an act. But today, everything hurt, even the smallest little lie that had lived inside her mind like a parasite. Anna just burst out crying. "Because the police are in with the mob and William is in with the mob and there is nothing I can do, but stay here."

"The mob?" Stefania stood up and walked to her daughter's side. "Jesus, Anna, I knew things weren't right here. Well, wait until I tell Papa about this. We'll see then what will be done. He will not stand for this."

She couldn't hold the tears back any longer. "Why? He's the reason I am in this mess to begin with."

"What? What do you mean? How can you say that?"

"Papa and Mr. Figerino forced me to marry William. They said if I didn't they would kill Tom."

"I can hardly believe that. You get your sweater and come with me. We are going home."

Anna followed blindly, not wanting to argue. When she got in her car to drive to Mama's house, William pulled in the driveway.

"Where do you think you are going?" he asked.

"We are going to my house for a little while," Stefania volunteered.

"I don't think so. Anna has a lot to do around here today." He walked over towards her car door. "Isn't that right, dear?" His smug little grin was poison.

"It's okay Mama." Anna said, "I'll see you a little later." Anna stepped out of the car and walked over to stand beside her husband.

"Are you sure honey?"

"Yes, Mama. I'll be fine."

Stefania felt the blood rise to her skin, but she left without saying anything. She knew it would just enrage the monster and she didn't want Anna to put up with any more than she had to already. So she did the only thing she thought she could, got in the car and drove off like a bat out of hell.

"What did she want?" said William.

"She just stopped by for a visit."

"Nosey busy body." William opened the door to the house and walked in. "You didn't tell her anything I hope for your and their sake."

"No, I didn't say anything." She shut and locked the door behind them. "What do you mean *their* sake?"

William walked towards the refrigerator but stopped. He didn't turn all the way around, but the look he threw over his shoulder silenced her heartbeats. He was a hungry snake that hissed with the voice of Death. "You know what I mean."

At the Sopoulos home that evening Anna's parent's had a serious talk.

"I was at Anna's today," said Mama.

"Oh, how is she?"

"Not well. George," she started hesitantly, "she had bruises all over her face. She wouldn't say, but I am pretty sure William beat her."

"God—No! I was afraid this would eventually happen."

"Then she told me…she told me that…" her hands were shaking too violently for her to hold her fork.

"What is it?"

With a softer voice than she thought possible, Mrs. Sopoulos somehow found the breath to say, "She said she couldn't go to the police because they are controlled by the mob, which you, William and Mr. Figerino are a part of. She said you forced her to marry William."

Mr. Sopoulos sighed and put his napkin down. "I am not part of the mob, but you are right, I did get them to force her to marry William."

"Why on Earth would you do such a thing!"

"I was just trying to do what was best for my daughter. She had fallen in love with that musician guy and I couldn't stand the thought of her bouncing from hotel to hotel to live." He clenched his fist. "That's no kind of life."

"And this is? What can we do to get her away from William?"

"I am not sure we can. I spoke to Mr. Figerino before the wedding and tried to stop it, but he said we had no choice now. I should have never made a deal with the devil. Maybe if I go back and explain what William has done, he will help me handle it."

"It's certainly worth a try, but be careful. I can't rest knowing our baby girl is being held hostage over there with that…that…”

“I know—”

໑໑໑໑

"Mr. Figerino, my daughter Anna, is being abused and beaten by her husband. I was hoping maybe you could speak with him and get him to stop. I normally wouldn't ask such a thing of you, but since you were involved in this arrangement from the start I thought—"

"You thought wrong! I will not involve myself in such matters. Maybe your daughter should listen to her husband and carry out his wishes. William has become a welcome guest in my home and I am sure that he would not have done this unless he was provoked. Now go and let me hear no more of it."

Suddenly George felt the same way as when he heard the mill was closing down. For someone to dismiss him like this, someone whom he thought had at least a shred of respect for him, it cut to the core. When George lost his job, he felt helpless, but today, he felt angry. "Then, I will take care of this myself," he said. "No man, I don't care whose welcome guest he is, is getting away with beating my daughter."

And with that he walked out and slammed the door.

Mr. Figerino pressed the intercom button. "Get William Bakalar on the phone...now."

໑໑໑໑

"William, this is Mr. Figerino, we have a problem."

"What is it Mr. Figerino?"

"I won't discuss it on the phone. Meet me at the store at 3 p.m.”

"Yes, sir."

Arriving home, George greeted Stefania.

"Well, what did he say?"

"He does not want to get involved in this and thinks William is justified in everything he does, so I guess I am going to have to take matters in my own hands. We have to get Anna out of there even if it means leaving our home and everything we have worked for."

"Do you really think we will have to leave?"

"I think if we don't our lives won't be worth a nickel!"

"Call Anna and tell her we will pick her up at 10 a.m. tomorrow morning. Tell her to pack light, but we are leaving for good."

CRCRCRCR

William walked in Mr. Figerino's office promptly at 3 p.m.

"So what's the problem, Mr. Figerino?"

"I am afraid your in-laws are going to cause us problems concerning your actions the other night. George Sopoulos was none too happy about you beating his daughter."

"How does he know...wait a minute, her mother was over at the house yesterday. I'll bet that barren bitch told her mama that I beat her. Wait 'til I get back home."

"I wouldn't concern myself with your wife right now. It is her parents that represent the biggest threat and that threat needs to be removed. Just do what needs to be done. You can deal with your wife later."

"Whatever you say Mr. Figerino. I will handle it."

The next morning after William left for work, Anna packed a small suitcase, waiting for her parents. It was 9 a.m. and Anna was shaking so hard that she had trouble calming her hands to drink her tea.

Meanwhile, George and Stefania loaded up the car and

headed to Anna's.

"I hope we don't have a confrontation with William when we get there," said Stefania. "It appears that he can become very violent."

"Just let me worry about that," said George patting his coat pocket. "I came prepared...just in case. No one is going to hurt my family and get away with it."

About half-way there, George noticed an unusual amount of play in the steering.

"Damn, I just got this thing inspected last week. We really don't have time for this."

Just then, the steering completely broke loose and the car became uncontrollable. Oncoming traffic whizzed by on the highway and the world became a swirling blur of headlights and horns.

"Oh, my God!" screamed Stefania, "….there's a truck!"

 C3C3C3C3

The morning passed with first 9:30, then 9:45 and 10:00, then 10:15. Papa was unusually punctual, but the clock then struck 10:30 when Anna heard a car pull into the driveway. But it was not her parents, it was William. She quickly threw the case under the bed.

"Hi, Sweetie. You sitting here waiting for me?"

"Actually, I was waiting on my parents to take me out to lunch, but they were supposed to be here at 10:00."

"Well, that is why I came home early as soon as I heard the news so I could tell you myself."

"What news?" Anna cried.

"Your mom and dad were driving down the road and lost control of their vehicle and crashed head on into a transfer truck. They were killed instantly."

Anna searched her heart to see if this was a lie, if William was just abusing her emotions today instead of her flesh.

And just then, she felt it. The world was different somehow, she felt truly and utterly alone. "No…" she whispered.

"Sometimes accidents happen, Sweetie. I am here for you, as I always am." As he put his arm around her, a darkness trickled through his touch and infected her bloodstream. He was telling a violent and malicious truth. Anna started to heave, drenching his new jacket.

"Goddamit!" William whined, recoiling to the bathroom to wipe off her stench.

☙☙☙☙

At the funeral, Anna was still numb inside. She just could not believe this was happening. It was so surreal. William put on the pretense of the bereaved and devoted husband. Anna's parents didn't have many friends, so it was a very small attendance.

As they were leaving the grave sight Anna overheard William tell his friend Sal in a hushed tone, "They should've left well enough alone. I just mean it pays to keep your mouth shut in this town. Sometimes accidents happen."

Anna couldn't believe her ears. Was William eluding that the accident wasn't an accident? Did he have something to do with it? The police said the steering rod broke, which made them lose control. Was it tampered with? The police said it was just an unfortunate accident. Sometimes accidents happen…maybe…Could he really have…suddenly Anna was no longer numb. She was filled with one singular and clearly identifiable emotion—fear.

CHAPTER 18

The years dragged on. The physical and mental abuse continued with Anna terrified to speak to anyone. Of course, she had no one to talk to...except Effie. Most days were spent in meditation and prayer to escape the horrors she faced every day when William would come home from work. She tried to make sure everything was just so, as to not set William off in a fit of rage and have to endure another beating. Anna had become extremely withdrawn, and yet, somehow much stronger. Without her realizing it, she was becoming awakened to her own supernatural abilities. She was beginning to visualize the person that she was destined to be, yet she did not fully understand it.

"Effie, I am having the strangest daydreams as of late. It's not like a dream when you sleep, but actually a vivid dream; a vision of people I have never seen and places I have never been. It is so real. Today, though, I actually saw and talked to Tom! He did not recognize me, nor remember who I was, but we both enjoyed the moment so much. There was such peace. Then, there was this man standing behind him, who appeared to be oriental, that said, 'Don't worry, you are fast approaching your destiny and will be reunited with Tom forever. You have a great many powers hidden inside of you that have not yet reached their potential, but they will very soon. Open your eyes and your heart to them. Love is the greatest power of all.' And Effie, then I suddenly jolted awake. Oh, if it was just true...that Tom and I could get back together and then we could—"

"You could what?" William's voice came from around the bedroom door.

Startled Anna said, "Oh, you scared me. I didn't hear you come in."

"Who were you talking to?" William said gruffly.

Anna was still holding Effie when William continued, "You are crazy as bat shit! You are sitting here talking to that fuckin' doll, aren't you...AREN'T YOU!"

Anna nodded and said quietly, "She is the only one I can talk to now that Mama is gone. She gave me Effie when I was a little girl and—"

"EFFIE" William taunted. "Just like you, another cheap looking little whore!" as he grabbed the doll and threw it against the wall, breaking Effie's porcelain face.

"Oops...sometimes accidents happen," said William as he moved toward Anna.

Anna suddenly felt something she had never felt before. It was a sudden charge of electrical current that ran through her whole body. She no longer had any control over her body as her spirit exited and rushed forth striking William in the chest propelling him into the wall and knocking him unconscious.

When William awoke, he found Anna in the kitchen preparing dinner. Shaken and bewildered he approached the table and sat. Not saying a word, he allowed Anna to serve him. Anna sat down across the table from him, placed her napkin in her lap and softly said, "It's ok, Sweetie, sometimes accidents happen."

William nervously eyed his plate of food, quietly got up and went out the door.

The next day Anna proceeded to glue Effie's damaged face. Looking at the cracked lines in the face she said, "We make quite a pair. With our battle scars and worry lines we could be twins. Maybe I should use some of this superglue to shut William's mouth once and for all."

Effie, or a spirit through her, suddenly spoke, "Two wrongs don't make a right. Two evil deeds do not produce good. Love is the key to all things, it conquers all. You must shed all ego and endure what is now so that when you are once again with your true twin, you will be able to reunite forever and ascend with the twelve."

Anna was completely taken aback. Maybe, she thought, she was crazy. Talking to dolls is one thing. Them talking back is quite another. But what she heard made her realize that she must continue down the path she had chosen. It was her vocation to endure her life with William as long as she must, but Anna continued to see things she didn't want to see and hear things that she didn't want to hear.

"Effie, I have just got to find a way out of here, but how?"

Then one night in 1996, Anna overheard a conversation between William and his goon buddy Sal, another "made man," that was supposed to be private.

"Sal, Michael Bilatto told me today that he wants you and me to help him on a job. He wants us to hit Ralph Goins."

"The fuckin' county prosecutor...Jesus H—"

"Shut your mouth! This came directly from Mr. Figerino himself. He wants it done quickly before Goins appoints that FBI guy that has been up our ass as chief investigator."

"Who? Kroner?"

"Yeah, that's the one."

"This is big, William."

"Where and when?"

"Next Thursday night at Goin's house. We'll meet Michael at Mr. Figerino's farm in Canfield and ride together."

Anna felt something stir within here that hadn't in a while—hope. The next morning she went to a pay phone a little way out of town. Over the years she had developed what any rational person would call intense paranoia.

"Federal Bureau of Investigation. How may I transfer

your call?"

With her heart pounding Anna stammered, "Agent Kroner, please."

"Hold, and I will transfer."

"Agent Kroner's office," a lady on the other end said.

"Is Agent Kroner available?"

"Not today, he is out of town. Could you tell me what this is about?"

"I overheard a plan to murder the Mahoning County Prosecutor and wanted to report it."

"I think you should come in right away and discuss it with Agent Kroner. Can you be here at 10 a.m. tomorrow morning?"

"Yes, I think I can."

"Ok. My name is Marge and I will see you at 10. May I ask your name?"

"It's Anna...Anna Bakalar."

"Alright, Mrs. Bakalar. We will expect you tomorrow."

The next day Anna hustled William out the door to "work" and she jumped in the car and headed for Canfield. It was close enough that she would get back in plenty of time and far enough away from anyone that might see her there.

Agent Kroner, himself, met her at the door of the field office and as they sat down, Anna was so jittery that she thought she was going to get sick.

"Would you like a cup of coffee?"

"Do you have tea?" Anna said as she sat down.

"Yes, certainly. Marge, would you get Mrs. Bakalar a cup of tea?"

"So, from what I understand, you heard this conversation between your husband and another man. They spoke of killing Mr. Goins, the county prosecutor, is that correct?"

"Yes."

"Do you believe it to be true?"

"Yes, that town is controlled by the mob and well, William, my husband, is a big part of it. He also said that a man named Michael Bilatto was going to help them and that Mr. Figerino had ordered them to do this," she continued.

"Leonard Figerino?...The Mafia Don? Are you sure that is what he said?"

"Yes, I heard him very clearly. They had mentioned something about meeting at his farm up here in Canfield."

"Why would you turn your husband in and get involved in this?"

"To escape, but I can't be involved."

"Miss, I am afraid you are already involved. You will have to testify when and if there is a trial."

"I can't. They will kill me, just like they killed my parents."

"We will offer you protection."

"How will you do that? The police and judges are all on the take. I am really terrified. I don't think I can—"

"You must if you ever want to be free of them."

"They will just find me and kill me."

"I can put you into protective custody and enter you into the witness protection program."

"We will move you to another city with a new name. Somewhere that you can't be found."

The 18-minute drive home seemed very long. Anna stopped by the store to get something for dinner as she didn't want to make William any madder than he normally was.

When she got home, William was there waiting.

"Where have you been?"

"To the store to get dinner. Look I got your favorite... lamb. I thought I'd make a stew."

"Why are you home so early?"

"I have to work late tonight and I wanted to get home and rest up a little."

"I didn't know you had to work tonight. You told me you would be working late next Thursday night, or I would have had dinner already fixed for you."

"Naw, we moved that late job to tonight to get it over with."

"Well, get in that kitchen and rattle them pots and pans. I'm starving."

Oh no, Anna thought. *How can I get word to Agent Kroner now! Mr. Goins is in grave danger. I will figure something out. I just have to.*

As Anna cooked she envisioned a new life far away from here, far away from this nightmare. It felt too good to be true, but it was finally happening.

William left around 9 o'clock. As soon as Anna was sure that he was gone, she jumped in her car and headed to a pay phone, hoping not to be spotted. She called Agent Kroner on the cell phone number he had given her.

"Hello," he said.

"Hello, this is Anna...Anna Bakalar."

"Yes, Mrs. Bakalar, go ahead?"

"They decided to do the job tonight, instead of next Thursday. William is on his way now!"

"Oh my god, I have to warn Ralph. Thank you for calling."

 C3C3C3C3

According to a statement later given in a plea agreement by William Bakalar:

Me, Sal and Michael left Mr. Figerino's farm and headed for for the prosecutor's home. When we arrived the lights were out and it appeared that no one was at home. I got out of the car and attached a speed loader to the revolver to make it shoot faster. Bilatto gave me the honor of carrying out the hit. I voice tested the walkie-talkies but did not get an answer. I tried again, but no answer. I couldn't believe this shit. I was being asked to pull off the mafia hit of the century and the fuckin' equipment didn't work. I went back to the car and said I couldn't do this hit without communication.

We regrouped down the street in a parking lot where we programmed two cell phones together and then went back to Goin's house. This time there were lights on in the kitchen and a car in the drive. Goins was talking on the phone.

I crept into the house and into the kitchen, carrying cocaine to plant on the body to make it look like a drug-related hit when I saw Goins standing there hanging up the phone. I rushed over to him and shot him in the stomach. He fell against the stove and I shot again hitting him in the forearm. As I started to finish him the fuckin' gun jammed. Hell! I panicked and ran out the back door heading through the woods. Stumbling to the car, I jumped in the back seat and huddled in the floorboard.

ෆෆෆෆ

"Is he dead?" Sal shouted.

"I'm not sure. I think so."

"What the fuck do you mean, you're not sure?"

"The gun jammed."

"We gotta go back and make sure. Why in the hell didn't you find a butcher knife and stab him to death for Christ's sake."

"Shit! What happened to the speed-loader?" Bilatto said.

"It must have fallen off."

"We have got to go back and find it, you fuckin' moron."

Just then the police scanner came on and said the police were on their way and that Goins was still alive. Police sirens could be heard off in the distance.

"We gotta get out of here...Drive!"

ෆෆෆෆ

Chapter 19

It was around 11:30, when Anna heard a loud knock at the door. It was Agent Kroner and some other men.

"We have to go. NOW!"

"Go where?"

"Grab some clothes and come on. We don't have much time."

Anna hurriedly packed and headed out with Agent Kroner.

As they sped off Kroner said, "We caught up with your husband and the other two men as they were heading away from Goins' home. They're in custody now, but your life is in extreme danger."

That shook Anna into reality. One of the arresting officers overheard Sal telling William that his wife was the only one that could have overheard that conversation about their plans and that they needed to have someone take care of the bitch.

Anna was whisked away into protective custody with a new name, Karli Roberts, and a new home as they moved her to another city...Carol Stream, IL, a suburb of Chicago. She continued to stay there until the trial began.

The trial dragged on for two more years as they traveled back and forth to Youngstown.

ಃಃಃಃ

"Officer Dolan, would you tell the court where you found this speed-loader?"

"I found it at the edge of the woods behind Prosecutor Goin's home."

"Please have the court mark this as exhibit F."

"Who's finger prints were found on the loader?"

"The lab found two sets that were positively identified as those of William Bakalar and Michael Bilatto."

"No further questions. The state now calls to the stand, Anna Bakalar."

"I object!" yelled the defense attorney. "A spouse cannot testify against her husband due to spousal privilege."

"The prosecution contends that this communication was not between Anna and William Bakalar, but instead, was an overheard conversation between Sal Harris and William Bakalar and is considered an observation by the spouse and therefore admissible."

"That is true." said the judge. "Overruled...as long as she waives spousal privilege, she may testify as to what she heard directly."

"Do you wish to waive that privilege, Mrs. Bakalar."

"It's Sopoulos, your honor. I am now divorced, and yes, I wish to waive my privilege."

"So be it, you may testify, but only those things that you heard directly."

The bailiff then said, "Will you swear to tell the truth and nothing but the truth so help you God?"

"Yes, of course I will."

"Ms. Sopoulos, what did you overhear at your home the night before Ralph Goins was shot?"

"I overheard my husband tell Sal Harris that they were to help Michael Bilatto kill Mr. Goins."

"You Bitch. You are gonna die!" yelled William. "I am going to have you killed!"

"Bailiff, remove that man from the courtroom." William

was whisked away cussing and screaming.

"Any further questions of this witness?"

"No, your honor."

"Alright then, Ms. Sopoulos, you are excused. You may step down."

Over the course of the next four years, the prosecutor made a plea agreement with William in exchange for his testimony. That, along with the FBI's deal with Leonard Figerino, convicted the chief of police, the outgoing prosecutor, the sheriff, the county engineer, members of the local police force, a city law director, several defense attorneys, politicians, judges, and a former assistant U.S. attorney for racketeering, murder and extortion. It seemed as if the entire city of Youngstown was on trial. William's plea agreement handed down two life sentences plus 20 yrs. for his part. He figured it was better than a needle.

"Good," Anna said, "I am finally rid of the bastard. It's finally over." She hugged Agent Kroner with tearful eyes and said, "Now maybe I can know what it's like to try and have a normal life." She started sobbing in his arms. "Thank you," is all she could manage to say.

"The Mafia may have left Youngstown, but they haven't forgotten you, Ms. Sopoulos. I am afraid you will have to spend the rest of your life in witness protection. You will be just fine as long as you don't bring attention to yourself."

After the whirlwind that the past few years had been for her, after all the nightmares and traveling, the torment and the constant anxiety, bringing attention to herself was the last thing she wanted to do. So there she sat in her little apartment in Carol Stream, alone. She thought in her mind that when all was said and done that she'd feel reborn, free to be anyone she'd ever hoped to be. But in the falling light of evening, in the stony silence of her Spartan home, she felt more like everything in her was already dead.

രുരുരുരു

CHAPTER 20

The long and grueling drive back to North Carolina was, thank God, uneventful. Tom kept wondering what he was going to be able to do once he got there. Job prospects were slim there too, but it was still his home.

He had a little left over from his parent's estate and from the sale of his father's business. That would hold him over for a little while until he could get acclimated and sort things out.

Tom wasn't the same man that he was when he left. Yes, in a negative sense he was still crippled, but, thanks to Master Bennie, he now had a new, positive direction in his life that most would consider supernatural ability. He was no longer the egotistical and arrogant 21-year-old that left this beach a few years ago with a major chip on his shoulder. No, now he was a much humbler and peaceful human being who realized that all in the universe was connected and deserved equal respect.

However, even though he had learned to overcome the deficiencies of his handicap through the use of portals to different dimensions, he still lived here in a three dimensional world, which required him to eat and therefore, to find employment.

As he approached Swansboro, he could begin to smell the salt air and hear the coastal sounds that had once been so familiar to him. He stopped and took a moment to watch as the boats came in to shore.

"God," he heard himself say out loud. Tom was over-come with a sense of reverence for the beauty and tranquility of the Bogue Sound. "Whatever possessed me to leave?" It was a question he asked to the stillness of the waters, to the golden sky of mystery, and to the dark stranger that used to hide inside his soul.

It was as if he was seeing the Crystal Coast for the first time, soaking in every image, sound and smell. Tom was so focused on his career before that he never took the time to smell the *frowers*, as Master Bennie put it.

After crossing the bridge into Emerald Isle, he navigated his way down Salterpath towards home. His home...His beach.

First stop...the Iron Steamer Pier. Time for lunch...time for a chili dog, or two.

"Two Chili Dogs, please."

The hairy-armed fry cook snorted. Without looking up he asked, "You want slaw?"

"Oh, no thank you." Tom spoke with the cheerfulness of a foreigner and didn't even mind when the cook muttered something about tourists and their tastes.

As he chomped down on one of the dogs, Tom thought of his old drummer, Chooch, who would hustle down to the pier as soon as they finished a gig and order a dozen dogs to snack on. People that heard that little detail about Chooch usually assumed he was a huge guy, but actually his name could have been String Bean.

One night he ordered his usual dozen and the guy behind him said, "Gotta a party goin' on?"

"Nope," said Chooch. "Just hungry."

The patron arched his eyebrows incredulously. "Hell boy, if you can eat all of them dogs I'll pay for 'em!" The guy rocked back on his heels, confident in his easy-money bet.

Chooch, equally confident, nodded without hesitation. Then he sat down and finished the dogs as the other fellow watched. After every bite, the man's jaw dropped a little lower. At first he was ribbing Chooch, taunting him a little bit, but by the ninth dog he was sweating.

Chooch, however, wasn't slowing down. He ate at the same methodical pace, making sure to chew adequately, wiping his mouth after each dog, occasionally refilling his coke.

By the eleventh dog, the man was muttering things like, "Ain't no fuckin way…no fuckin way."

By the twelfth, the man had his wallet out, already resigned to the fact that he'd made a wager with no upside.

"I can't believe you ate the whole dozen, but here you go. I promised to pay for them and I always keep my word, although, I gotta say, I think you'll be paying for them in the long run," the guy said, laughing.

As soon as Chooch got the handful of cash and thanked the gentlemen he raised his hand toward the cook and said, "Another dozen chili dogs, please...this time with a little more mustard."

Tom laughed to himself while he remembered thinking the guy was going to faint.

Tom strolled casually along eating his lunch, stopping on the dock to soak it all in. He looked over to an old man fishing off the pier. "Nothing like the smell of chum and chili dogs in the morning, huh?"

The old man muttered something unintelligible, but didn't look up.

"Good to be back," Tom said quietly with a smile.

Next stop, the Ramada Inn. Tom decided to walk down the beach and breathe in a few more memories. Oh, that salt air in the September breeze and the feel of sand between your toes. A great time to be at the beach. Seagulls now took up the space where the tourists had been. All of the gulls were lined up in rows looking toward one bird facing them as if in a meeting.

He remembered the tired old joke his Dad would always

tell him. "That one must be the Chairman of the Bird." Tom could hear his old man's voice and he smiled.

Gazing down, he saw a starfish lying in the sand by his feet. He reached down and tossed it back in the ocean. Maybe it would have new life...maybe Tom would have new life, too.

Looking off in the sunset, he thought he saw someone coming toward him..a sudden deja vu moment that disappeared as soon as it came. He just shrugged it off.

As he was walking back toward the inn, he noticed that Melvin was gathering up the umbrellas and chairs as he did every day. Tom went to greet him.

"Hey, old man. Remember me?"

Melvin squinted at the sunlight recognizing him saying, "Tom! You had better watch that 'old man' shit." He started to laugh but then noticed Tom's cane and crooked gait. "It seems you are a lot worse off than me. What in the world happened?"

"Car accident out in L.A. a couple of years ago. But I'm ok now, except for the leg."

"Too bad...I guess you won't be entertaining anymore. What are you doing now?"

"Well," he said hesitantly, "I'm not too sure." Tom studied the old hotel and thought of those days with fondness. "I have got to find work somewhere, but my prospects are kinda limited." As he heard the words come from his mouth, Tom felt a sudden bitterness try to creep into his heart, but he was aware of it before the seed of self-doubt could take root.

Instead of allowing darkness to swallow him as it once had, Tom used the principles of redirection that Master Bennie taught him. He smiled into the sun and said, "How about you Melvin? Got any ideas for me? I bet I can fold chairs with the best of 'em!"

"Maybe—" Melvin squinted, taken aback by the brightness of Tom's smile. It's as if he was looking into the eyes of a much kinder and wiser Tom than he'd ever known. Melvin thought of some of the Sunday School stories he used to teach the kids, stories about people being touched by God in some way. "You know, St. Andrews Episcopal Church over in Morehead is looking for someone that can play the organ and piano as well as direct a choir. It's not a night club gig but—"

"But it's better than the job I have now." Tom chuckled and turned out his empty pockets for dramatic effect.

"Very true. So you think you might be interested in applying?"

"Absolutely! I used to play in the church when I was younger and I'm good at working with singers. Do you know anyone over there?"

"Well I'm actually on the board of trustees...I'll see if I can get you an interview."

"Fantastic. Thanks so much, Melvin. I knew coming back to my roots wouldn't let me down."

Melvin patted Tom on the shoulder and shook his hand. Something about his aura was just totally different than he remembered. It made him want to just keep smiling. "Where are you staying, son?"

"Nowhere yet. I just got back in town."

"You know you're welcome to stay here at the inn until you get back on your feet."

"Now that's really fantastic. Thanks Melvin."

Melvin smiled and continued stacking chairs and folding umbrellas.

Tom followed suit and helped as best he could. After a few moments Tom said, "Maybe when you uh…I mean, when you talk to the church, maybe don't use my stage name. Tom Marks could still carry a bit of a stigma here in the Bible Belt."

"I see your point—" Melvin laughed. "Trouble is, I'm not

sure you've ever told me your real name."

Tom stuck out his hand and said, "Thomas Marcus Banos, but I go by Mark Banos, good to meet you!"

"All right, Mark, I'll see what I can do."

As it turned out, it only took a few weeks for the board to approve of Mark, now going exclusively by his given name, as the new choir director at St. Andrews. Mark felt the position to be very fulfilling in a spiritual and emotional sense, but it was also very low on the pay scale. Still, it paid the rent and kept him going and the congregation seemed to be very appreciative.

It was during this time that he also met a nice young lady at church. She was a sweet girl that liked to walk on the beach and sit and talk about all kinds of interesting things. Patty was an avid boater and liked her Schlitz beer and fast Corvettes. She and Mark would take her Vette down the dirt roads to picnic at Cedar Island on Sunday afternoons after church. She'd place a hair brush against the accelerator to hold it down as she steered with her feet so they could sit on the T-top roof drinking beer. Yeah, maybe she was a little crazy, too.

It was a particularly beautiful Sunday afternoon on this one trip to the island. The place was pretty much deserted in the early spring...nothing but shade trees and reeds. They spread out a picnic blanket under a tree and drank a few more beers when she asked, "Want a piece?"

As Mark moved closer to her she leaned over impishly and said, "of chicken!"

Mark said, "Oh" with a disappointed smile.

"Now Mr. Banos, what else could you have thought I meant?"

And with that Mark took his cue and kissed her. She returned a long deep kiss that would have knocked Mark off his feet if he hadn't already been laying down. And then she jumped on top of him as they wrestled on the blanket, frantically ripping clothes from one another's bodies.

They rhythmically consumed one another, melting together under the hot sun, finally gasping as they collapsed in each other's arms.

The sound of the wind stirring through the reeds returned to their ears, and they were conscious of the world once more.

"Oh, Mr. Banos, it was about time!"

Mark assumed what she meant by that was that he had had repeated opportunities to take advantage of her, but for some reason had ignored her advances. Maybe, or maybe the advances were just too subtle and southern belle-like. Seems like timing is everything.

A few weeks later, she decided to move in and shared Mark's small apartment. He didn't remember asking her to move in, but it didn't seem to matter.

Patty cooked meager dinners that included things like Mushroom Stroganoff and Rice-a-Roni. This was fine with Mark as he had long lived on "Cup of Noodles," lovingly referred to as *Cup of Crap* on the road, as a constant dietary supplement.

Mark liked Patty for her companionship, but he really didn't love her. He didn't love the touch of his fingertips brushing hair from her face, he didn't love the sound of her breath lulling him to sleep, he didn't love the thought of the two of their souls commingling to form an eternity between their two hearts.

The reason he didn't love any of these things is because, well, they didn't exist. Of course, Tom wasn't necessarily consciously aware of any of this, all he knew was there was just something missing.

The truth is, Patty had all the depth of a kiddie pool. It didn't really matter though, as not only did she have fine culinary skills, but she also, well, let's just say that she had enough ass-sets to keep Mark occupied.

A few days turned into months and months into years. Mark was still at the church, Patty was still at the apartment and life continued its circle dance.

Then as Mark approached year 15 of this never-ending conundrum, the most peculiar things started to take place. Mark became more and more lethargic and his grooming habits, which had always been impeccable, seemed not to matter anymore. He let his beard grow out and never bothered to cut his hair. He also bathed infrequently allowing his musk to permeate the apartment. He didn't seem to be able to focus on anything and completed his daily tasks by simply going through the motions without putting in much thought or effort.

"Did you take a bath today?" Patty inquired.

"I mean...had one yesterday," Mark replied.

"A shower a day keeps the lice away," said Patty.

"I don't see no need. Why don't you come a little closer, I feel like performing some magic," Mark chided.

"I don't see no need, David Copafeel," Patty retorted. "Besides you've had too much scotch again to even make it around the bases, so don't bother. I'm going out for a while. You will have to fix your own dinner if you want something other than your liquid diet."

"Whatever I fix couldn't be worse than the banquet in a box that you would serve," Tom snorted.

"Bastard!" she shouted slamming the door.

A few days later, Chivas, his golden retriever and constant companion, died suddenly for no apparent reason. The vet could not find anything wrong that could have caused his sudden demise. He was only five years old.

Then came the big blow. Melvin had left the board of trustees and the church had voted not to continue Mark's contract as he was no longer a good fit for the church. He played too loud, he was disrespectful to the pastor, he wasn't there on time and his musical selections were uninteresting...

none of which he thought were true.

"Oh well, fuck 'em," he said pouring himself another drink.

Patty, who had just heard the news about Mark being terminated, arrived home.

"I heard the church let you go. I'm sorry, but you brought it on yourself. You just haven't been yourself this whole year, letting yourself go like you have," said Patty.

"I don't understand what you mean. Ungrateful bunch of hypocrites. They were lucky to have someone as talented as me in their Podunk little church. Why I—"

"Look, I have something to tell you before this goes any further. I'm leaving."

"What—?"

"I'm leaving...I want a little something more than living in this cramped apartment, cooking, cleaning and copulating with Mr. Clean. Gary asked me to move to Arizona with him and I have decided that it would be my best option."

"Gary? The guitar player in the band at church? When did this happen?"

"On about drink 147—"

"You smart mouthed bitch...take your shit and get out!" Mark shouted. "And don't let the door hit you in the ass on the way out."

And she left.

It seemed as if one turd after another dropped from the sky, and poor Mark was the tidy bowl man. Mark was getting more and more depressed when he heard a knock at the door.

"What now, huh?" he shouted at the door. "Landlord here to kick me out or milkman here to blame me for a kid?"

But when he opened the door, he was greeted by a familiar voice. "Hi Tommysan."

"Oh, my God!" Mark gasped.

"Not God, Bennie. How are you?"

"Come in, Come in!" Mark stumbled through the den and motioned towards the couch. "Good and you? What are you doing here?"

"I tell later, you fix tea now, then we talk. It has been rong trip. I had to take plane to Raleigh. That took seven hours. Then I jump puddle pooper to New Bern and then take taxi here. Why you live so far away? Bennie, how you say, fuckin' tired!"

Tom started to comment, but Bennie interrupted.

"Phew! What that smell?" said Master Bennie waving his hand in front of his nose.

"What smell?" Tom looked around like he was going to see a green cloud. "I don't smell anything."

"Skunk don't smell his own hole first. When last time you have bath?"

"I don't know...sometime this week I think."

"You no think shit...you no know shit...but you smell like shit...you look like shit. Go take bath, then we talk."

After Mark cleaned himself up, they drank tea and chit-chatted a long while. Then Master Bennie said, "I come to see friend in trouble, one who needs my help."

"Oh, who is that?"

"You!"

"Me! You traveled all the way across the country to help me because you had a feeling that—"

"Not feeling, me know! Besides, I wanted some Eastern Carolina Bar-B-Que with hot slaw."

"I have had a sudden rash of bad luck. Is that what you are referring to?"

"Aye, more than bad luck from what I see. You have never looked this disheveled. What have you been involved in since you left LA?" inquired Master Bennie.

"Well...for the past 15 years or so I have been working for a church and—"

"Church?" exclaimed Bennie. "You go church? Church

186

can be good and sometimes not so good. One body with 200 minds can cause great confusion. Just as a person can pray for you to get well, a person can also pray for you to get sick. Has anyone ever had anything against you there?"

"Well, there was a disagreement with a couple of the deacons over allowing the children to play instruments in the band. The kids weren't very good, but I figured it was more important to encourage them to participate so they could grow both musically and spiritually, given time. The debate did get a little heated, but then subsided."

"That's because they knew there was another way to defeat you, even though the rest of the church was on your side. Remember, Jesus said where two or more are gathered…" Bennie trailed off and nodded. "Can be for good or not so good," he said finally. I fear that you are suffering from a severe psychic backlash. I can sense the negativity all around you. You must get help right away"

"How did this happen?" Tom asked.

"Don't know for sure, but I told you long time ago that using your gift is both a blessing and a curse. Because you are sensitive to the hidden world around you, you also are vulnerable to hidden enemies. You will often encounter NHE that will try to terrorize you. This time I believe you have encountered a vampire that was drawn to you by your deacon friend's prayers."

"A vampire? Like Dracula?"

Bennie leaned over to grab Mark's cane and whacked him over the head with it.

"Ow! What the hell was that for?"

"Interrupting! Life not like movie, Tommysan. Real life, real evil."

"Fine, jeez. I get it…but what's a…what did you call it? An en-ay-chee?"

"NHE, stupid. Three letters. Non-Human Entity can come in many shapes, you seem to have found a psychic vampire, one that drains the positive life force out of you and everyone that is around you and turns everything in your life that is positive into something very negative. I am sure you have heard the phrase, *sucking the life out of you.* Have you not been waking very tired as of late, not caring about anything? Did you recently lose a pet or a girlfriend?"

"Yes, but how did you know?"

"Me, know much… you, not so much. That's why you need help."

"How can you help me?"

"No can help you this time. But I know of someone who I think can. She is a gifted spiritual healer named Karli Roberts. In Chicago. Here, you call." Bennie produced a business card from his front shirt pocket. It featured a name, a number, and a strange symmetrical symbol.

"Are you sure that she can fix this?" Mark studied the card with doubt.

Bennie folded his arms and tilted his head downward. "No."

"No, what do you mean no? What if she can't?"

"You dead man."

"Great, but why didn't you just call me with her number instead of coming all this way?"

"Told you, Carolina Bar-B-Que! And I wanted to see you before the funeral, heh, heh."

"Whose funeral?"

"Hopefully not yours. Now let's eat, your treat."

So they drove down to the Big Oaks Drive-In in Salterpath and ate BBQ.

"Damn good BBQ", Master Bennie said after devouring the second chopped sandwich. "Why they put vinegar sauce on it?"

"East Carolina BBQ." Mark explained.

"Ha! I from East, Tommysan, we no have vinegar pigs!" He laughed at his own joke for a long time. "I like East. But

I like your East, too. OK, I think I stay awhile." He scratched his head and pulled a crumpled map from his back pocket. "You know Holiday Inn?"

"No Holiday Inn for you, Sensei. You will be staying with me."

"We come eat more East Carolina BBQ?"

"Yes."

"Then me stay with you...Thank you. We go home now, shave, cut hair. You still look like shit...you no longer smell like shit...keep take bath. No become plick again."

Master Bennie stayed with Mark for the next month working with him, helping him to ground himself and again, heal his Chakras before getting help from Miss Roberts. Master Bennie explained that it was very important for Mark to cleanse himself completely before trying to heal his spirit.

As he drove Master Bennie back to the airport, Mark reflected on what a close and dear friend he had become and that this may very well be the last time that he would see him. He had always treated Tom like a son. As Master Bennie said goodbye he added, "You know my name used to be Mark too, before I ascended. I wrote a short book once, maybe you have read it."

"I don't think so—"

Handing him a small ice pack container Mark said, "Here is something for when you get back to California."

Grinning Master Bennie said, "East Carolina Bar-B-Que?"

"And hot slaw," Mark said.

Mark may have been imagining it, but he swore he could see moisture in Master Bennie's eyes as he said, "I love you, son. I will see you again when you take your rightful place. You know, your birth parents were right in naming you. Your name has always been Thomas."

Mark said, "I doubt it," as the two shared a final embrace.

Chapter 21

When Mark got back home he glanced at the number written on a piece of paper laying by the phone. Picking the piece of paper up, he looked at it again, laid it down and poured himself a drink. As he sat there relishing the taste of the scotch, he again picked up the paper and twirled it around in his fingers. "Oh, what the hell," Mark muttered, "what have I got to lose. Damn near lost everything already." So, he picked up the phone and dialed the number.

A young lady's voice answered, "Stop, don't call anyone else. I will call you back in ten minutes."

"Hello? What do you mean don't—"

But she had already hung up.

"Strange reception," Mark said to the dial tone. What the hell had Bennie done to him now?

She called him back in almost ten minutes on the dot.

"Hello, my name is Karli. How are you Mr. Banos?"

"Not so good…wait, how…how did you know my name? And my number I didn't--"

"I know much, and not so much," the young lady said.

He couldn't help but laugh. "Definitely sounds like a friend of Master Bennie's."

"Well, Mr. Banos, why don't you—"

"Sorry, it's Mark. The last name bit was a neat trick, but you can call me Mark."

He could hear her speaking through a smile on the other end. "Why don't you tell me why you think you're calling?"

Mark looked down at his scotch and swirled it around. "Well, a friend told me to call. He said you might be able to help me."

"It's possible, but not certain. Ultimately you have to help yourself…but I'll see what I can do." The more she spoke, the more she reminded him of someone not just wise like his sensei, but someone comforting…someone nostalgic. "I see that there is a lot of negativity surrounding you causing you a lot of pain and despair. Someone or something is trying to prevent you from succeeding in your life."

Mark was taken aback by this. "Why? Do the deacons hate me that much?"

"Deacons?"

"Nevermind."

"The truth is, I don't know why. There are evil things in other worlds that come into ours and try to make our lives miserable. I have a strong sense that feels whatever it is has connected with you, and is literally draining your life from you. It seems to be creating a great deal of confusion."

"You can say that again." Mark finished off his drink and rubbed his eyes. "What can we do?"

"We cannot destroy it, but we can trick it."

"Trick it, huh? How?"

"Leave that to me."

"And how much will it cost?"

"$10,000!" she said.

"Whoa! I'm not sure—"

"Just kidding. The material I need are just $95; God provides for me."

"That's it?"

"Yes. Hurry now and send it to me."

"What is your address?"

"…311 Blackhawk Drive, Carol Stream, Illinois. Hurry as it will take several days to prepare."

"Ok. Talk to you soon." As he was about to hang up the

phone, he wanted to say something else. He felt that whatever it was was really important, something his heart needed to say, but by the time he thought to say it, he had forgotten.

"Weird," Mark said as he put the phone back on the receiver. She seemed to know everything about him without him saying a word. He couldn't wrap his mind around how mysteriously familiar she sounded.

Mark hurried and sent her the money as instructed. About eight days later a package arrived. It was from Karli.

He quickly opened the box. There was a candle in the shape of a man and a note to call her as soon as he opened the box.

"Hello Mark," she said. "Did you receive the package I sent?"

"Yes."

"Good?" she said. "Follow my instructions to the letter."

"Yes ma'am, psychic witch doctor."

"Mark, this is serious. Pay attention if you want this to work."

"Ok, sorry. I'll be serious."

"I want you to light the candle once in the morning and then once in the evening, at the exact same time of the day. It is to be lit for three minutes, no more no less. Sit quietly and meditate while doing this and then extinguish the candle. Do this until the candle is no more. The spirit will see you disappearing as the candle burns gradually and think you no longer exist."

"Pretty slick, Miss Karli."

She laughed and said, "You're funny." That familiarity struck Mark again. Weird.

"How did you learn all about this kind of stuff?"

"I have always had an intuitive gift that has allowed me to discern things...to see things as they really are. Since moving to Chicago, I aligned myself with the Church and its sisterhood helped me to dedicate my talents to God, in a different way...teaching me to meditate and navigate through portals in different dimensions of space and time, helping me to be able to heal others in need, such as yourself."

"That's very interesting. I had a similar experience after a bad car accident. It seems that we might be following the same path. It appears that we have a lot in common."

"Maybe...you never know," said Karli.

As Mark continued with her plan, he called her every day, sometimes twice a day, so he could tell her of his progress. At least, that's what he told himself. The truth was Mark wasn't quite sure why he felt so compelled to call her, but all he wanted to do was hear her voice. They talked about many things, what he had done, what he was doing now, her likes and dislikes.

Mark asked one time what she looked like and she told him that she had blonde hair and brown eyes.

Mark said, "Oh, that's sexy," before he thought to stop himself. Strange, he thought that he suddenly felt her blush.

She said, "And I weigh 300 pounds."

"Sounds good to me, more to appreciate." They both laughed a perfect unison.

She was pretty evasive not to reveal too much about herself, except that she was a devout Roman Catholic and worked with the church, helping with the children.

One day, she asked Mark more about what he did and he told her about performing and explained a little more of how that car accident had prevented him from doing that anymore.

She said, "Oh, I would have loved to have heard you sing. Maybe one day you will sing for me?"

"Maybe," I said, "But you know, I did make some recordings way back when. They're not too good by today's standards, but they hit the charts in the day. I will send you one."

"Oh, that would be great."

As they were speaking, she was preparing lamb stew.

Mark then mentioned to her his philosophy on Greek men and cooking and she laughed and said, "Yes, that is very true, but isn't Banos Greek?"

"Yes," he said, "but I am a great cook!" and they laughed again. Then she quickly snapped, "Hiney!"

"What did you call me?

She laughed and said, "No, not you, my son, Vincent. He was trying to reach the stove and that was an old Greek term we used in my family for many years that meant stop what you are doing, NOW!"

"Whew, for a minute, I thought you got mad at me. You never told me you had a son. I didn't know you were married."

"I'm not, Vincent was alone, dropped off at the church and I eventually adopted him."

"How old is he?"

"Three.'"

"I'll bet he is a handful."

"Sometimes more than you know." She laughed again.

"I love working with kids. I had a children's and youth choir at church and we had some great times together," said Mark.

"Maybe you should teach!"

"Teach? I don't have my certification or a degree."

"You could always go back to school. You will be good at it. I just know it."

Then she said, "Sorry to cut things short, but I must go and finish supper. Goodbye, Mark."

Again, as he started to hang up the phone, he wanted to say something. Something urgent. But by the time the message from his heart was translated in his brain and sent to his lips, it transformed into a mess of formless breath.

Mark was starting to feel better and better as the days passed by. He believed he was finally getting rid of his funk and that Karli's cure was finally working. Or was it Karli that was working?

For the first time that he could remember, Mark really seemed to have a connection with this voice on the other end. A woman that he had never met and yet, it seemed as if he had known her his whole life. An emptiness that had filled him for the past twenty years was gone. All he could think of was Karli.

<h1 style="text-align:center">Chapter 22</h1>

When Karli arrived home from the grocery store, her hands were loaded down with two giant paper bags, her son, Vincent, tagging along by the tail of her shirt, and her cold fingers desperately fumbling to find the deadbolt key, then the door key. While searching through her bag, she inadvertently tripped over a small, brown package when she stepped into the house.

A string of very old and very proud Greek expletives, ones that Vinny would be mimicking in no time, spewed from her mouth as carrots and celery flew from her bags and she came crashing down on top of the rest of her haul. Thankfully, as expected, she landed on top of the carton of a dozen eggs she'd just purchased to cushion her fall. God works in mysterious ways, indeed.

After she scrambled to pick up her items, shooed Vinny off to play with his toys, and mopped up the muck she'd splatted across the floor, Karli finally noticed the box that had come in the mail for her. Normally, Karli was just excited as anyone to open mail, but today, she tore at the packaging tape a little more aggressively like any sensible person does when they blame inanimate objects for their own clumsiness.

When she calmed down enough to notice the address on the other side of the box (she had been tearing at the bottom or the corners or whatever she could rip) all momentary anger dissipated—her eyes traced the letters that formed the name MARK BANOS written carefully on the return line.

Karli opened the small package now like she was a child celebrating Christmas. Inside was a cassette tape of one of his albums. Just as he had promised to send. As she peered in the box a sudden rush of emotions overcame her.

"Oh, my God..." Karli screamed.

For a moment, time suspended itself, took a small coffee break, if you will. In this negative zone between time, Karli followed her mind's eye back through the whirlwind of Youngstown, the beaches they used to own, the sunsets and moonlit walks, the stars shining between their eyes and the whispers that echoed between their hearts. And in an instant, it was gone, restrained to the contents of a simple box, the weight of a marker on cardboard.

The truth is, even though Karli was an excellent psychic, she couldn't always see *everything* that was coming. Sometimes they were boxes on her doorstep, sometimes they were memories that weighed on her constantly like an alternate gravity.

Time came back from pouring that coffee, unaware that he'd picked possibly the worst time to leave his post.

Karli allowed her lips to make the shapes that she'd abandoned so many years before. "It's Tom..." she whispered. As she looked at the picture on the front of the cassette tape, she read the words, *Tom Marks Live!*

As she hurriedly played the tape, the first song was "If" by bread, the same song he had sung for her that night at the beach, the same song that she'd dreamed about so many times. As the song continued to play, her tears began to flow, recalling the memories of that special night and how he had given her a single red rose when he had finished. She thought her heart would explode. How did he find his way back to her and why didn't Karli know?

The voice was so familiar, but she only saw him as Mark Banos. Psychics only discern the real truth, so she guessed she wouldn't have realized he used a pseudonym. If he had just told her his real name in the beginning, that he was Greek, maybe this tragedy might have been prevented. Maybe, she—

The phone rang and it was Mark.

"Mark! Hi, I just got your tape and it was absolutely beautiful…I…"

"I am so glad you liked it!"

"Liked it? I loved it!"

Mark smiled. "It's been a long time since I've shared that music with anyone." Suddenly he felt an old familiar tingle in his left ear, something he had not felt since before he even met Master Bennie. It was like seeing a silhouette of a memory. Familiar, but he couldn't place where it had happened before.

"It's like you are looking right through me when you sing, I remember—" and then she caught herself.

"Remember what? Did you see me perform somewhere?"

Karli could barely handle the pressure of her own wish. Years ago she had prayed that Mark could forget about her. Now that she was here in Chicago, her new life and new identity, the safety of her child depended on the certainty that Mark could never discover her secret. Against every fiber of her desire, she said, "No, I meant I remember some of the songs."

"Oh. Well, I…" Mark trailed off for a moment. He couldn't help but feel he was walking through some kind of fog, unsure if he was moving closer to his destination or farther away. He shook it off. "I just wanted to report that your patient seems to be fit as a fiddle, thanks to you."

Karli took a deep breath. "Not so much me, but through God's help."

"You know, patients always fall in love with their doctors." Mark caught himself wrapping the phone cord around his finger like a high schooler. There was another tingle in his ear, this time more electric, more familiar.

"Oh, Tom," Karli slipped again, "I mean Mark, sorry, Mark—" she felt herself blush.

"That's fine," Mark laughed, "I went by that name for half of my life. My full name is Thomas Marcus Banos, but Mom used to call me Tom Mark, especially if she got angry with me. It was just natural to use it as a stage name. What is your middle name?"

"Anna," she said without thinking.

"I think I used to know an Anna, but can't remember. I meet so many people…Karli Anna Roberts." He loved the way the name sounded coming from his mouth.

"Mark I—" she hesitated. Karli thought of everything that made up her life now, she thought of the constant fear she'd endured for those first few years and the relative security she'd finally achieved.

"Yes?" Mark's question felt like he had just cast a line off the pier and was waiting all day for a bite.

"I'm sorry…that this happened to you. And I hope that everything turns out the way it should, the way God has planned."

Mark smiled. It wasn't the response he was hoping for or even expecting, but it felt sincere. "Thank you," he said in a low tone.

The other end was silent save for a strangely familiar breathing pattern.

"Well, I guess I should be heading on. You'll be happy to know I took your advice and enrolled in a few college courses." He laughed, "my first class begins in a half hour, so I better hurry to give all the kids plenty of time to crack jokes about the OMOC—old man on campus!" He waited for a response, a repartee, but he only heard that tranquil and warm silence. "Wish me luck."

I wish you love, Mark Banos. I wish you love.

CHAPTER 23

Christmas was fast approaching and since Mark had no one except his phone-a-friend in Carol Stream, he focused on finding gifts for them.

Vinnie was easy. Mark purchased him a game called Gator Golf, which seemed like it would be fun and was age appropriate. Karli was not so easy, since he had never met her, knew very little about her and, if he were being honest, it couldn't be something too personal or she might think he was some kind of pervert stalker.

She did mention once that she collected dolls, so Mark went to several shops to see what he could find. In a small boutique, a flashy looking Spanish girl, caught his eye. Not a Spanish girl, but a Spanish girl doll, made of fine porcelain. She was dancing the Flamingo and fanning her skirt.

"$200! Yikes!" Mark realized he was thinking loudly enough for the shopkeeper to stare at him. He laughed nervously and scratched his neck.

It was a gift for someone very special, after all, so he whipped "the ol' Massa Card" out of his pocket and didn't give it a second thought. He got a call a few days later from a very excited young lady.

Karli was screaming into the phone, "My Doll, My Doll! I love my doll! Thank you so much. You shouldn't have. Thank you, Thank you, Thank you!"

"You are entirely welcome. Least I could do for you putting up with me."

"My pleasure, dear sir. And Vincent loves his little golf set, although I told him he's not to play with it in the house."

"Good idea."

"You do such nice things for me. It has been a very long time since someone has been so nice."

"Easy to be nice to such a beautiful woman."

"Ah, you don't know what I look like. I told you I weighed 300 pounds! I am an old ugly Greek woman."

"Oh, I don't think so. You have nothing but beauty about you. I can feel it coming through the wires." Mark laughed but then realized he was actually being serious. He tried to adjust his tone to get Karli to realize this too. "Actually, ever since you first picked up the phone, I knew there was something different about you, something I just couldn't explain. It's like I have known you from a past life." He cleared his throat. "I mean, am I being crazy here?"

"Maybe," said Karli.

"I think more than maybe. But sometimes the truth is what's so insane. I think, Karli...well, the *truth* is" he said as he gulped, "I'm falling in love with you."

Without hesitation she said, "I love you too, Tom."

A burning sensation hit Mark's ear stronger than ever before. He was no longer in any state to separate his subconscious desires from his conscious actions. In fact, he wasn't in a state of control at all…more like a state of rapture. "Will you marry me?"

"Yes," she said, "of course, I will."

All of a sudden his ear was bouncing and burning. His blood felt like it was pulsing with sunlight. It was as if he was projecting into the astral plane but actually taking his physical body with him—a corporeal entity in an inner dimensional realm of spiritual bliss. He was jumping excitedly around the room when she suddenly said. "Call me tomorrow, there is someone at the door."

As he hung up, her image was suddenly revealed to Mark.

"Anna?" Mark said reaching out to her.

Then it all came rushing back to him. Karli Anna—Sopoulos! Mark then remembered those summer days in 1975, walking on the beach, going to Ohio, asking her to marry him. Why hadn't he remembered these things all these years? Why didn't he marry her before? Why can't he remember more?

Suddenly the psychic bliss in which he was basking turned to a murk of utter confusion and pain—how could he have abandoned his one true love? How could he feel so foreign in the confines of his own mind? What was happening to him and how could he be sure it wouldn't happen all over again?

Mark fell to his knees both fearful and full of gratitude. One hand pressed hard against his forehead as the pain of half of life's memories rushed through his skull, and his other hand clenched his heart, so overwhelmed with the miracle of rediscovering the greatest joy God had ever blessed him with.

"Anna..." he said softly. Tears formed in his eyes as the picture of his double-life came into focus. "My Sopie!"

CHAPTER 24

When Karli hung up the phone she instinctively told Vincent to go to his room. "Close the door and play, ok, sweetie?" She took a breath and peaked through the peephole of her apartment door. On the other side was a man whose face she'd never forget, but a man she hardly recognized after so many years.

"Agent Kroner!" she said as she swung the door open, still beaming from Mark's call. "It has been a very long time."

The older more grizzled looking FBI veteran stood in the hallway holding his badge next to his face, momentarily caught off guard by her chipperness.

"Come in, sit down," she said motioning toward the living room.

"Thank you," said Kroner as he molded himself into the sofa. He glanced nervously around the room fidgeting with the brim of the hat in his hand.

"Mind if I smoke?" asked Kroner. "Should've nixed the habit years ago I guess, but it is still one of my little indulgences."

"I'm sorry to admit it, but I still smoke as well...gives me something to do to fill the lonely nights," she said lighting up.

He took a deep inhale, and watched pensively as the smoke that came pouring out his nostrils. "Sorry to just barge in on you like this. I know seeing me probably doesn't dredge up any pleasant memories."

Karli laughed, "On the contrary," she moved an ash tray closer towards the coffee table where he was sitting, "you're the person I associate with one of the happiest days of my life."

Agent Kroner smiled a little, but just a little. Anybody could see it had become a foreign expression for him.

Anna stood up again, "Can I get you some coffee? Tea?"

"No, no. it's fine…" he stammered.

"Well then, what exactly brings you to our quaint little town? It's great to see you but, I doubt you came all this way just to catch up. Is everything alright?"

Taking a long drag on his cigarette he says, "I'm afraid not. I have some bad news. Evidently the mob has been keeping pretty close tabs on anyone you may have been acquainted with in the past. They found your name and address on a box in your old boy friend's trash can in NC and put two and two together. I'm afraid you and your son's lives aren't worth a nickel if you stay here. We are going to have to move you in the morning." He tried to sound like he was talking about strictly business, but Agent Kroner couldn't help but look around the room and see the photographs, the kid's toys, smell the air of a home-cooked meal.

"Move me?" Karli was stunned—she had expected this day to come many years ago. When it didn't, she allowed part of her psyche to rest easy. The news coming now was like waking prematurely from a dream. "Where?"

"I am not telling you or anyone, not even those on my staff. You will know when we get there. And make absolutely sure that you tell no one, especially your ex-boyfriend as I am sure his line is tapped." He said as he stood, "Please, get yourselves packed quickly."

Karli started welling up and then burst into tears clinging to Agent Kroner as she continued, "But Tom and I just got back together after all of these years. He asked me to marry him. I can't do this to him again. How will he find me?"

"Look," he said softly, trying to return some semblance of a warm embrace, "I know this is a very hard decision for you, but I can assure you, if you don't move they will find you and kill you and the boy." He pulled away and left his hands atop Karli's shoulders. "Hit men do not care about anything other than fulfilling the contract for their employer. If I let you contact your boyfriend, they will follow him here and kill him as well. There is no good solution, except to leave and to do so now."

Karli stepped back and wiped her eyes. She took a deep breath and tried to set aside her childishness. She too looked around the house she'd learned to call home. She thought of Vinnie. Immediately, Karli found herself in a frame of mind geared toward action instead of nostalgia.

Agent Kroner said, "I will see you early tomorrow morning...try to get some rest. I will have someone stay outside and watch over you tonight. Don't worry...things have a way of working out." And he left.

The nightmare begins again.

Karli began packing up what she could as she tried to hold back the tears. She bathed and put Vincent to bed, deciding to just tell him tomorrow they were just going on an adventure. All she could think about was Mark. He again asked her to marry him and again she would have to make the choice to forgo her happiness. Why?

Just as before, she only acted to protect the ones she loved.

After packing, and finally letting her tears cascade in full force, she fell into a deep trance-like sleep. Around 3 a.m. she reached semi-consciousness and became aware of someone's presence in her room. Somehow, this presence didn't trigger any kind of anxiety, it wasn't some kind of spooky intrusion. Soon, she felt a brush against her cheek and a familiar tenderness that she had only felt once before. Karli felt someone snuggle up behind her softly stroking her hair.

Then she heard a whisper, "It will be fine, you will be safe, I will come and find you. You are my forever love. Do not be afraid. We are one for all eternity." And then he was gone, leaving her his gentle peace. She awoke knowing complete and total unconditional love and acceptance.

ଔଔଔଔଔ

Excitedly, Mark spent the rest of the evening rummaging through a shoebox of old photographs until he came upon one...The One, he was looking for. It was a picture of Anna, the one she had given to him at the beach. A little crumpled and faded, but recognizable as the girl he had seen in his vision. He held it tightly in his hand trying to pull more memories from it, but to no avail. He just couldn't remember more than a few details about their relationship. Why couldn't he remember?

The next morning he called Karli to tell her of his revelation. The answering machine picked up as it often did, but with a different message.

"Hello, this is Sopie…

Mark was immediately struck with the oddity of the message. She always called herself Karli. No one ever called her Sopie. That was his pet name for her.

The message continued, "I have to go right now, but know that I will always hold you in my heart and you will always be in my thoughts and prayers. God Bless you, I love you. Goodbye."

"What?" Mark felt his blood pumping. "Fuck!" He threw the phone against the wall and broke down. "NOT AGAIN…" The warmth of tears covered his palms. But after awhile, when his anger subsided, Mark realized something important. *She must know too*, he thought. Since the name was changed to Sopie, and he was the only one that ever called her that…maybe…just maybe…

Of course, Mark did exactly what he knew he probably shouldn't do and jumped in the car and took off for Chicago. But 1,500 miles with no sleep is never a good idea.

He arrived in Carol Stream early the following morning and ran to her door, but there was no sign of anyone living there. She was already long gone.

Mark went to several of the local parishes to inquire about her, but no one seemed to know her, or that she was involved with the children, or so they said. It was as if she was a memory long-since forgotten, a dream that had been written off as illusion.

There was no choice for Mark but to return, broken-hearted, to North Carolina and start again. He just couldn't make any sense out of this. Rolling everything around in his head over and over. Questioning over and over.

Why would she just up and leave without even a goodbye?
Why would she agree to marry me and then disappear?
Why can't I remember anything from before?
Why?
Why?
Why?
What else didn't make sense was someone thinking they could stay up for two days and begin day three without any sleep. Add pain and anguish to that mix and you have a recipe for disaster.

Mark was heading into the mountains of West Virginia when there began a light drizzle. Roads get slick fast when it rains just a little, and to complete the disaster formula, there was a 400 foot drop-off on both sides of the road. All of a sudden the car started to skid uncontrollably toward the right shoulder.

"I can't pull it back!" he cried. Then, there was an eerie silence that fell. There was no sound from the car, no rumble of the road. He dropped both hands from the wheel, unsure of what to do, afraid for his life. Just then, something or someone took over control of the car and veered it safely back into the driving lane. The silence ended and Mark took control back over the steering and brought the car to a stop. His heart was still pounding as he saw Anna's face appear as a reflection in his rearview mirror. He turned, but no trace of her was left. She had slipped back through the psychic portal as quickly as she came.

Mark put his head in his hands and burst into tears. He had never felt more alone. The air was silent and heavy, but the white noise of the radio crept into earshot. Her voice could softly be heard through the static.

"I will always be with you and protect you," Karli said as she faded from his life again.

Chapter 25

Back safely at home in Carolina, Mark again sat alone in his apartment. The small apartment seemed to have grown much larger with the emptiness he had inside. All he could seem to do was think of Karli...of Anna. Of how close they had gotten for a second time only to lose her once again.

He, again, began to look at Anna's photograph searching for hidden answers locked away in his mind. Every day he would pull out the photograph and look deeply into her eyes hoping an answer would come. Mark would play that song "If" over and over until he just couldn't take it anymore...day in and day out. Nights were the toughest, but somehow he hoped she would feel what he felt and find her way back...*IF.*

Stupid, stupid, stupid!

Mark continued on for the next few years, taking odd jobs here and there, ending each day with his ritual sob session. He quit taking classes as he no longer felt as if there was any point. Eking out his meager existence, he barely made it through each day. His heart was completely broken.

But one night he had a dream...a vision. As he awoke on the couch his dog, Chivas, licked his face and said, *"You will be on the path to your final destiny very soon. I will help lead you, my friend."* And then he was pulled back to the earthly dimension with a sudden jolt. Now Mark stared at the empty scotch bottles littering his night stand and thought he had really lost it. Or had he? Reality, after all, is a figment of our imagination. It is what we believe to be real, no matter which dimension we are traveling through.

"Yeah, I'm having a conversation with a dog that's dead-...I need some serious professional help," he said into the phone. "That's right, yes." He nodded and jotted down an address. "Sure, yep, uh-huh. ok, Tuesday sounds great." He hung up.

After years of fixating on his problem and becoming more and more depressed, Mark found himself sitting in the waiting room at the office of Dr. Miki MkDabbs, PsyD. Glancing around the room at the diplomas he noticed that Dr. MkDabbs was not only a clinical psychologist but a certified hypnotist as well. Mark decided that he would look into regression hypnosis to see if there was any chance he could restore his lost memories. He had a friend in high school that had repressed her memories from childhood and a hypnotist had helped her. He thought maybe this guy could help him too.

After completing a mountain of paperwork, he was finally led in to see the doctor.

"Right this way Mr. Banos," said the nurse. "The doctor will be with you in a minute."

Mark sat in a small room in a reclining chair waiting. While thinking about how he would explain all of this to the doctor, in came Dr. MkDabbs. He appeared to be in his early 40s. A tall, slender man with dark rimmed glasses. As expected.

"Hello, Mr. Banos, I'm Dr. MkDabbs. What can I do for you today?"

"Hi Doc...and it's Mark. Pleased to me you." He extended his hand.

"Ok, Mark...tell me a little about why you have come to see me."

"Well, to be honest, I guess I am suffering from depression. You see, my girlfriend whom I met thirty years ago disappeared and I am afraid she's all I can think about. I am having trouble sleeping and when I do I have the strangest dreams."

"Oh, that is nothing unusual, after all you have been together for thirty years."

"No, we met thirty years ago. Now she's disappeared again."

"Again?"

"Well, maybe I had better tell you the whole story," said Mark. "Pull up a chair, it's a rather long one."

Then Mark began to tell the doctor the whole story, as he knew it... how they met, asking her to marry him after only seeing her once, the trip to Youngstown, her sending him away, finding her again during a phone conversation, and her agreeing to marry him a second time and then disappearing.

"Up until several years ago, I didn't even remember her at all, not even her name. But once I asked her to marry me on the phone, a vision of her face came to me and I remembered bits and pieces of our earlier time together. I have remembered no more since, although I did dig up her picture from a box of old photos. It was the one she gave me at the beach the first time we met. Am I ready for the straight jacket now, Doc?"

"Not quite yet," the doctor said laughing, "but your story does sound like a cross between "Somewhere in Time" and "The Twilight Zone." It seems to me that with you being able to remember everything, with the exception of this one event, that we should try regression hypnosis. Have you ever been hypnotized before?"

"No, but I had a friend who got a lot of relief from hypnosis as she was able to recover her memories as a child. What do you think caused this? Why can't I remember?"

"It could have been from your accident or this memory may just be too painful for you to remember. It is your brain's way of protecting you from a memory that might be harmful to you. Don't worry, you will be in complete control during the session and if I see that a reappearing memory becomes too painful for you, I will bring you out of the hypnosis. I will not let you suffer any pain."

"When do we start?"

"Right now, if you are ready."

"I'm ready, let's get started."

"Ok, I want you to lie back and relax. I will introduce some of the details you do remember as triggers to stimulate your memory. Take five deep breathes and then close your eyes. Listen to nothing except my voice. Empty your mind of all thoughts."

As Dr. MkDabbs tapped Mark's wrist he said, "You're going deeper, deeper...inhale and hold it...exhale...deeper and deeper...inhale and hold it...exhale...going deeper and deeper. You are now entering a garden with beautiful flowers all around you. Take a moment to notice the brilliant colors. You see a bench in the garden. Sit and relax a while. It feels so good, just sitting there looking at the plants and flowers. You notice a house up the path a little further. You get up and head toward the house, feeling very much at peace. When you reach the house, you go up on the porch and there is the door to the house. You gently open the door and walk in. You see a beautiful foyer with many fine paintings and objects of art. It is a beautiful home. It feels good for you to be here. So, so good. You notice a grand staircase leading down. You can't see what is at the bottom, so you begin to descend down, down, down...Counting the remaining stairs as you descend. 10, 9, 8, down, down, down, 7, 6, 5, 4, 3 almost there, 2 and 1. You see another doorway. This door leads to a data room that holds a record of every event you have had in your life. It is here you will find that which you are seeking. You open the door and a brilliant light comes forth and slowly ebbs as you enter. You see stacks and stacks of books. You are to look for one labeled 1975. Have you located the book?"

"Yes."

"Good. Now turn the page until you reach June."

"I found it."

"Good. Do you see the night club at the beach you and your band were performing at?"

"Yes."

"What are you doing now?"

"Rehearsing. It is the afternoon and the bar is closed."

"Find where you were running on the beach."

"I found it."

"Did you meet someone?"

"No."

"Go back to the club that night. See if you see anyone new that you didn't know before."

"No."

"Go to the next day. Do you see a girl named Anna in a black bikini in your hotel room?"

"No. All of the pages of the book are blank."

"Are you in love with a girl named Anna?"

"Yes, but I don't know who Anna is."

Seeing Mark become more and more agitated, the doctor slowly brought him out of the session.

"I want you to close the book now and put it back on the shelf. Walk out of the door and gently close it behind you. Now walk back up the staircase, slowly ascending. As you reach the top you will again enter the foyer above. Once there, you will walk through the door entering the garden. Walk back down the path from which you came. I am going to count to five. As I do you will become more and more awake, feeling refreshed and relaxed. 1, 2 waking now, feeling so good, so refreshed. 3, 4 almost awake, remembering everything that occurred while you were asleep and 5. How do you feel Mark?"

"Nice, but I don't remember any more than I did. Why

do I not remember?"

"It could be because your brain is keeping you from re-membering as a protection mechanism, or it could be that you have some false memories that have taken the place of the real memories."

Mark felt the light in the room go out as he heard that phrase.

"False memories?"

What does that even mean? If he couldn't trust his own mind to recall the events of his life accurately, how could he even be sure that he was alive at all?

The doctor kept speaking but Mark could hardly focus.

"It is hard to tell, but you definitely have what is called retrograde amnesia, the inability to have memory-access to this past event prior to the accident or trauma from the event itself. One big problem with this is Anna herself could tell you what happened and you might not remember five min-utes later what she had told you as your mind may reject the truth as being a false memory."

No…no that couldn't be right. A flash of an image scratched at Mark's mind…it's like he could view the corner of a jigsaw puzzle. He saw a screen door obscuring her face, a grey afternoon and a coldness of steel. What if this was it? What if there was no bigger picture, that everything in his life had been invented to protect him. Mark stared down at his leg, his cane, he wondered about his inter-dimensional knowledge, about Master Bennie, about how long he'd been in this room, how long these fluorescent lights…

"The thing that disturbs me is that while you didn't re-member anything about meeting Anna, you were very em-phatic about still being in love with her. After only knowing each other for two weeks and meeting only once, you asked her to marry you and she accepted. I could dismiss this as the impetuousness of youth, however, you again asked her to marry you on the phone, never meeting this lady in person and not realizing it was Anna, and she accepted. You were both in your forties. That is just strange. I have never seen anything quite like this."

Dr. MkDabbs began edging away, a picture on an etch-a-sketch being rattled back into oblivion. The room was turning black, and Mark was trying to remember his parents' faces. Had he ever even been born? What was his life, really? Could he actually sing or play music, did he ever really live on the west coast? Mark looked down at his hands and wondered for the longest time what his real name was. This was the feeling of everything he assumed to be rock bottom suddenly turning into quicksand.

"However," Dr. MkDabbs continued. His voice was like a whisper at the end of a long dark hallway now. "One of my colleagues had an unusual case where a metaphysical occurrence called 'Twin Flames' were on the verge of reuniting." The doctor laughed, "I used to write all of that stuff off as nonsense, but to hear such a well-respected member of the community speak with such passion about these two subjects…anyway, as she explained it, one flame was running from the other, while only the other one was awakened to their destiny of being reunited."

On the edge of total oblivion, Mark heard a word, and saw a light. It was as if a new and certain universe was being created right before his very eyes. In a moment, he found a voice, he knew from that voice that he had a mouth, a throat, and a body. Mark said the phrase, "Twin Flames?" He felt the familiarity of these words and he knew without a doubt that it wasn't the first time his mind had entertained the thought. It didn't matter if he imagined Master Bennie or the beach, or anything else because he *knew* that he had heard of this one thing…this one very important thing. He clung to it so tightly.

"Yes, that's right. It is very rare to see this occurrence, but it does happen, so maybe—"

"Doc," Mark said hoarsely, returning to the reality he had accepted long ago as being truthful, "you will find this odd, but a very good friend of mine from California, who is very well-versed in such things, told me that I was destined to meet my twin and explained the relationship in great detail. Then, he told me that the time was not yet right, but it was drawing near." Mark sat up in his chair a little more. "It's been many years since we last spoke so…maybe, Anna is MY twin and for whatever reason she is running from me right now. If that is the case, I know that I am destined to be reunited with her. It doesn't make it easier, but there's some comfort in knowing."

"Maybe that will give you peace." Dr. MkDabbs stood and smiled. "Good luck on your journey, Mark."

"Thanks, Doc. Maybe at least I will be able to continue on, knowing there is a reason for all of this and eventually a resolution."

"You know, there's what I like to refer to as the three R's of human existence. Remembrance, realization, and revelation. Each one has a specific tie to our past, present, and future. Maybe you've exhausted your mind's ability to recall past events, but hopefully it will allow you to realize your present goals. Perhaps these goals will reveal your future destiny."

Mark smiled. He was taken aback by the profound simplicity of what the good doctor had shared. "Jeez, Doc, how'd you get to be so smart?"

He laughed, "Good schooling I suppose. Maybe you should try and transfer some of your intuitive and spiritual knowledge into the world of academia? You mentioned that you had dreams of pursuing a degree didn't you?"

"Well, I did and I guess I was enjoying myself. But I couldn't stop thinking of Anna when I was there…she was the one that pushed me in that direction."

"Hmm…it's starting to sound like maybe you're the flame

running in the wrong direction. What better way to reunite with your twin than to follow the path she placed you on?"

Mark had not considered this. It followed every philosophical tenet that Master Bennie had taught him about flow and balance, but he had been blinded by his grief to assess the situation.

"I would concentrate on your educational goals for now. I have a feeling everything else will start to fall into place rather quickly if you just go on with your plans."

So, Mark continued with his education and finally got his degree and certification to teach, Class of 2004. Now the hard part...to find a job. After all, by now he was already fifty and had to find a school that was willing to take a chance on him at his age.

After sending out what seemed to be a hundred resumes and receiving enough rejection letters to repaper his apartment, there came an offer from a school in Louisiana. It seemed that the local Catholic high school, Holy Cross, was in desperate need of a band instructor and Mark could start this fall.

New Orleans...well, that was one city he had never been to, so after careful consideration for about two minutes, he decided to go. He decided that the prospects around Atlantic Beach were mighty slim and the change of scenery might do him good. He could try it for a year. If he didn't like it he could always come home.

So Mark started to dance and sing, "I'm off to Alabama with a banjo on my knee, heading for Louisiana my true love for to see."

Yeah, if that were only true...

Chapter 26

Mark's trip out to Louisiana was not so bad as he took I-10 instead of I-20, a much more southerly approach that followed the gulf coast. Gulfport was a familiar landscape that allowed him to start to feel at home as he approached New Orleans. Only 78 more miles due west.

He entered the city around one o'clock in the afternoon and decided to stay at The Avenue Hotel until he could find a place. Hopefully, someone at the school could guide him in that direction. At least this place had a kitchenette which would save him on meals and was within walking distance of where all the action was.

It was still early, so he decided to go to the French Quarter and see what was going on. Mark was one to try and get a bead on the heartbeat of strange new cities. He went to several shops, picked up some scotch, of course, and ate a Muffuletta sandwich at the Central Grocery Co. This was a local delicacy that those in Carolina call a Poor Boy sandwich. It was a little different though, with a chopped olive relish and put on a round piece of bread the size of a hub cap. Definitely filling. He then feasted his eyes on a place called *The Cigar Factory* where they made hand rolled cigars.

"Where y'at?" the store owner bellowed.

Mark looked a little puzzled. "I guessin' I'm at The Cigar Factory," he responded.

"Non, non......I mean how you be?"

"Oh, fine...just looking around to see if you have any

panetellas."

"Oh, but of course, the finest!"

"I would like a couple and a cutter, if you don't mind."

"Certainement!" The tobacco-tanned creole bagged the cigars and rang him up. "That will be $23.76."

As Mark was paying he noticed several chess tables at the entrance to the store.

"Can anyone play? I mean, is this like a lounge?"

"If you can play, you can bring in a bottle and drink and smoke your cigars too, s'il vous plait."

"Now that's a novelty, I'm in. It looks like me and Mr. Macallen are going to kill a couple of hours here. Anybody free for a game?"

"Hey Coonass," the shop keep yelled across the room to a fella just walking in the store. This fella wants to play some chess, you interested?"

"Always up for de game. Hi, my name is Pete," he extended his hand toward Mark. "You desire to play?"

"Hi Pete, I'm Mark, and certainement," he said with a smile as he sat clipping his cigar, lighting up and pouring himself a round of scotch.

"Why did the store owner call you Coonass? Is that a nickname or something?"

"No, that is either the finest or worst thing you can call a Cajun, depending on how you say it. You can just call me Pete."

Pete looked up and asked, "You ever play before?"

"Sure", he said, "As often as I can find someone to play."

"Yeah, it mighty hard to find folks to play these days," he said. "Everyone in a hurry." Pete pulled out a rolling paper from his front pocket and licked his lips. "Chess, it take time, see? And patience."

He poured a palm full of tobacco into the paper and rolled it loosely, but carefully. "But not too much time...see what I mean?" He licked the freshly rolled cigarette and made his third move. "Checkmate!" Pete sat back in his chair, his grin glowing like the devil's through a lit match.

Mark couldn't fuckin' believe it. That old Ragin' Cajun had just beaten him in three moves.

"That was pretty sweet, Pete. You didn't even give me time to finish my drink," Mark said as he gulped it down.

"Yeah, Bobby Fischer thought it pretty good too," he said as he started laughing.

"Well, I have had enough schooling for one day. Another time Pete?"

"Anytime, Mr. Mark," said Pete still cackling through smoke and sulfur. "Anytime. I see you real soon, non?"

Mark took the remaining plantation style panetella and headed back to his room. Or at least that was his intention until a fellow came up to him and sprayed soap on his shoes. "Looks like you need polishing," he said proceeding to wipe them down, right before he shook Mark down. "That'll be $20..$10 for the shine and $10 for my rhyme!"

"I don't think so." Mark started to walk away.

"Hey, you gotta pay up."

Mark continued to take another step when the guy grabbed his arm.

"Man, you gotta pay; I did my work."

It was time to introduce Mr. Shoeshine to Mark's friend, *The Bear.* Without a word, Mark slowly turned to face his aggressor. As Mark turned he began to envision a large razor-clawed beast coming up behind the guy. He began drilling his mind into his adversary's, keeping his focus directly beyond the guy's right shoulder.

The fella quickly looked and looked back, with Mark still staring right through him. His eyes glazed over in bewilderment as he became confused and began to tremble. Finally after a minute of tense silence, he let loose of Mark's arm, turned and said, "Man, you just ain't worth it."

That was the first time Mark had ever had to use The Bear

as taught to him by Master Bennie. Thank God it worked. It would have been a shame to have had to shove it up his ass over a lousy twenty bucks.

Mark decided that was enough excitement in *The Big Easy* for one day. He went back to the hotel for a little shut-eye before he began his new life.

C3CBCBCB

Preparing the classroom was a new chore for Mark. Bulletin boards, readying uniforms and instruments for the fall, going to what seemed like endless teacher's meetings for two weeks and then finally, the first day of school.

Thankfully, he had met what turned out to be a lifelong friend in Marty, the art teacher. They both came from a similar artsy background, plus Marty loved to eat and drink... which was great as far as Mark was concerned. It had been a long time since anyone had hung out with him. First time out, they went to Drago's in the French Quarter for drinks and oysters.

"Without a doubt these are the finest oysters, bar none, no pun intended, that I have ever eaten. In Carolina the oysters for the most part are packed in brine and very bitter and nauseating." Mark continued, "Marty, you're not originally from here are you?"

"No, could you tell by my Tarheel accent?"

"No, it was the fact that I could understand you at all!" They both laughed.

"You know, I'm from Coastal Carolina," and Mark told him a little of the journey that had brought him there.

"Me, I'm not far, not far at all! I was raised in Havelock," said Marty.

"Wow, small world."

All of a sudden Marty yelled, "Man, you talk about sumptin' fittiin' to eat," using his best Fat Harold imitation as he scoffed down another oyster.

"Yeah, these are a lot better than those that you get in Carolina. These is oysters!" Mark laughed.

That Saturday night, they went to K-Paul's Kitchen for the Shrimp and Crawfish Etouffee. "Never had shrimp fixed this way before, with a roux, but it is quite delicious. But me being from the coast I can't help but think it needs some Old Bay, plus where we come from shrimp doesn't hit the water. We cook everything in a steam pot."

"Dat be true but down here it always be with de roux," Marty said as he guzzled another Blue Moon. "At least de booze be de same," using his finest Cajunese.

"Woo-ee…I guarantee!" Mark countered.

ᘓᘓᘓᘓ

They had many fine such evenings in The Big Easy. Sometimes they wondered how they managed to stay out of the obits or not get fired from their cushy day jobs as they liked to call them.

It was football season and Mark had become pretty tied up practicing drills with the marching band every day after school. He really hadn't put much thought into working with a marching band when he filled out the job application. He wasn't thinking high school. But, as luck would have it, one of his sophomore students stepped up and became his assistant. He showed the marching steps to the others and even helped get the equipment and uniforms organized.

"Son, you have been a godsend this season. I couldn't have done it without you."

"No problem, Mr. B. I like helping you with the band and, who knows, maybe I'll decide to teach music when I graduate."

"Well, I hope you like being poor!" Mark said laughing.

"By the way, have you seen my day-planner anywhere, I

seemed to have misplaced it. I never loose track of anything that important. I could have sworn it was on my desk when we went out to the field."

"No, I haven't. Do you want me to search for it?"

"No, I'm sure it will turn up," said Mark hesitantly as a sudden strangeness overcame him.

"Did you always teach school, Mr. B?"

"No, originally I started out as an entertainer, but I had a car accident that crippled me and prevented me from performing. I didn't get my degree until I was 50, so let that be a lesson to you...always be prepared for the unforeseen and get your education early. That way you always have something to fall back on if your dreams suddenly disappear."

"I hear you. Mom is always saying the same thing everyday...over and over."

"Listen to your mom. She sounds like a smart lady."

"Ok, later Mr. B; I've got to head home."

"Thanks again for your help."

C3C3C3C3

Then one afternoon just before school let out for Christmas break, Mark heard a familiar shout from behind him.

"Yo, Mr. B! Waz up?" Marty said.

"You are!" he shot back, "How the hell are ya?"

"If I was any better I would be twins."

"Hey, when we get off," Mark said as they got a little closer, "why don't we go toss a few?"

"And then a few more? Count me in."

They took off and hit a few of the bars on Bourbon St known for great jazz and topless women. "I'm getting hungry. Let's go eat," Mark declared.

"Sure, you wanna get some Cajun food."

"No, I have had enough of that shit since I got here...not bad, but they boil everything."

226

"Yeah, I know. I'm getting a little sick of their itsy bitsy lobster, myself."

"I was thinkin' chicken? I saw this place on the Food Network called Wille Mae's over in Treme and it looked so good."

"Treme...isn't that a dangerous neighborhood?"

"I don't think so or the Food Network folks wouldn't have gone there...but you can be my bodyguard," Mark said laughing.

"Oh, what the hell! Sounds good to me."

"Come on, you've been drinking. I'll drive."

"What the piss? You've been drinking too!"

"Yeah, but I got fifteen years of drinking on you. Besides I am a cripple, they probably won't expect me to walk a straight line," Mark said with a grin. "Let's go."

It was around six when they got to Willie Mae's. The place reminded Mark of some of the old seafood taverns back home. The signs outside probably were put up in the 1950s. Actually, it looked just like Skeeter's Place in North Myrtle Beach, where they served barbecue mullet sandwiches with the tails still on. They decided that this would be a treat.

"Mr. B, I see you only treat your friends to the finest cuisine."

"Oh yeah, nothing too good for a fellow Carolinian," Mark said with a chuckle.

They met some of the warmest folks Mark had seen since moving to New Orleans or New Awlins as they say in Treme.

"We'll have the fried chicken and red beans," Mark said.

"Yes, sir," said the waitress. "Would you like something to drink with that?"

"Yes, ma'am," interjected Marty quickly. "I'll have a Blue Moon."

"No Blue Moons here, but I can offer you a NOLA Blonde."

"Ok, sounds good. Can I get a beer, too?" quipped Marty.

The waitress laughed and said, "And for you sir?"

"That's fine with me, too," Mark said.

After polishing off a couple of beers, their food arrived. "This is the best food I have eaten since I got here. A real switch from the past few months."

"I agree, Mr. B. This is fabulous and I am already stuffed."

"You ready to go?"

"Not until I get one more piece of that corn bread."

"You ready now?" Mark said after watching Marty devour the muffin. "It's getting dark and I believe we might not want to be down here after dark."

"Right!"

They paid their tab and bid their adieus. They were walking back to their car mighty *sassified,* when Mark noticed three young men with hoodies following them pretty close behind. While Marty was continuing to jabber, Mark noticed that they sped up their pace. Muggers do some pretty stupid shit when they see a cripple. Easy prey...sometimes.

One of them went in front of Mark and Marty, blocking their way. The other two came from behind.

"Evening, gentlemen," Mark said with just the slightest bit of sarcasm.

"Shut up old man. Give me yo money!" he demanded.

Before he could utter another word, Mark knocked him unconscious with his cane, hooked the cane around the second man's arm breaking it with a snap and threw him to the ground stomping his head with his good foot. He was out. The third man had something that glistened in the moonlight in his hand. The impetuous lad was running towards Mark with a knife.

"Now I'm sure your mama taught you not to run with sharp scissors," Mark commented as the weapon went sailing across the street as he went sailing into a nearby building. "Same thing with knives, kid."

The entire surgical procedure lasted about seven seconds, if Mark counted correctly.

"Now Marty, you were saying?"

"Jesus H. Jones, Mr. B, what the fuck was that?"

"Oh, just a little luck, I suppose."

Marty was a statue with his jaw on the ground. "Bull-shit. You looked a little more than lucky."

Mark moved over to the first mugger. "Well, maybe it was a little training too. Ji Pang E...something a friend taught me when I became disabled, but please don't tell anybody about this. Surprise is my weapon."

Marty ran his hand through his hair and looked around to survey the scene. "Jesus…you can count on me, but holy shit! What are you doing now?"

Mark knelt beside the first victim. "Oh, I don't want these boys to suffer."

"Wait, what are you going to do, finish them off?" Marty started to inch away from the man he was beginning to think might be some sort of ruthless crippled vigilante.

"Oh no!" Mark laughed. "I am going to revive them, otherwise they might sustain permanent injuries."

"Are you out of your fuckin' mind. Didn't they just try to kill us?"

"Yes, but I think they have learned their lesson for today. I was always taught to heal first, fight second. It is important for my spirit's karma that I don't harm people."

And with that he revived all three who quickly took off running as soon as they awoke.

"See they learned a good lesson. Maybe next time it will save a cripple who does not have my skills. I guarantee they will tell their friends."

"I suppose," said Marty.

They then got in Mark's car and headed back.

Mark soon realized that this was a crazy ass city. He had only been there a few months and had been accosted twice.

He never had to use his martial arts techniques anywhere since Master Bennie shaped the way that he now looked at things. The city seemed to have eyes. Mark always felt like he was being watched. Mark decided that this place would warrant a more cautious look.

Mark and Marty got through their first year of teaching at Holy Cross. It was a good and rewarding year. Teaching was pretty exciting for Mark and he enjoyed being involved playing music again and working with the kids. He wished he had done it sooner.

The last day of school, once again, *The Boys* decided to go have a conversation...their code word for a drink. That day they must've had more than a few as Mark's tab was $70. As they staggered out of the bar, Marty took a step off of the curb and heard a horrible snap.

"Fuck!" Marty yelled. Mark looked down and there was Marty withering in pain. He had broken his ankle.

"I'll get my car." He whipped his car next to the curb, almost taking Marty out.

"Jesus, Mr B. You want me to drive?"

"Hell to the no, never!" as they raced to the nearest hospital ER, which was Charity Hospital on Tulane Ave.

The triage personnel started to work on Marty as soon as they arrived, taking x-rays, drawing blood and asking fifty-eleven different questions for his medical history.

"What difference does it make if my sexual functions are normal?" Marty bellowed. "The only thing getting fucked here is my ankle! Shit!"

When the doctor finally arrived, he confirmed that it was a compound fracture and he would have to have a cast made. This was going to take awhile.

"Why don't you go get a cup of coffee, Mr. Banos? The cafeteria is next to the flower and gift shop downstairs. You can wait there and I will call you on your cell phone when Chuckles is ready," said the nurse.

Mark liked her bedside manner.

"Great," he said. "Marty, I'll be back to pick you up in a few."

"Don't worry about me, I'm feelin' no pain!" Demoral will do that to a guy. "Arrrgh!" he winced as a nurse prodded at his foot.

So Mark ambled on downstairs toward the cafeteria. Going in, he poured himself a cup of java and sat down to wait…and wait. The minutes trickled by into a half hour. "Man, the coffee at hospitals suck," he said to someone else in the cafeteria as he poured a second cup. As he sipped, he started to watch the parade of doctors and nurses passing by. One of the security guards that passed by looked strangely familiar, but he was sure he didn't know him. Maybe, he thought, it was one of the guys that was in the ER while they were working on Marty. Strange though, Mark was fixated on the guard's face for quite awhile, that is, until another face caught his attention.

He spied a woman out of the corner of his eye leaving the gift shop carrying a small package. Catching a glimpse of something she was wearing around her neck, he realized it was a necklace…a very familiar necklace…one he had seen many times as a child.

Quickly he hobbled inside the flower shop, picked up one red rose and threw some money on the counter and sped out the door.

The woman was almost halfway down the corridor so he yelled, "HINEY!"

She stopped in her tracks and turned at the sound of Mark's voice in total bewilderment.

"Hi ya, Sopie," Mark said as their eyes locked. Seeing the red rose she started to weep and run toward him. Mark's ear again was on fire as he heard an instrumental version of Bread's *"If"* in the background over the hospital's Muzak.

He no sooner asked, "Will you marry me?

"Yes, of course I will," she said and hugged him and said, "Yes, yes, yes!"

Their spirits collided and joined as one. An entity that would never be pulled apart again. Mark would never forget the look in those eyes. Oh, those beautiful brown eyes...joy and love overflowing.

Finally, his beautiful Anna was in his arms again and this time it was forever...although forever is never long enough...

Chapter 27

Mark's cell phone rang. "Oh, it's Marty," he said with disappointment. "He must be ready to go"

"Marty? Who's Marty?" Anna put her hand on Mark's chest to see if he were truly there.

Laughing, Mark said, "He's just a clumsy friend who broke his ankle. I have to give him a ride home." He took her hands into his own. "Come with us."

"Oh, I wish I could, but my son is here having a procedure done and is in recovery now."

"It's Vinnie, isn't it?"

"Yes," she said with a smile. "Your memory is very good."

Mark wanted to make a joke about amnesia, but he decided to let it slide. Jubilance will do that to a guy's sense of humor.

"Oh, I cannot wait for you to meet him, but I must go… he's waiting for me." Anna reached into her purse and pulled out a pen and an old cough drop wrapper. "This is my address and phone number. Why don't you come by around 8:30 tonight and we'll talk then."

"Sounds great," Mark said as he pulled her in close for one more precious hug. As he made his way down the hallway to the ER, he shouted back, "I love you!"

"I love you, too!" she said and then more quietly, "with all of my heart and soul."

Marty was up hobbling around on his new crutches, still feeling no pain with all the dope (and booze) he had in him.

"Now if we run into trouble while we are out I can Gee-pangy them with these." He waived his crutches in the air like a madman.

Mark smiled and motioned to the nurses that his friend was nuts. Moving a little closer to Marty, he whispered, "that's Ji Pang E and let's keep that between us, ok?"

"Ok, Mr. B!" Marty saluted Mark as he often does, but this time he nearly toppled over the hospital bed.

On the ride home Mark told Marty, "Thank you for breaking your ankle today. I will be forever in your debt. Would you consider being my best man?"

"Best man? What are you talking about...you're getting married? To who?"

"The love of my life these last 30 some years. I never would have found her again if you hadn't broken your ankle. It's a long story...but not today, we gotta get you home and off of that foot."

So, Mark dropped Marty off at his house and headed back to his apartment.

The clock could not possibly move slower. Tick, tick, tick went the seconds. Mark was like a kid at Christmas and this was to be the best Christmas ever!

Finally it was 8 o'clock. He jumped up and headed downstairs, out the door. He was in such a hurry that he didn't notice the fellow outside in front of him.

"Oops! I'm so sorry. I didn't see you. Are you alright?"

"Right as rain, no problem Mr. Mark."

As Mark looked up it was Pete from over at the Cigar Factory.

"Well, Hi Pete. How's it going?"

"Great! Ready for another game?"

"Not right now," he said laughing, "I am late for a date."

"Is that so? Well, have a good time and don't forget ol' Pete. You come and play soon."

Mark said goodbye and hurried to his car. He felt a

strangeness in the air for a fraction of a second, something unsettling, but he didn't linger on it long. Instead, he gave in to the magnetism of his heart and allowed himself to be pulled toward Marigny, where Anna lived. It wasn't a long drive, but it seemed like it took forever. Mark is usually a very patient person, but he just couldn't wait to see her. He stopped on the way to get a bottle of wine, a merlot, she liked red. Finally he arrived at his destination...

As Mark climbed the stairs, an eerie nervousness creeped into him as a chill ran up his spine. He shook it off and then as he got closer his left ear started to tingle and the door flew open.

"Hi sweetheart," she said. "Come in!"

As he walked through the door, he handed her the wine.

"How did you know? I love merlot!"

Mark recognized "The Wedding Song" by Kenny G, one of their favorites, playing in the background as he gazed into her tear-filled, brown eyes. "I just knew—"

Then they embraced, and kissed. Needless to say, the wine went unopened. They fell to the floor wrapped in each other's arms, shedding their garments as they fell...a gentle thud on the thick rug.

"I love you so much darling, I have been waiting for so long."

"Oh Mark, I just knew you would find me. I love you."

She moaned in pleasure and anguish and he began to kiss her lips, her face, her small breasts reaching down with his hand between her legs rubbing slowly then moving back up again.

She rolled over, pulling Mark on top. Her inner thighs were so silky, moistened by her nectar. She writhed with desire as she said, "Mark, I want you—"

Their spirits became as one, finally in the physical realm. As he glided in and out of her, she gently began to moan.

The pleasure surmounted anything he had ever encountered before or since. Here was this angel, surrendering herself to him willingly. Conjoined twins, as they were so long ago. He was in heaven. And then, they both collapsed in each other's arms.

CMCMCMCM

"Good Morning, Sweetheart," she said, bringing him a cup of black coffee. A sudden deja vu moment flashed by Mark. Was this a dream? A memory? Mark felt a rush of anxiety, insecurity, fear that what he had finally encountered after all these years was just another illusion.

But then she touched his face, and everything was fine again.

They snuggled up in the bed and talked a long while — laughing and crying as they spoke of their long journey. And as they did, she finally told him a little of what had happened to her in Youngstown, her testifying against the mob and being in a witness protection program. At least that explains why she had to leave Chicago so abruptly, without a trace.

"At least, you are safe now. Aren't you?"

"For the time being. There is always a chance they will eventually find me, but for now, it's seems we're okay. I was told that they will never give up, but I have to have a life, too."

"We need to find ourselves the Priest!" Mark laughed.

"Why didn't we get married before? What happened to us in Youngstown?"

Just then the phone rang and it was the hospital.

"They are ready to release Vinnie. You will have to meet him and get his permission to marry me," she joked.

"Of course I will. Come on, let's get dressed."

CMCMCMCM

Mark and Anna arrived at the hospital a short time later. All either of them could do was smile, at everybody and everything. They walked down the hall holding hands until they reached Vinnie's room. Once there, Anna suggested, "Wait here," and she went in.

"Hi Mom," said Vincent, his mouth still swollen from the wisdom teeth extraction.

"Hey my little chip monk, how are you feeling?"

"A little swollen."

"I see that. Are you ready to go?"

"Absolutely!"

Vincent, very observantly, said, "Mom, you look different today, so happy. What are you smiling so much about?"

"Oh, I have someone that I want you to meet. Mark Banos is an old, old friend of mine and I found out yesterday, that he lives here in town. Would it be okay for him to come in so he can meet you?"

"Sure Mom, why not?"

With that she went to get Mark and take him in to meet Vinnie.

"Hello, Mr. Banos, I am pleased to meet you," as he extended his right hand with a wink.

"Hello Vincent, it is my pleasure," Mark said, taking his hand. "I have heard so much about you and have so looked forward to meeting you."

The little three year old that Mark had heard playing in the background during their phone conversations twelve years earlier had certainly grown, and grown into a very polite young man and that in and of itself was a rarity these days.

"So, what do you do, Mr. Banos?"

"Oh, I teach music at Holy Cross Catholic High School."

"Holy Cross! I go to Holy Cross and play in the band there."

"No kidding! What instrument?"

"Baritone Horn!"

"JUST LIKE MOM DID!" they both chimed in, finally letting Anna in on their little joke.

"You two knew each other, all the time! And you—" as she punched Mark.

"Yes, I realized when I walked in the room that this was my Vincent from the marching band. He played along real well." Mark let out a long belly laugh at Anna's surprise. "Truthfully though, he's been a constant help to me this year, staying late, helping me get things sorted out for the next rehearsal, game or competition. He talked about his Mom, but never mentioned you by name, and I never saw you around the school. Vinnie and I have become about as well acquainted as you and I, but maybe not quite."

Anna said, "Well, that sure makes this a lot easier. Honey, Mr. Banos has something he wants to ask you."

Vinnie said, "Oh, are you going to ask me if you can marry Mom? Well, heck yeah!"

And the trio started to laugh.

"As soon as I get well, I think we ought to spend some quality family time," Vinnie joked.

"I agree, what do you think Anna?"

"Most definitely!"

"Well, I think a few days down in Gulfport would be nice. What say you guys?"

"Yes!" resounded Anna and Vinnie.

A few weeks later, the three headed to the Mississippi Coast. Mark booked a place at the Legacy Tower, which had an excellent view of the beach. It was a two-bedroom villa with two baths, full kitchen, and a balcony overlooking the ocean.

"Wow!" exclaimed Vinnie. "This is way cool. I even have a hot tub!"

"Oh, Mark, this is absolutely paradise. I wish we could stay here forever."

"Maybe not *here* forever, but you can count on us being together forever."

The next day Mark rented a Hobie Cat and they sailed along the shoreline. Mark purposely put Anna up front. The first wake they hit, Anna was drenched.

She stood up and said, "Ok, hotshot...payback time," as she flipped the Cat so they were all soaked.

After rolling the sailboat back upright they all climbed aboard laughing.

"That will teach you to mess with a tough broad from up north."

"Oh, I think maybe not so tough," as Mark gave her a kiss on the cheek.

That afternoon, they wandered through the local shops with their pocket sucking temptations at every turn. Of course, Anna couldn't resist the doll shop and Mark couldn't resist whipping the ol' Massa Card back out.

As they stopped to get some ice cream, once again Mark felt this uncanny chill in the air and a feeling that he was being watched as he noticed someone disappearing into the crowd.

"What is it, Mark?"

"Oh, nothing. Let's go," he dismissed. He'd been feeling this way more and more lately, but Mark was sure that he was just on edge. After thirty years of chasing after a dream, it's only natural to be hyper-sensitive to the threat of losing it.

Mark knew never to dismiss his intuitions, but maybe it was just better this way. Maybe if he and Anna were destined to exist in a constant chase and be chased dynamic, he should just enjoy the bliss of togetherness while it was at hand. Or maybe he was just being paranoid. The only thing he knew for certain was that he was happy, and it had been a long time since he could say that with any confidence.

The next morning he got Vinnie up early to go surf fishing. They didn't have much luck until around 9:30 when—

"Mark! Look...I have something." Vinnie's pole danced up and down.

"Give him a little slack and ease him in."

"It's a big one!" said Vinnie as he fought with the fish.

"It's huge!" Mark said as he saw him reel in a large Spanish Mackerel. "That's supper tonight!"

They brought their catch up for Anna. "What am I supposed to do with that?"

"It's dinner! Clean it and cook it!"

"Yeah Mom, I did all the hard work catching it."

"And what did you do Mr. Banos? I don't see any fish in *your* bucket."

"Well, I—"

"I thought so. Then how about you be Mr. Mom and clean it and cook it! If you're lucky, I'll take KP duty...if dinner's tasty, that is." She winked and giggled at the surprise scrawled on Mark's face.

After spending most of the afternoon playing on the beach and laying in the sun, they went back to the condo to eat an absolutely wonderful meal from Vinnie's trophy fish. They then spent the rest of the evening playing board games.

On their last evening Vinnie suddenly jumped up and said, "Oh, look at the time. I am so tired. Guess I will go to bed."

And he exited, leaving Anna and Mark to a little time to themselves on the balcony, sipping wine and allowing the gentle breeze of summer to take them far away.

"This is so peaceful," Anna said. "I have not felt this much peace in a long, long time. It's been good for Vinnie, too. He really likes you and enjoys spending time with you."

"I enjoy him, too. You have done a remarkable job with him, especially after all you have been through."

Mark put his arm around Anna as the breeze turned chilly.

"I hate the thought of leaving tomorrow," she said.

"I hate to go, too, but we have a lot to do when we get

back. I guess we can't just lay in the sun day after day."

"Why not?"

"Yeah, why not?" He leaned over to kiss her. "Come on. Let's go in and get some shut-eye. Mornings always come early."

The three of them got very close in those few days of leisure. Anna had not rested nor taken Vinnie on vacation before. She didn't make a whole lot of money and she was afraid to leave home too often. Mark, also, had not had a vacation in some time. Vacations always brought back memories of that beach they were on so long ago.

As they drove back Mark said, "Now look, here it is August and we haven't even talked to the Priest! You are not getting away from me again!"

"You're right," said Anna, "We need to do that." She laughed again. That laugh which was so happy, so free. The two of them had come so very far to get to this moment in time.

And time…They had plenty. They had the rest of their lives.

ೞೞೞೞ

"Wait, wait!" cried Sonny. For a long time he had been lulled into a trance by the old man's narrative, but this last bit slapped him back to reality. "If you finally met Anna again after all those years, surely she filled in the blanks in your memory. What gives?"

"No Sonny, I am afraid not and if she did, I simply don't remember. If you recall, the doctor said that she might tell me things from the past that my mind would simply dismiss as false memories."

"I'm just saying that my first priority would have been to ask some questions, to fill in those gaps. I mean, the way you talked about the amnesia…"

"I very well may have asked questions, but there's no way of knowing now what I've forgotten, what my mind rejected…In any case, we had waited so long and the passion for the future was so strong that we never dwelled on the past."

Old Mr. B smiled and looked out his window. "Master Bennie explained to me earlier that 'our past was the future' but I was too stupid to listen and understand. Maybe I still am to some extent."

The Old Man shook his head and returned his thoughts to Sonny. "Bottom line is we spent our whole lives trying to help others by sharing the love that we had by living in the now. It's just like Miki MkDabbs once wrote, "*realization is the first step on the path to revelation.*"

"I guess but—"

"And it's like me and the greats like Yogi Berra always say, 'you can never forget what you can't remember!'"

Sonny laughed. "You're a crazy old man. But what about—"

"Now Sonny," Mr. B interrupted, "I love you, but pipe down so I can finish the story.

CHAPTER 28

The skies blackened that Monday, the morning of August 29th. It was mostly a voluntary evacuation the days before. Now, everyone in New Orleans was ordered to leave immediately. It seemed inevitable that Katrina was headed right for the city. All anyone could do was sit and wait.

Thankfully, Marty had driven Vinnie to the safety of Crossett in Arkansas on Saturday. It looked especially bad for those in and around the area where Anna lived. Anna didn't care if she lost everything. She didn't have any real possessions of value other than Mark and Vinnie. Of course, she just had to stay. There were children at Charity Hospital that couldn't be moved. So she volunteered to stay and help, as was her custom. Mark also volunteered to stay and help her.

When the hurricane reached the Mississippi coastline it was a Category 3 and nothing to play with. Years ago, Mark remembered going to "*Last Day on Earth Parties*," as they called them, during the big storms back at the beach. The foolishness of youth. Mark was old enough now to see the signs—this was not going to be a party.

As they approached the hospital Mark said, "Anna I love you, please don't go anywhere without me."

"I will be by your side, tonight, forever and always," she said with tender sincerity."

Mark could hear a trust in her voice like he was hearing himself say the words. It didn't take the effort to discern meaning from Anna's words that it did from anyone else's because, well, because it's like he understood her before she ever spoke. It's like every idea or emotion one had the other felt intuitively.

She put a hand on his arm. "Let's get busy and see what we can do to protect the children."

Inside, they monitored the radio closely to check on the quickly advancing storm. Earlier in the morning the east side of the Industrial Canal failed. The 9th District was a rushing torrent moving houses from their foundations.

6:10 a.m. Katrina makes landfall at Buros. A wall of water 21 feet high crossed the Mississippi River and its levees into most of Plaquesmines Parrish.

"Mark this doesn't look good," Anna said. She looked at the children all confined to their beds. "If these levees don't hold, this hospital will flood and we will have no place to go."

"I agree, but for right now with the children being in the shape they are in, our only option is to sit tight and ride it out."

7:00 a.m. Levee wall panels on the west side of Industrial Canal breach. Desire area and the neighborhoods of St. Claude, St. Roch and the 7th Ward wash away.

As the hurricane hit, the winds were ferocious at 100-140 mile an hour gusts. No one dared to venture outside. Mark and Anna huddled with the children inside, providing comfort as they could. Mark sang songs with them to keep their fears to a minimum, but it was a scary time. Water was coming in from the basement and flooded up to the first floor. They decided that they had to move the children higher to the second floor.

"Alright everyone," Anna said, "follow the leader up

the stairs." The ones who could walk did as they were instructed, and the loving couple did their best to help those that couldn't. Many of the hospital staff were still there, but many had left to protect and secure their own families. New Orleans was already becoming a wild frontier.

Then they heard the news. Another set of panel walls on a nearby levee had failed and water was flooding the parish. They had no choice but to move the children from the hospital.

8:14 a.m. The National Weather service issues a flash flood warning for Orleans Parrish and St. Bernard's Parrish citing a breach on both sides of the Industrial Canal. Water is expected to rise 3-8 feet and you are advised to move to higher ground immediately.

"Anna, we have got to somehow get these children to the Super Dome where an emergency last option shelter has been set up. No matter what condition they are in."

"But how, Mark? How?"

"I noticed that they keep the transport vans on the second level of the parking garage. Maybe we can use those. We can take a look and come back and get the other volunteers to help evacuate the children."

Anna and Mark made their way outside to the garage to get the vans ready while there was still a road to drive on. As they rushed through the pouring rain toward the first transport, Mark saw someone in a security guard's uniform on the parking deck above them.

CRACK!

Mark heard the sickening sound of a gunshot as the assassin's bullet whizzed by his head. "Anna, get down!" Mark screamed as he looked up to see a familiar face chambering another bullet in his rifle, readying to take aim for another shot."

Pete…

"Pete!" he yelled, "What the fuck?" A red flame seared through every vessel in his body. An angry horde of yellow jackets came swarming from his eyes and circumnavigated the hitman's head and torso. Pete flapped wildly at the bees to no avail. Mark's spirit separated from his body without a second thought and flew at Pete. Mark's ghastly form shot through him like a bolt of lightning. The instant contact was something faster than the human body could comprehend— the rush of energy made light-speed look like a snail's pace. Pete's corporeal form exploded into one gigantic fireball and disintegrated.

"Checkmate...Coonass."

As Mark's spirit emerged from the bloody mess, Pete was no more, or so he thought. Then he heard Master Bennie's voice, "Be careful not to kill him for his spirit will fight you to keep you from returning to your body."

Suddenly, Pete's spirit was holding onto Mark in a grip that was impossible to break.

He struggled and struggled to free himself, panicking, "No, stop it you psycho," he screamed, "I have to get back to Anna and the children!" Mark used all his might and fought relentlessly.

Pete's grip tightened as he pulled Mark farther toward the dark abode. Mark fought hard, but as he did Pete's grip just kept getting tighter and tighter. Mark could hear Master Bennie's voice again, "Water is formless, put it in a vase, it becomes the vase; heat it and it evaporates into the air. Be like water and evaporate and become air. You no be there."

Mark relaxed and envisioned himself an inferno, and as

he did he could feel himself becoming smaller and Pete's grip loosening. As Mark began to disappear, he suddenly heard the howling of what he thought was the hound of the Baskervilles. Chivas appeared from out of nowhere, ripping and tearing at his attacker. Then Mark felt this strong but gentle force around his waist, the same force that took control of his car years earlier. Suddenly, he was jolted back into his body, shaken but still alive.

As Mark reentered his body, he turned only to find Anna lying motionless on the ground...

Epilogue

"Bullshit," the young man said with a ring of incredulity. "It's all just bullshit, isn't it Big Guy?"

"Yes, Sonny," the old man said with tears in his eyes. "Of course…" his voice could barely make out the words, every syllable was like exhaling a ghost. "Of course it is," he whispered.

The sound of her voice came from his lips—the closest thing he'd had to a kiss in a very long time. It tasted like death.

Before Sonny realized it, the old man had fallen asleep, but he didn't seem to be resting. His face was tight and frozen in a expression of intense thought. It was as if his mind were clutching a memory as tightly as he held that shining coin necklace in his fist.

Hours later, after Sonny had left, after all other living souls had vacated to the land of peaceful dreams, the old man awoke to a living nightmare. The room was spinning darkness, the bathroom was a hundred miles away. "Damn," he muttered, "not now…"

Old Mr. Banos staggered as best he could to the edge of the tub, head arched towards the toilet bowl. He gagged and coughed on shadows, vomiting blood and bile and a lifetime of sick energy from the depths of his being.

But the fit stopped as suddenly as it had started.

Trembling, Mr. Banos felt a burning in his throat and an overwhelming sense of panic. The phrase, "living on borrowed time" blinked in his mind like a neon light flickering in the window of a dingy bar. He wiped a crimson stain from the corner of his mouth and massaged his near lifeless legs. After a long struggle to get back to the bed, he could finally have a real night's rest.

The next morning was a sunrise of clarity.

"Hello, Marty?"

On the other end of the line was a familiar voice. "Yep, it's me Big B. What's up?

"I am," he said with a dusty chuckle, "at least for the moment."

"What are you doing this early in the morning? They change the time for the bingo tournament?"

"Something like that—look, I need a favor."

"Sure, just name it."

The old man peered around the corner to make sure no one was coming then hunched over with the phone to conceal his voice. "Do you still own a vehicle?"

"Yeah I've got the old S-10, but you know that thing's not street legal anymore because of the gas engine."

"Piss, Marty, that doesn't matter—we're outlaws. I don't need to go far, but I do need a ride."

"A ride? Are you kidding? We wouldn't make it five miles with this thing before getting pulled over."

"It's just a ticket—don't worry I'll bill the home for it."

"Is that right? So not only are they going to let you leave for God knows where but they're also going to pay any charges or legal fees you accrue?" Marty paused for a moment to laugh. "Sounds like a sweet deal, really. They got any open beds over your way?"

"Look, I've got a plan, Ok? Just come in the afternoon and I'll tell them I have a dentist appointment."

Marty's voice raised at least an octave higher. "But you don't have any teeth!"

"Well then," the old man said, "I'll just tell 'em I'm pregnant and I need to see an OB—STAT!"

"You've really lost it now. Seriously, how do you expect we're going to pull this little caper off—that is, *if* I decide to help you?"

"You just let me worry about that, Ok?" The old man changed his tone to show he was being serious. "Marty, this just might be it my friend, you understand? So are you in or what?"

A pause. A sigh. "Well, just where is it you're trying to go?"

"Where else? Only one of the classiest stools this side of the Mississippi. I want us to have one last quick *conversation* before last call."

"A bar?" Marty sounded dumbfounded at first, but then, something gripped him. All of a sudden it was as if the old man were the most persuasive man in the world. "Jeez," he finally said, "I guess I can't refuse one more round with my oldest friend. Count me in. When are we breaking you out of there?"

"Day after tomorrow," the old man said. "Well wait, on second thought, better make that tomorrow. A man in my condition doesn't know how many tomorrows he's got left in this world."

"What time then?"

"Well, five o'clock of course! Nah, better make that right after lunch so they'll be too busy to notice I've disappeared."

"All right, sounds like a plan. I'll see you at one."

’ଓଓଓଓ

The next day, when John came in with the usual pig slop, he stopped and stared for a minute. "What are you doing all dressed up today Mr. B?”

“Unfortunately, I’ve got to attend my niece’s funeral at three. She brought such sweetness to life,” the old man said. “Always put a smile on people’s faces, that one…such a comfort to have around.” Mr. B let his voice quaver a bit and even summoned a single tear for his little performance.”

John was taken aback at the “genuine” show of emotion. He thought Mr. B was actually showing a sensitive side for once. “I’m so sorry to hear that…did she suffer long?”

“No, thank God, she passed rather suddenly the other night.”

If you don’t mind me asking, what was her name? I’ll put her on the prayer list at church.”

“That’s sweet of you John. Her name was Ivanna. Ivanna Macallan”

“Macallan? I thought you were Greek?”

“That’s her married name…and, actually, it was my wife’s niece. But imagine that, a Greek marrying a Scot…no accounting for taste, but I guess it turned out fine for eighteen years.”

Marty arrived to escort Mr. B to the “funeral” promptly at one. He wheeled the old man out to the back parking lot just before the administrator noticed he was missing.

“Where’s Mr. B?” Sally asked John as she made her rounds.

“He just left for the funeral. His wife’s niece, you know?” John spoke matter-of-factly as Sally would have already known since she signs off on most every trip or appointment. This shouldn’t be news to her.

“Oh, Sopie Banos was such a wonderful person,” she said with admiration. “She and Mr. Banos moved here from Toronto about twenty years ago and jumped right into helping this community with their talents and donations. I remember when they dedicated the local children’s hospital—you know, St. Agnes downtown? Both worked day in and day out to get that place up and running. She volunteered for hours over there with the children. Heck, she volunteered just about everywhere in town, even here!"

"Is that right?" John asked. "All that was before my time."

"Yes, I suppose it was. I never knew them to have any close friends, although a Mr. Kroner would drop by now and again. And of course his grandson, who also moved to live here a few years ago, came to visit everyday. Well Mrs. Banos passed about four years or so ago. I never could figure out for the life of me how she could put up with that crotchety old Mr. Banos. But maybe he wasn't quite the same then… they always seemed so devoted to one another and the New Bern area. I guess he didn't have time to be such a grump."

John laughed. "Hard to imagine that old geezer in love… she must have been something special."

"Certainly was. Any woman that can turn a man like that old coot into a generous, kind-hearted, animal loving, baby kissing, philanthropist has some kind of magic about her I can tell you that! I even heard a rumor that the old coot spearheaded the raising of more than $387 million dollars to completely gut and renovate the Charity Hospital in New Orleans back in 2018 just as the city was planning to tear it down. It is now one of the most up to date modern hospitals in the United States and the second largest.

The folks in the neighboring parrish sure were grateful as it saved their homes from being demolished to build a new hospital. Of course, it is just gossip."

"I guess he just misses her is all. He seemed real torn up about the niece."

"What was her name again? It's strange, but I don't know if I remember meeting her."

"Let's see…it was Wynona…or wait, Ivanne? No, no, it was Ivanna Macallan. That's it.

Sally raised her eyebrows to the ceiling. "Ivanna…Macallan…you MORON. Her name was 'I Wanna Macallan' as in scotch! He just escaped to get a drink! Call security and see if we can track him down before he gets himself hurt."

ଓଓଓଓ

By the time security reviewed the tapes and made the appropriate phone calls, Mr. B was zooming down highway 70 in the passenger seat of Marty's pickup. The pair headed east toward the beach of the old man's youth, the beach where he first met Anna…

"So where to Mr. B?"

"Pine Knoll Shores," he yelled over the roaring engine.

"What? That's all the way down on the coast?"

"Marty, I thought you were an art teacher…what's up with the geography lesson here? I know where it is. It's where my favorite bar happens to sit."

After an audible sigh, the faithful friend said, "I thought you said this was going to be a quick trip?" Marty looked over to the feeble looking old man in his passenger seat, staring out the window at the world passing him by. After a moment, he finally just said, "Ok boss, Pine Knoll Shores it is."

After about an hour drive (one that would have been only 45 minutes had the duo not been stopped as Marty predicted) they reached their destination. As the beat up truck rolled onward toward the coast, Old Mr. Banos felt like time was slowing down, like the outside world faded away and he was slipping back into a time from long ago.

He couldn't help but think of all the crazy things he did as a young man, how stupid it was of him to take off for Ohio and back over a two day period. He could hardly fathom how he had the strength or stubbornness to leave the beach at 2 a.m. on a Sunday and arrive back at 5 p.m. the following Tuesday ready to perform on stage.

Even now, he thought it all sounded preposterous. He couldn't help but think how funny it was that the most ridiculous things you do in your youth could end up being some of the most important events of your life.

It would have been nice, he thought, to have those real memories in his later years. Master Bennie had eluded to the fact that once one Twin left this earthly plain, the other would gradually regress until they too passed on and once again were reunited. Maybe that is why the old man couldn't remember his past.

It doesn't really seem to matter much now. It would have been nice if he and Anna had discussed the past…but that wasn't the case. That just isn't what Twin Flames do. The two of them burned so brightly with one another that they only had time to illuminate the world around them. And Old Mr. Banos, even in his days of most solemn grief, he knew that the world needed that love more than he did. He wouldn't dare be that selfish.

Besides, Vincent was a real comfort in the years after Anna's death—he and the old man even made some cash producing a few syndicated cable shows. He and Vincent had formed a new type of cable-less television company years earlier using WiFi and had made millions soon after Vinnie graduated from college with an engineering degree.

But Vincent now had a life and a wife of his own back in Toronto. And as much as the old man enjoyed his time in Canada, this was his true home. This coast, this salt air, this land of tides and summer love—this is where he belonged.

The old man rolled the window down. "That ocean air feels so good, Marty."

"It better," he said in a low grumble. "This trip's already cost me $5,000 for a stupid abuse of a natural resource fine that I TOLD YOU we were going to get! And, that doesn't include the additional $900 I spent to front for the gas. Plus, $75 because this truck gets eight miles to the gallon going on a field trip to the beach. Jeez!"

"Yeah, but at least that cop was nice, huh? Didn't even

try to shove his billy club up your ass. And as far as the ticket and the gas goes, just put it on my tab." He laughed, "Smell that salt air?"

"What's that? Oh, I thought you were just sharting again old man."

"Hey, watch that 'old man' shit or I'll rap you with my cane."

"You gonna Geepangy your faithful driver and loyal friend?" he laughed.

"I might just have to you old drunk! Now turn here so we can make happy hour."

ෆෆෆෆ

The Atlantic Beach Tavern. The happiest place on Earth.

The two walked in and, with Marty's help, Old Mr. B didn't have to use the cane or walker. The old man sat down at a bar stool and breathed in the comforting smell of stale smoke and mildewed carpet. "Chivas and water please," said Mr. B.

The bartender looked at the old man bewildered and said, "Did you say Chardonnay and water?"

Trying desperately to be polite and not slam the little twerp's head into a cocktail glass, Old Mr. B said, "No, son, Chivas and water. Scotch, I want scotch."

"Oh," the young man said, "Sorry, we just don't have much call for scotch these days." The tow-headed kid poked around under the bar and slid some things around on the shelf. "We have Johnny Walker Red," he called up from the floor.

"That'll do."

The kid popped up bottle in hand and asked, "So how much do you want?"

"How much do you want to give me?" Old Mr. Banos couldn't remember a trip to the bar that was ever this complicated.

The kid thought hard for awhile. "Well," he said finally, "I guess as much as you want to pay for."

After another minute or two of this kind of nonsense, the kid poured the scotch into a 6 ounce plastic cup and splashed some water across it.

"All right sir, that'll be $45."

"Wait, what do you want, Marty? It's on me."

"You don't have to do that Mr. B, I got—"

"I said it's on me! Now are you going to stand their stammering or are you gonna shut up and order a drink?"

"I'll have a Blue Moon."

The old man laughed. He knew what Marty really meant was he'd have about ten or twelve Blue Moons. *Not on my goddamned tab* he thought.

"Ok," the bartender said, "that'll be $65."

Old Mr. B handed the kid a debit card. He stood there and stared at the thing.

"You want to start a tab?"

"Nah, just cash me out."

"Sorry, but, we've got a $100 minimum on cards."

"Jeez kid, I'm planning on leaving a tip you know?"

Hesitantly, he took the card and agreed. "All right then."

While the kid was ringing up the bill, old Mr. Banos noticed that, across the bar, a haggard looking old fisherman had spilt his beer. Without a moment's hesitation, he reached over the bar for a dirty towel, sopped up the puddle of booze, and rang out the rag back into his glass.

Classic Beach tavern.

When the kid brought their drinks, Mr. Banos looked over to his pal and said "Marty, you remember the time we had a conversation at the bar in town and both drank Blue Moons until we couldn't walk?"

"Yeah," he said with a laugh, "Which time?"

"The time when I had just gotten back from Toronto

and you still had the job at West Carteret High. After you finished up those asinine teacher work day meetings you and I zipped off to the bar early."

"Maybe, buddy. Sometimes I think we had a little too much fun because it's getting hard to remember it all."

"Well that time you drank six to my one and somehow I got stuck paying the tab…$75!" The old man half-punched Marty in the arm. "That was pretty high back in those days 'cuz beers were still 75 cent each!"

"Hmm…" Marty scratched his head. "I'm no great mathematician, but I do believe that's about a hundred beers!"

"Yeah, good thing we were driving because we sure as hell couldn't walk."

"That's for sure." Marty took a sip of his beer and watched as the old man sipped his drink. "So, I gotta ask, what's with this scotch and water shit? You've always been a top shelf kind of guy. Why make one last great escape for that piss?"

The old man laughed. "As you just saw, the top shelf here is still under the bar. The fact is, this just tastes like memories. I used to come here back in '75 all the time and this is what I drank then. The way I figure it, if this is the end of the line, I want to have one more sorry ass drink with my sorry ass friend." The old man laughed and coughed a little slapping Marty on the back. "After all, it's not about taste now—it's just about the nostalgia. The good times."

"Come on Big B, quit talking like you're dying and drink like a man."

The old man took a big gulp and wiped the moisture from his mustache. "We're all dying my friend, some just quicker than others. No one in my family ever lived past sixty. So, as far as I'm concerned, I'm living on borrowed time."

"Ah horse piss," Marty said, "there you go with that curse and superstition shit again."

"Hey, you should listen to your elders better. We're all dying, but we're all living too. When your ear hairs start turning white and your neck skin hangs down like a turkey's, you don't think about all the neat shit you've bought and sold over the years? You start thinking about all the things you've done, all the people you've spent quality time with, even if they're shitheads like you, Marty."

The devoted friend just threw up his hand to that little remark and took another sip of his drink.

"The places you've been, the adventures you've had, the people you meet along the way, that's what really matters. At the end of the day, it's just like Monopoly, all the pieces just go back in the box."

The two friends sat in the solemnity of the dive bar for a few moments, drinking in their final piece of shared time together. Sipping it, savoring it.

After a while, Marty decided the best thing to say was nothing. Instead, he just put his arm around the old man and patted him on the shoulder.

Mr. B laughed. "This feels familiar—yep, same sweaty arm I had to throw around me every time I carried your happy ass out of one of these places."

The two of them laughed together.

"Hell, I bet I carried you out of more bars than you carried me in!"

Wiping his eyes, Marty said, "Dat true, dat very true." After they composed themselves and ordered a couple more drinks, Marty spoke a little more seriously. "You know, I don't want to sound too mushy here or anything, but you've always been kind of like a dad to me."

Without missing a beat, the old man said, "Well your dad must have been really fucked up."

The two of them roared with laughter now, so much so that everyone else in the bar (all three of them) began to notice.

"I'm serious," Marty said. "I used to spend many a day with my dad at the VFW bar and shoot the shit just like we're doing now. When he passed away, you were really there for me. I'll never forget that."

Old Mr. B nodded his head. "I like to think we needed each other, Marty." He reached into his pants pocket and pulled out something small and shiny clenched in his fist. "If you don't mind, I'm going to need you one more time."

Marty raised his eyebrows. "Anything, just ask."

The old man held out his hand revealing a coin on a gold chain. "Give this to Sonny for me."

Marty looked confused, but took the jewelry. "Why not just give it to him yourself?" He studied the coin—it had two heads. One male; one female. It was warped in some weird way though, the female side had some strange fold in the metal.

"Look pal, I think we both know that I didn't buy a ticket for the return flight today. Make sure you give him the instructions I am about to tell you exactly as I tell you. Promise me?"

Seeing that the old man was deadly serious, Marty nodded his head in agreement. "No problem Big B!"

After whispering something in his ear, the old man tried to stand abruptly. "Well, it's five o'clock. Time for the real party to begin!" The old man downed what was left in his plastic cup and instructed his buddy to follow suit.

Mr. B showed Marty how to get further down Salterpath until they rolled up to the old resort. There it was, all seven floors of it looking much less grand by contemporary standards.

"What are you doing here?" Marty joked, "Getting us a nice room?"

The old man smiled. "Unfortunately not, my friend. Just let me off here—I've got to make the rest of this trip alone."

"But you can barely walk! What are you talking about, let me help—"

"Marty—" he said to interrupt, "barely walking is nothing new to me or you." He laughed a little and said, "Barely just means go slower, stumble more, tumble every now and again. Like I said, nothing new."

Marty just sighed and shook his head.

Old Mr. B half-fell out of the antique truck and shut the door behind him. "You're sorry as skunk shit, Marty. But I love you anyway."

Soon, the rumbling of the gas engine faded away into the sounds of the ocean breeze, the caw of the gulls, and the whispering sunset. Old Mr. B hobbled towards the dunes and found a seat where he could look out over the sea and the sands. Of course, Melvin was still the only one down there, folding up all the beach chairs and taking down all the umbrellas with as much vigor as he'd had seventy-three years ago.

"Jesus tap-dancing Christ," Mr. B said to himself. Melvin had to be a hundred and five years old by now.

Some people have it all, he thought.

In the misty orange haze, the ocean seemed to call out to the old man. Every wave retreating from the shore was a finger slowing gesturing for him to come closer. He sat for what felt like hours, enjoying the peacefulness of a never-ending invitation to come back home.

Waiting, just waiting, praying to any god that would listen.

The stirring breeze carried a voice, perhaps his own, but perhaps someone else's entirely. It was faint, but he could hear the words clearly enough…*remember me.*

Off in the distance, the sunlight danced from the glittering waves. Light breathed life, and from the radiant reflection, a young girl appeared…beautiful, translucent, familiar…

ෆෆෆෆ

Not long after Sally had discovered Old Mr. Banos had

escaped, Sonny arrived for his usual visit. Much to his surprise, his grandfather was nowhere to be found. At first he assumed the old man was in the dining room since it was near five.

In his room, Sonny noticed a puzzle box that looked strangely similar to one he'd seen before. Resting on top of it was an old photograph of a stunning, young woman. After studying it for quite awhile, he realized that the puzzle box was just like the one his grandmother had…could this be her in the picture?

Sticking out from the underside of the box was a newspaper clipping from The Times-Picayune of Greater New Orleans. The date was August 2005.

In an apparent random act of violence in the aftermath of Hurricane Katrina, the bodies of a local music teacher and a social worker were found shot dead in West Jefferson last night. Mark Banos and Karli Roberts were reported as trying to rescue children from Charity Hospital when the incident occurred. According to local authorities, the shooter disappeared without a trace in the chaos. Currently there are no leads as to the whereabouts of the perpetrator. Similar acts of senseless violence have plagued New Orleans in the weeks following the…

Sonny couldn't believe what he was reading. "Shot dead?" he said to himself.

He couldn't wait around, so he decided to just head over to the dining room to ask his Big Guy how he and his grandmother managed to come back from the dead. It didn't take him long to realize that the old man wasn't in there either. Outdone and frustrated, Sonny spotted John. "Where the hell is my Big guy…I mean, where is Mr. Banos?"

After a lengthy explanation and mention of "Ivanna Macallan" and a "friend with a pickup truck," Sonny knew exactly where his grandfather had gone.

As he rushed out the door, Sally tried to stop him saying, "Sonny, I was just about to call you once the police looked over our tapes and—"

Without breaking his stride, Sonny said exactly what his Big Guy would have—"Blow it out your ass, Sally!"

The forty-five minute drive took twenty. "Crazy old shit," Sonny muttered as he weaved in and out of traffic. He was lucky not to get pulled over as he zoomed through Havelock and Newport. He drove absent-mindedly, as if the car and his body knew automatically how to reach their destination. All he could think of was the worst, but he didn't feel angry or upset, he simply felt excluded. Why Marty? Why not him? Didn't he deserve to say goodbye if he had to say it at all?

Before long, Sonny was turning down Salterpath and approaching Pine Knoll Shores. There was no question in his mind that he'd find his Big Guy there—ever since his grandmother passed away he could see it in the old man's face. This was the place that was pulling him, the tide was calling him back to the place where he first met his true love.

Squealing tires in the parking lot of the Ramada, Sonny hopped out of the car and ran towards the beach. When he hiked to the top of the sand dune, he wasn't at all surprised at what he found. There the old man lay, as if in a perfect dream, finally at rest.

"They're together now," a voice said from behind, "your grandad and his Sopie." In all his hurry, Sonny hadn't even noticed Marty standing there.

Normally when people say things like that, hollow sentiments at funerals, niceties to the grieving survivors, it sounds like bullshit. Normally, when Sonny had heard these kinds of remarks in his life, he felt his hair stand on end and his blood boil, but not this time. This time, it wasn't just bullshit people say—it was the truth.

Sonny started to tear up…he was too late to say goodbye. "You really think they are? My Big Guy and grandmother?"

Marty stepped closer and put his arms around the young man. "Yes, of course they are, Sonny boy. Of course they are."

Sonny let his frustration and sadness pour out, but, truthfully, he wasn't exactly sad. He liked having the old man around, but he hated knowing he had to live a life of misery. In a way, he was happy to see him here instead of in some gray-scale hospital room.

After a while, Marty said, "He asked me to give you this when he was gone…I thought he was being a little silly you know, but I guess he knew something was coming." Marty handed over Anna's necklace.

Sonny turned the coin necklace over and over in his hand searching for some meaning. The faces on both sides seemed so serious. The man's was facing right and the woman's facing left—it's as if they were always looking for each other but always together at the same time. The crease on the woman's face felt so strange between his fingers…

"Now listen close because he told me to say these words exactly."

Sonny stared up intently, hoping for something, anything to make some sense of this.

"He said to give this necklace to your first born grandson, that death was nothing more than another chance at life and that—" Marty stopped to clear his throat. He couldn't help but feel a chill in the air and got a little choked up.

"What?" Sonny demanded. He was hungry for answers.

"He said that he'd *see you then*."

A silence fell on the two of them as they stared at the old man sleeping in the sand, dreaming of all the love he'd ever felt and given in this world. One by one, the sounds returned to them. The salt water rushing over the sand, the gulls flapping their wings overhead, and the coastal current of souls slowly rising towards the stars.

ೞೞೞೞ

The old man separated from his feeble body one last time

with no intention of returning. The last thing he felt was the curve of his lips, a smile of gratitude for Master Bennie. Not many people get to die with dignity, and his body was thankful.

There was no sound, no sensation of being. There was only a flood of purple light, and a feeling of timelessness. In a brilliant flash of white, the no longer old man blinked his eyes and saw a starfish lying on the beach. He reached down with a now boyish arm and tossed it back into the sea. Walking back to the shore, he stooped down to continue building a sandcastle with a little girl. Once they put the final touches on the last tower, the little girl said, "This will make it perfect."

She pulled a shining coin from her pocket and pressed it into the sand. The shining metal talisman glowed a bright orange, revealing not one face, but two, staring at one another eye to eye.

The little boy and little girl joined hands and walked down the sand towards the light in the distance.

"Will you still marry me?" the little girl asked.

"Yes, Anna, of course I will."

As they walked, they grew with every step. Mark became taller, more muscular. Anna transformed into the beautiful young woman from the summer they met. As they walked closer, they shared one last passionate kiss, aging together as they had in life, but in a matter of seconds. Soon, as their bodies reached their final forms of old age, the two intertwined and became one. They walked as a single body, with four legs, four arms, and two faces—one looking east and one west.

They were totally different and, yet, somehow the same. They were finally now a unification of opposites, the embodiment of the yin and yang coin they once possessed. This was the moment when they could rise to the realm of the ascended masters, but only with each other—only with each becoming the other.

With a few more steps, the sands all fell away beneath their feet, the ocean swallowed itself, and all things physical dissolved—all mortal illusions were revealed and dispelled.

All that was left was one self, and an infinity of stars paling in comparison.

"...Then one by one, the stars would all go out and you and I would simply fly away."

About the Author

Spencer Michaels is the pen name of the father-son writing team comprised of Michael and Spencer Bennington. When friends ask how the collaboration began, son Spencer is quick to joke that his dad, Michael, guilted him into becoming a writing partner. That wry sense of humor smacks of modesty as Spencer is also an Adjunct Professor of English and a doctoral student at the University of South Florida and works as a freelance writer.

One might say that entertaining is in Michael Bennington's blood. Prior to becoming a novelist, he worked as a professional musician for over 50 years playing varied venues from night clubs to coliseums and even recorded CDs and served as back up to nationally known recording artists. He shared his love of music as a teacher at Sacred Heart Catholic School for 13 years before retiring in 2012. He says that these days his music is limited to playing at his church where he serves as choir director.

Spencer's first book was inspired by what he believes is an inspiration to many a writer...the love of a beautiful woman. He also credits the stories his dad told about his early days as a nightclub entertainer with sparking his imagination.

Michael notes that his love of writing began rather accidentally when he suffered a stroke. Not being one to rest on his laurels, Michael launched into writing and convinced Spencer to jump on board as his partner. Michael lists The Baltimore Orioles as his other passion, along with single malt scotch. He jokes that those wondering what to get him for Christmas might consider Yamazaki, an 18-year-old Japanese Whisky Sherry Cask he has his eye on.

Originally from Denton, Maryland, Michael and his wife, Susie, have called Danville, Virginia their home for the past 40 years. Spencer describes his birthplace as being "more than soupy grits and snaggle-tooths," but also the perfect blend of Southern home splendor, small town community and big city dreams. Although Michael remains in Danville, Spencer plans to relocate to Tampa, Florida and wonders if "gator wrasslin'" is in his future as he is an accomplished Tae Kwon Do instructor.

In addition to son Spencer, Michael and Susie, have one other son, Miki, two grandchildren, and a Sheltie named Luci, who the family considers their only daughter.

Stay in touch with Spencer Michaels here…
Twitter - @SMichaelsBooks
Facebook - SpencerMichaelsBooks
Website - https://spencermichaelsbooks.com/

9 781630 991104